"I say you will remain here and here you will remain," Angus said.

Mary sniffed. "Humph."

Angus couldn't believe it. She'd *sniffed* at him, dismissing him completely. How dare she? By God, he would show her who was boss and what he would and would not stand for. He lifted her higher in his arms and kissed her. *You swore you wouldn't kiss her again,* his logical side whispered in his ear. *You should have a care.*

The logical side was probably right, but the lusty side of him was fighting to overrule it. His body was achingly aware of the softness of her curves, of the full press of her breasts against his chest.

Somehow, some way, he would conquer this woman, bend her to his will, and he already knew there was one way—and one way only—to silence her infuriating speech. However, if he kissed her again, he didn't know if he'd have the strength to step away.

His captive took matters into her own hands. Held prisoner against his chest, her eyes flashing daggers, she grasped his collar and planted a kiss upon his surprised lips.

Angus felt the pressure of her soft lips with a ferocious mixture of pleasure and fury that dissolved his self-control with one fell blow. Giving in to the passion, he tightened his arms about her and deepened the kiss.

Turn the page for rave reviews of Karen Hawkins . . .

TO CATCH A HIGHLANDER

"Love and laughter, poignancy and emotional intensity, endearing characters, and a charming plot are the ingredients in Hawkins's utterly delightful tale."
—*Romantic Times*

"Karen Hawkins's best book to date! Fast, sensual, and brilliant, it tantalizes and pleases all in the same breath. . . . This is romance at its best!"
—Romance and More

TO SCOTLAND, WITH LOVE

"Hawkins bring another hardheaded MacLean brother and a sassy miss together in a sensual battle of the sexes. Her humor, intelligent characters, and story are simply delightful."
—*Romantic Times*

HOW TO ABDUCT A HIGHLAND LORD

"Hawkins takes a fiery Scot lass and a wastrel lord and puts them together in a match made in, well, not heaven, but one that's heated, exciting, and touching. Hawkins excels at taking tried-and-true plotlines and turning them into fresh, vibrant books."
—*Romantic Times*

"In *How to Abduct a Highland Lord*, the characters are as wonderful as the story. . . . [It] is laced with passion and drama, and with its wonderfully romantic and thrilling ending, it's a story you don't want to miss!"
—JoyfullyReviewed

KAREN HAWKINS

One Night in Scotland

POCKET **STAR** BOOKS

New York   London   Toronto   Sydney

Pocket Star Books
A Division of Simon & Schuster, Inc.
1230 Avenue of the Americas
New York, NY 10020

This book is a work of fiction. Names, characters, places, and incidents either are products of the author's imagination or are used fictitiously. Any resemblance to actual events or locales or persons, living or dead, is entirely coincidental.

Cover illustration by Craig White. Hand lettering by Ron Zinn. Designed by Esther Paradelo

Manufactured in the United States of America

ISBN-13: 978-1-61664-971-5

For Nate, aka Hot Cop

Thank you for being so patient with
my nearly constant state of "deadline dementia,"
which is occasionally broken by the famed
"pre-release jitters," closely followed by
a (very short) period of "book release euphoria."

You make my soul grin.

Acknowledgments

Special thanks to: Waldo, a magnificent personal trainer; Sue, a wonderkind of a personal assistant; and Julietta, a slightly paranoid but dedicated chef.

Thank you for contributing so many great tips and hints on fitness and organization, as well as hundreds of incredible (and easy!) recipes, to my new website, www.karenhawkins.com.

Because of you guys, www.karenhawkins.com rocks!

One Night in Scotland

Luxor, Egypt
April 12, 1822

Dearest Family,

I write this in haste. As of last Tuesday, I am still in Egypt, the "guest" of a sufi who will not allow me to leave until I return an artifact I legitimately purchased from an antiquities dealer in Cairo.

It galls me to return it, but it appears I must. William, as soon as you can, set out for Scotland to New Slains Castle and request my friend, the Earl of Erroll, to commend the artifact to your care. Then make all haste to deliver it to my trusty (if annoying) assistant, Miss Jane Smythe-Haughton, whom you met on your last visit. She is currently housed with the consulate in Malfi and awaits your arrival.

Mother, do not worry. I have been in worse fixes and escaped unscathed. I fully intend on continuing that tradition.

Yours,
Michael

ONE

Aberdeenshire, Scotland
May 12, 1822

The inn's wide oak door slammed open, the icy wind swirling snow across the uneven, rough plank floor. Almost as one, the inhabitants of the room looked at the newcomer, a heavily bundled-up young lady obviously offended by the dire weather.

Shivering from head to toe, Mary Hurst grabbed the door with both gloved hands and struggled to close it. Her maid appeared and they finally secured the door, both panting from the effort. "Thank you, Abigail."

"Ye're welcome, miss." Abigail rubbed her arms and looked around the room with interest. "Gor', miss, there do be a lot o' folks in this establishment."

Mary undid the scarf that covered her chin and ears from the harsh elements and blinked at the gazes locked upon her. The harsh weather had driven all other travelers inside the only available inn on this

particular stretch of long and lonely Scottish road-
way.

Mary stepped through the wide arch that led to the
common room. "I've never been so cold in all of my
life."

Abigail rubbed her gloved hands together. "Aye, 'tis
as cold as a witch's teat!"

Mary's face warmed to a hot burn as the two farmers and a well-bundled tradesman who sat around a
table by the window guffawed. A clergyman who sat at
the long buffet table sent Abigail a hard stare before he
hunkered down over his plate. Meanwhile, in the far
corner, two rough-looking laborers chuckled boister-
ously, winking when Mary sent a reprimanding glance
their way.

"Abigail, please watch your language."

Unabashed, Abigail grinned. "Aye, miss."

She unwound her muffler and looked about the
room with interest, her broad face brightening with an
even broader smile.

"Gor', miss, do look at all the *gentlemans!*"

Mary turned a stern stare on her enthusiastic maid.
"Abigail, ladies do not stare in admiration at strangers.
So let's *not* look at all of the gentlemen."

Abigail's smile dimmed. "Very well, miss, but—"

"No 'buts.'" Mary removed her scarf, shaking off
the melting snow. As she did so, she caught the gaze
of the final occupant of the taproom. Dressed head
to toe in unrelenting black, the man sat in the only
chair beside the crackling fireplace. Larger than any
other man in the room, he had broad shoulders and

long legs that made even the heavy chair seem too small.

He was still wrapped in his coat and a heavy muffler partially concealed his face. That was a pity, for he had a most striking appearance: dark hair that fell over a noble brow; a strong, acquiline nose; and pale green eyes that caught and held her gaze.

Abigail said in an audible whisper, "Miss, I thought we wasn't supposed to stare at the gentlemans."

Mary's face burned, certain that the man had heard her maid's unwelcome comment, but he merely favored them both with an indifferent glance before turning his gaze back to the snapping fire, his face a study of disdainful boredom.

Piqued by such an obvious dismissal, Mary turned her back on the stranger and yanked off her wool-lined gloves.

It was a most inhospitable welcome. There were no available chairs and not one of the male occupants had stood when she and her maid entered, much less offered up their seats.

But she could endure this and more for her brother. *This is for Michael. I cannot let him down.*

She had a special place in her heart for her youngest brother. He had been sickly from the time of his birth until well into his teens, when, miraculously, he had ceased catching every illness that came through their village. Within a year, he'd lost his worrisome cough, gained a golden tan, and grown four inches.

Though he'd recovered fully, the long years he'd been ill had shaped him in many ways. The hours he'd been forced to lie upon the couch had left him with little to do but devour book after book. When his health had improved enough that he could attend school, he found he was far ahead of his classmates and, somewhere along the way, had become a scholar.

To his family's surprise, he'd taken his fluent Greek and Latin, his advanced knowledge of sciences and histories, and had become the one thing none of them had expected . . . an Egyptologist.

Mary said the word in her mind, savoring it. It was a new term, come to usage only since Napoleon's Nile campaign. His troops had ravaged the Nile valley, and after Napoleon's defeat, their acquisition of a large number of ancient Egyptian treasures had enriched the coffers of the British Museum. Michael was a member of Britain's Royal Society, an organization founded in 1660 and comprised of energetic scientists who valued empirical evidence over everything else. The members took their role as the leading experts in the study of Egyptian artifacts very seriously indeed.

But Michael hadn't joined the society just to search for Egyptian artifacts. He was on a special quest that only the family knew about: to recover the Hurst Amulet, which had been stolen from an ancestor and gifted to Queen Elizabeth I. History suggested that the intrepid queen came to fear the amulet, thinking it possessed magical qualities, and had passed it on to a courier from a foreign land.

The problem was, no one knew which land. Over the years, Michael had become convinced that the amulet had ended up in Egypt, and he was determined to find it.

Mary was eager to hear what new clue Michael had unearthed. His life was so exciting, she thought wistfully. He was doing the very things she wished she could do—adventuring, exploring, finding and purchasing historical artifacts for private and public collections. She, meanwhile, was the sole child left at home, and the care of their parents had fallen on her.

Not that she regretted it. She loved her parents and the vicarage, but sometimes her soul longed for excitement.

Right now, though, she could do with a lot *less* adventure, and a lot *more* warmth. Her hands and feet were freezing; she couldn't feel her toes at all.

She straightened her shoulders and gazed about the inn's common room in the way she imagined Michael would, coolly and without fear, meeting the gaze of every man present.

The farmers and tradesman in the corner lost their grins immediately, dropping their heads and muttering to one another under their breath. The clergyman turned bright red, then sniffed and returned to reading his well-worn Bible. The rough laborers stopped guffawing and shifted uncomfortably in their seats. Only the darkly garbed man by the fireplace didn't acknowledge her, but continued contemplating the flames as if searching the glow for the last book of Ramesses.

Fortunately, she didn't need him to pay attention to her. She'd tamed the common room with just one look. "Come, Abigail. Let's bespeak a hot meal and see to hiring an escort to New Slains Castle."

The clergyman's head snapped in their direction.

"New Slains?" Thin and slight, he was almost swallowed by his frock coat and slouched muffler.

"Yes, New Slains Castle."

"Och, ye canno' wish to go there."

"But I do. I must speak with the Earl of Erroll."

"But—" His gaze flickered past her, then back. "The road is impassable. No one will take ye there."

"Someone will have to, for I've very important business to conduct with the earl. Besides, the roads cannot be that bad; the ostler said it had only been snowing an hour or less."

"Yes, but before that it was raining, so there's sure to be ice. The road is very steep in places and treacherous."

Abigail made a distressed noise. "Miss, mayhap we'd best bespeak a room fer a night or two until—"

"No." She'd come so far to fetch the item Michael needed to win his freedom, and she wasn't about to give up.

"But, miss, ye'd have t' have yer head up yer arse to—"

"Abigail!" *This* is what came of traveling with a companion one had barely met.

Normally when Mary traveled, she took one of the serving girls who helped clean the vicarage, both well trained and genteel. Unfortunately, influenza had raced through their small hamlet just before Michael's urgent letter had arrived and both maids were ill. Mary had been left with no choice but to accept the only available female willing to travel to Scotland on such short notice, her groom's niece.

Abigail blinked in mild surprise. "What's toward, miss?"

"That phrase is vulgar."

"Th' one about stickin' yer head up—"

"Yes. It's not an appropriate expression."

"Nay? Even when 'tis the truth?"

One of the farmers snickered loudly. Mary glared at him until he covered his mouth, though his shoulders still shook.

"It's not proper *ever*." She tucked her gloves into her pocket. "Now, we must find the landlord and—"

The outer door opened and a short, squat man came into the entry hall behind them. He was swaddled in a huge coat, a prodigious number of mufflers, and a thick woolen cap. Stomping his boots upon the floor, he paused on seeing Mary and her maid standing in the common room. "G'day. Can I help ye? I be Mr. MacEllis." The thick Scottish brogue was barely understandable.

Mary dipped a curtsy. "I am Mary Hurst and this is my maid, Abigail. We would like to bespeak a private parlor, if one is available."

He *tsk*ed. "Och, miss, we dinna have such a thing. 'Tis the common room or none."

Mary forced a smile. "Fine, then. We'll find some chairs here. We'd like some dinner as well. We haven't eaten since this morning."

"I'll bring ye out some Cullen Skink." At Mary's blank look, he explained, "'Tis stew made of finnan haddock, potatoes, onions, and whatnot."

"Ah! That would be lovely." It sounded appetizing and she loved stew, especially on cold days. "All we need is a seat, then."

The innkeeper went into the common room and looked around. His gaze flickered over the farmers and tradesmen and fell upon the gentleman by the fire. "Why, 'tis—"

"MacEllis, there you are," the man said in a deep, rumbling voice. "I came to try your whiskey, if you've any left."

The innkeeper shot a side-glance at Mary and her maid. "O' course we do, er—"

"Mr. Hay."

"Mr. Hay, then. I'll bring ye a good tipple."

"Thank you. After, of course, you've seated your new guests."

"Aye." The innkeeper turned toward the wide bench by the buffet table. "Vicar Turnbill, would ye mind scootin' yerself down a wee bit? We've guests, as ye can see."

The vicar looked as if he did indeed mind, but he gathered his Bible and plate and slid to the far end of the table, where he sat stiff-backed as if afraid his very air might be tainted by their presence.

The innkeeper gestured to the plank bench. "There ye go, miss! I'll fetch yer stew and some bread." With that he hurried off, leaving them alone with the men in the common room once again.

"Oh, I do hope there is a lot of stew, fer I'm hungry enough to eat a hog's head all by meself." Abigail swung her cape from her shoulders and hung it on a peg by the door.

If every eye had been fastened upon them before, they were glued now, for Abigail's plain gray gown accentuated her astounding figure.

Abigail smoothed down her gown as she cast a winsome glance at the clergyman. The scrawny man gulped, his Adam's apple bobbing as he turned bright red. With a sputtered deprecation, he ducked his head into his Bible.

Abigail grinned as she took her seat, making certain she was facing the men in the room, whom she now favored with a simper.

Mary clutched her pelisse tighter and wished she could toss a muffler over Abigail. Never had there been such an attention-seeking maid. Resigning herself to the inevitable comments and stares, Mary took her seat at the end of the table.

As she did so, she found herself meeting the sardonic gaze of the stranger by the fire, his green eyes glinting with mockery. Her face heated and she resolutely looked away.

Mary wished she could teach Abigail a bit of decorum, but the girl was addicted to the attention her figure solicited, and Mary couldn't completely blame her.

Mary wouldn't mind being so blessed herself. She had the ample breasts, but the rest of her was ample as well.

It wasn't that she was fat, but she was *healthy*. She lacked both the slender, willowy figure favored by fashion and the hourglass figure that Abigail enjoyed. Mary's shape was more . . . squarish, a shape enhanced very little by the current style of gowns with their tiny puffed sleeves and waistlines directly beneath the breasts.

Stop thinking about such silly things! You need to focus on your mission.

Her throat tightened at the thought of her brother. His letter had assured them that he was well, but she knew from experience that his letters were often carefully edited for their parents' eyes. Later on, when it was just him and Mary, he would tell her the *real* tales of danger and deception, excitement and—sometimes—tedium.

She knew more than any of their other siblings just how far some of Michael's letters were from the real truth, and it frightened her now in a way it never had before.

He was not doing well; she could feel it in her heart.

It would be a relief when they finally reached their destination, recovered the artifact from the earl, and met up with William, who should be sailing from France now to meet them at the dock in Whitby. William had gone to collect one of Michael's best friends and compatriots, Jean-Francois Champollion, to serve as a guide for the delivery of the artifact to Michael's captor. No one knew Egypt like Champollion.

If everything went as planned, Michael would be free within the next six weeks—which was far too long to be a captive, but the best they could do.

The innkeeper returned carrying two bowls of steaming stew and a hunk of thick bread already buttered. Despite her worry for her brother, Mary's rumbling stomach welcomed the lovely stew.

As she ate, the travails of the last few weeks seemed to melt into insignificance. She was truly blessed to be able to make such a journey. Had either of her other brothers been home, it would have fallen to William or Robert to make the trip. Fortunately, Mary had been the only one available. Eager to go, she had overridden her parents' objections with a calm assuredness that she hadn't always felt once the journey had begun.

Their travels had been far more difficult than she'd expected. They'd suffered a broken wheel on their third day, and then faced two days of slogging rain that had left the roads treacherously muddy and travel painfully slow. There were times she'd thought it would be faster to walk than remain in the creeping carriage.

Then, as they'd passed through Aberdeen, the rain had turned into snow, which had made traveling impossible until it eased up and the road became visible once more.

Abigail hadn't helped, either. The woman had chattered nonstop about things Mary had never done or thought to do—lies she'd told, men she'd allowed to kiss her, and how she'd once stolen a penny from a man who hadn't bought her a big-enough present.

Mary was certain Abigail had a good heart but wished the maid possessed more moral refinement. *Oh no, I'm beginning to sound just like Father. That will never do. What I should do is focus on solving the latest dilemma of our travels.*

Mary pushed her empty bowl away and collected her courage. "Excuse me, please." Her crisp voice interrupted the low murmured conversation of the others in the common room.

She waited until all except the dark stranger by the fireplace turned her way.

She cleared her throat. "*Excuse* me."

He slowly turned his head and regarded her with a cool stare.

Much better. "I beg your pardon, but my maid and I need a guide to the castle."

Silence settled upon the company, an odd, heavy sort of stilted air.

The innkeeper, who'd been brushing the coats hanging on pegs by the door, blinked. His gaze flickered past Mary and then back. "And why do ye wish to go to the castle?"

"I must speak to the earl."

"I dinna know aboot that. The earl dinna take well to visitors."

"Aye," said a man by the window. "He's a recluse."

His friend added, "He ne'er comes to Aberdeen, neither. Not seen 'im there once't."

That was disheartening.

Abigail put down her spoon. "Why's that? He ain't maimed, is he?"

An awkward silence followed this.

MacEllis cleared his throat nervously. "O' course the earl ain't maimed. He's—"

"Scarred," came the deep and rich voice of the dark stranger. "He was injured in a fire many years ago. He does not like being seen."

Abigail wrinkled her nose. "Disfigured, is he? Pity, that."

"It doesn't matter," Mary said impatiently. "I *must* speak with him. 'Tis a matter of grave import. My brother's *life* depends upon it."

A cold smile flickered across the man's face. "That is certainly dramatic."

She met his gaze evenly. "It's true, too."

"Does the earl know this brother of yours?"

"Yes. My brother is Michael Hurst."

The innkeeper started. "Michael Hurst? The adventurer as writes them articles in the *Morning Post*?"

"You've heard of him, then."

"Aye," MacEllis said in a reverent tone. "The vicar borrows the paper from Lord Erroll and reads us Hurst's adventures e'ery time one is in the paper."

The vicar fairly beamed. "The columns are very well written. Hurst is a modern-day hero."

Several of the men nodded.

Mary smiled, feeling proud. Only she and Michael knew the truth about his columns: that she had written every one of them.

As Michael's exploits became more well-known, the editor of the *Morning Post* had approached Michael at a meeting of the Royal Society and requested that he submit to the newspaper a personal account of one of his trips to acquire an historical artifact. Between trips at the time, Michael had agreed to do so, but within two days was offered the opportunity to embark on yet another adventure.

As a result, the story was never written, but the editor refused to allow the matter to die. He wrote constantly asking for the promised article.

On a whim, Mary offered to pen it to quiet the editor's clamor. Michael had encouraged her, saying she could keep the profits if she promised to write him taller than his mere six feet one inch. Laughing, she'd agreed. She'd not only made him taller, but she'd used her fertile imagination to push the story far beyond the boundaries of reality.

The resulting article was a huge success and the editor had demanded more stories. With a bank check for an astonishing five pounds in her hand and Michael's encouragement, Mary had done so.

The innkeeper cleared his throat, doubt plain on his broad face. "Miss, meanin' no disrespect, but ye canno' be Michael Hurst's sister. He dinna have any."

Her smile faded. "He does, too. He has three, in fact."

One of the men by the window said in a voice of authority, "He dinna mention a sister in his columns."

She narrowed her gaze and said in a sharp tone, "He doesn't mention his mother or father, either, yet I can assure you he was not found as a fully formed babe beneath a cabbage leaf."

This caused some snorts of amusement. But it was the quick, appreciative glance from the dark stranger that made her smile.

"Hurst has had some amazin' adventures." MacEllis rubbed his chin and eyed her thoughtfully. "Did he really wrestle a python wit' his bare hands?"

"Yes." But Mother didn't know about that one; Michael had hidden the newspaper when it arrived.

The vicar leaned forward, his thin face alight. "If—when ye see Mr. Hurst, pray tell him that we here in Aberdeen are faithful followers of his."

"I'll mention it to him the next time I see him." *Please God, let that soon. What if he doesn't come home—ever?*

She had to swallow a lump in her throat before she could speak again. "It's because of my brother that I *must* see the Earl of Erroll."

The innkeeper shifted uneasily from one foot to the other, his gaze flickering past her and then back. "Miss, ye canno' just—"

"I will take you," said a deep voice, husky with a Scottish accent.

Mary turned toward the dark stranger. "*You?*"

He stood and she realized how truly large he was. He was larger than any other man in the room, even larger than her brother William, who stood at six feet three inches.

Abigail let out her breath in a whoosh and said in a whisper that was no whisper at all, "Whooo, missus, but he's a fine un, ain't he?"

There was no disguising the admiration in her tone, and Mary had to agree.

The emerald eyes glinted at her; his hard, fine mouth was firm above his scarf; his black hair was a stark contrast to his golden skin. "I happen to be traveling up the cliff road and I can take you directly to the castle." One brow lifted. "If you wish."

Mary collected herself. There was something about the man's husky dark voice that sent a shiver of almost recognition through her. "How much will you charge for the assistance?"

"How much do you have to pay?" he answered without hesitation.

Abigail giggled. "Gor', but ye do be a cheeky one!"

The man's gaze flicked across Abigail but seemed to

find nothing of interest, for it returned immediately to Mary. "We shall have to leave immediately. I've no wish to arrive at my own destination late."

Mary was relieved that he wasn't impressed with Abigail's busty charms; that could have made their trip even less comfortable.

She gripped her hands together. It was a bit of a risk to allow this stranger to escort them, but what choice did she have? It was either pay this man to assist them, or stay here and perhaps be snowed in for days. And Michael was counting on her.

Green eyes narrowed in impatience. "Well? Do you wish to go to New Slains or not? I don't have all day to stand here whilst you make up your mind."

"I appreciate the offer, Mr. Hay. I will pay you two shillings to drive us to the castle."

"Fine." He strode to the door, moving with an easy grace.

Mary stepped forward. "But—we can't leave this very second."

He stopped and pinned her with a hard look. "Why not?"

"Our horses have not yet rested and—"

"I shall have your things transferred to *my* carriage. My horses are rested and ready to go."

"But I don't think we should—"

The door closed behind him.

"There ye go, miss," Mr. MacEllis said, looking satisfied. "I'll pack ye a wee mite t' eat upon the road. It'll take ye three hours at least to reach the castle, maybe more in this weather."

Mary supposed there was little she could do; she just wished she didn't get such an ominous shivery feeling from the stranger. There was something about him—the way his eyes rested upon her, the manner in which he moved . . . He was a man's man, bold and hard, with little time for the frivolities or warmth of life. Her only reassurance was that his voice was more cultured than those of the other men here. Yet his clothes were too common for him to be the earl's social equal. Perhaps he was a landowner who lived near the earl? That was possible. Still . . .

She turned to the clergyman and moved closer so they wouldn't be overheard. "Excuse me, sir."

He looked up, his gaze suspicious. "Yes, miss?"

"I hate to bother you, but . . . the gentleman who is taking us to the castle. I—I don't know him and I was hoping you—" She could see from the man's confused expression that she was muddying the waters with her hesitation. "Sir, would you vouch for him? Will I and my maid be safe?"

He looked astounded. "God bless ye, o' course ye'll be safe! Why, he's—" The clergyman nodded his head. "Ye need have no fear. He's a good mon, he is."

Her fears calmed, Mary dipped a curtsy. "So I thought, too, but I wished to be certain. Thank you, sir."

She hurried back to the door, where Abigail was shaking out her damp cloak. Mary realized that her unease with the stranger was merely because of her own fears and worries, not because of the stranger's character.

"Well, miss, this worked out well." Abigail tugged her cloak about her shoulders. "I wish we could sleep

here a mite before we pressed on. I'm powerful tired,
I am."

"So am I, but at least we're not hungry. We must be
grateful for what we have." As Michael was fond of saying, *Excitement is never comfortable. When it comes, you just hang
on and hope you don't fall off.*

"Come, Abigail." Mary gripped her cloak closed and
shoved open the heavy door. "I wish to make certain our
trunks are transferred and not set in the snow where
they might get wet." She stepped out into the windy, icy
snow, which stung her face.

"Lor', miss! 'Tis horrible weather."

So it was, but one did what one could. *Michael, just
hold on. I will not let you down.* Head down, she trudged
toward the large coach that sat on the other side of the
inn yard, noting with surprise that her trunks were already lashed to the back. Their rescuer was nowhere in
sight, but a small, spry fellow in a heavy black wool coat
opened the door and gestured for them to enter.

Mary hesitated, staring at the darkened interior
for a second. Then, putting her head down against the
weather, she climbed in.

Letter from Michael to his sister Mary, from a caravan heading for the Sahara Desert:

I can't thank you enough for sending the books I left beside the bed when I was visiting at Michaelmas. What would I do without you looking after me?

Mary, I know you feel that you are tied down with Mother and Father growing older, but you forget that they themselves have always been travelers. If they had the chance to go somewhere, they would take it and they would expect the same of you. Traveling is a family affliction and we all have it.

One day, when I've finished my search for the elusive Hurst Amulet, I want to take you to see pyramids so high your neck will hurt for trying to see the top, rivers so black and deep that you would believe in the River Styx, and verdant fields set among miles of desert sand as if magically transported there.

One day, Mary, we shall see all of that and more.

Two

Three hours later, as snow swirled across the white-covered road and piled in high drifts to either side, the carriage creaked around the final bend of the cliff road and passed through the large stone gates of the castle. They bumped and swayed as the dirt road turned into cobblestones.

Mary lifted the leather curtain and stared up at the huge stone building. New Slains was an amazingly beautiful castle, more of a palace. Several stories high, it soared above them, the large multi-paned windows sparkling in gray-mortared granite walls. The building was impressive and well appointed with rich details about the windows and the huge wide oak doors. Yet it was the further wing that caught her attention. Blackened with soot, the roof completely open to the falling snow, it was a complete ruin. Black-streaked walls were framed by thickly smeared lines where wood shutters had once rested, while half-charred timbers stuck up from the snow like giant bones. Though the damage was not new, no attempt had been made to fix it. Someone had boarded up the windows and chained closed the charred doors, but that was all.

The sight of this damaged and neglected wing was in odd contrast to the smooth gray perfection of the rest of the castle, the overall effect ominous. Mary shivered a little at the sight.

A moan pulled her back into the carriage. She patted Abigail's knee. "Are you still feeling ill?"

Abigail leaned forward, her arms crossed about her stomach, her face pale and pulled. "Gor', tell me we've reached the castle, miss!"

"We have. We should stop any second."

Abigail looked past Mary to the castle walls outside, her pained expression brightening a bit. "I've never been in a castle afore, miss. It's so big, isn't it? I—" She peered more closely out the window as they passed a window streaked with soot. "Why, it's naught but a ruin! It's done burned down."

"Only one wing. The rest of the castle appears to be in excellent condition." She wished she could ask about the circumstances that had led to such destruction, but their escort had offered little in the way of explanation. In fact, though he'd efficiently seen to their luggage, he'd said not a word but had climbed upon the coach seat with his assistant and they'd set off immediately.

She had to admit she'd been a little disappointed that he hadn't attempted to at least see how they were faring. But hour after hour had passed and the carriage slowed only when the way grew excessively steep or slick, and she and Abigail were left quite alone.

Finally, the carriage turned sharply and pulled up to the wide oak doors, the carriage jolting as it stopped. Abigail sighed with relief. "Gor', miss, I've ne'er been on such a horrid road."

"It was very narrow and bumpy, wasn't it?"

"Aye, and straight off the cliff in places." Abigail drew a shuddering breath. "Thank goodness we're here."

Mary couldn't agree more. Between the dangerously winding road, the rapidly deteriorating weather, and Abigail's moaning, the trip had not been pleasant. It would have been even more unpleasant if they hadn't been in such a surprisingly luxurious carriage, complete with well-sprung leather seat-backs, a foot warmer, and red velvet trim on the thick cushions.

The carriage had to be the possession of a very wealthy family. She didn't know why Mr. Hay had agreed to help them, or what his connection was to New Slains Castle—if he even had one. Perhaps now her questions would be answered.

She waited until the door swung open and the dark stranger appeared, large and imposing, his coat covered in snow, his muffler wrapped about his neck and covering the lower half of his face until only his green eyes showed.

His cool gaze flickered across Abigail, taking in her pinched expression, and then on to Mary, who met his indifferent gaze with an interested one of her own. He reached down and unlatched the steps, making sure they were in place before he stepped back to allow them to alight.

As Mary gathered her cloak, the front doors to the castle creaked open and several impressively liveried footmen rushed down the stone steps toward the carriage. Mr. Hay turned to speak to them, his voice muffled by his scarf and the wind.

The footmen halted, looking uncertain. He snapped another order, and two of the footmen rushed forward to take the trunks, while the rest moved respectfully out of the way.

Their coachman/guide turned and held out his gloved hand to Mary. "You have arrived at New Slains Castle."

His voice washed over her like the brush of dark velvet. "Thank you," she returned, aware of how mundane her own voice sounded next to his.

She knew very little about Scottish accents, but his was different from the ones she'd thus far encountered. It was fainter, more hidden, rounding out a word here and there. It was also far more attractive, and she had to suppress an inane desire to make him speak more.

He lifted a brow and she realized he was still holding out his hand. She gathered her skirts and finally placed her hand in his.

Though their hands were separated by their gloves, she still felt something odd, a wave of awareness, as if just by that firm clasp, something momentous was about to occur. It was a silly thing to feel, and an even sillier one to believe, but she couldn't deny it was there. She withdrew her hand as quickly as she could, her face heated.

She couldn't shake the feeling that she somehow knew this man, or of him, though the idea was preposterous. She'd never met him before and would likely never see him again. Her reaction was simply a combination of exhaustion and gratitude that he'd assisted her.

As she took a step toward the castle entryway, her boot hit a patch of ice. For a second she wavered, struggling to catch her balance when a strong hand grasped hers once again, an arm slipping about her waist.

Instantly, the world steadied. Mary found herself staring up into the stranger's eyes, aware of her heart thundering madly in her throat. It was a heady feeling, whatever it was, and she allowed her fingers to tighten over his. His green gaze locked onto hers with an intensity that let her know that he, too, felt that tingle of awareness.

Heat flew through her and she was aware of how her shoulder pressed against his broad chest, how strong his arm was where it encircled her waist, warming her the same way a cup of delicious hot chocolate might.

Just as suddenly as he'd caught her, he released her and stepped away. "The stone is icy. Watch your step."

She nodded mutely, wondering at how skin prickled with heat. *Good God, what is this? I have never been so affected.*

She had to know what it was. Without a word, Mary reached out and took his hand once again and waited. It took less than a second for her body to tingle again. Amazed, she looked up at him and tightened her fingers on his.

His brows snapped down as his gaze flickered to

where her hand was swallowed by his larger one. "You shouldn't—"

"Miss?" Abigail called weakly as she stood in the doorway of the coach. "I think I might be sick after all."

With a muffled curse, Mr. Hay released Mary's hand and reached out to assist an obviously weak-kneed Abigail to the ground.

Mary rubbed her tingling hand, her heart beating irregularly. *Goodness, that was certainly interesting.* She didn't know what it meant, but she hoped she'd find out.

"Lud, miss, I'm done fer." Abigail shivered miserably as their rescuer handed her over to the nearest footman. "I'd give me left teat fer some hot stew and a fire to sit beside."

The stranger's eyes quirked—had that been a smile? Mary couldn't be sure.

"Abigail didn't enjoy the winding road," Mary explained.

"So I see. You look well enough, though."

"I'm an excellent traveler. I just wish I had the opportunity to do more."

He sent her a curious glance.

"La, miss!" Abigail shivered. "If me left teat ain't enough fer a cup o' stew, I'll offer me right one as well, and—"

"Abigail, *please!*" Mary pretended not to notice the astounded gaze of the footman.

Their rescuer's eyes blazed with humor. "I'm sure the earl is at least hospitable enough that you'll find yourself before a warm fire *and* some hot stew and still keep your, ah, personal possessions."

Mary murmured, "We can only hope."

He shot her a quick glance, his face warmed with laughter.

Mary's breath caught in her throat. *Good God, he's beautiful when he smiles.*

There was no other word for it. His stern face relaxed, his fine lips curved from their harsh line into a warm and generous smile, and his eyes crinkled in the most amazing way. He was like two different men.

Their rescuer turned to the waiting footmen. "Take these trunks inside and escort the ladies to the library. They wish an audience."

There was a scurry of activity as his requests were fulfilled.

Mary raised her brows. He was certainly cavalier in how he spoke to another man's servants. Though he hadn't been any less cavalier in his treatment of her and Abigail, really.

The closest footman bowed. "My l—"

"I will return to the stables with the coach." He favored Mary and Abigail with a faint bow. "Good evening, ladies." With that far-too-brief farewell, he turned and proceeded to the carriage.

"Wait!" The word sprang from Mary's lips before she knew what she was about. Standing in the courtyard, surrounded by the exquisitely outfitted footmen in the shade of a massive castle, her only companion a coach-sick maid, the awkwardness of her mission came crashing upon her.

She was about to enter this forbidding abode to ask a desperately needed favor from a man she'd never met.

For a moment, she wanted to somehow borrow some of the easy strength that seemed to sit on their rescuer's broad shoulders.

She hurried up to Mr. Hay, who stood beside the front wheel. She gulped at the cool curiosity in his gaze. "Pardon me, but . . . will you wait for us? We shouldn't be long, for I only need to ask the earl a question, and then we'll wish to return to—"

"No."

"I will pay—"

"You may keep your money."

Her shoulders sagged. "But how will I get back to our carriage at the inn?"

He shrugged. "If you request it, the earl will arrange a return ride to the inn."

"Very well." The snow drifted between them, the faint wind tossing their cloaks around their ankles. There was less than two feet between them, yet it seemed as wide as the North Sea. "I—I wish you'd stay."

His brows lowered. "Why?"

Her face heated. "I don't know anyone here, and it would be nice to see one friendly face."

"You think *I* have a friendly face?" His voice could not convey more surprise.

She looked directly at him. No, he didn't have a friendly face. His expression was too cold, his gaze too piercing. Even more to the point, his muffler was still pulled about his chin and jaw and kept her from clearly seeing his entire expression. "You have a friendly face when you laugh. Right now you look . . ." She tilted her head to one side. "Rather sour, as if you'd just eaten something you didn't like."

His lips twitched. "You don't pull any punches, do you?"

"Should I?"

"No. Not with me." He regarded her for a moment, then said abruptly, "You are afraid to speak to the earl."

"No . . . yes. I mean, I—I don't know him and I must have his help."

"For what?"

She shook her head. "It's a complicated story and I— Please, if you could just stay until I've had a chance to speak to him. It would be comforting to know we had a way back to our carriage." She wondered at her sudden lack of spirit. *I'm just tired. I need to collect myself; Michael would never be so foolish.*

"I told you that I must go. Erroll will see to it that you're taken to your carriage." He turned away to climb into the seat.

She placed a hand on his arm. "Wait. Please."

He looked down at her gloved hand before turning to face her. "I am not staying."

"I know, but . . . perhaps you could help me in another way. What do you know of the earl?"

He shrugged. "Just what I've heard."

"Is he kind?"

Mr. Hay's expression hardened. "No."

"Oh." That was too bad. "I don't suppose you have any hints as to how to best approach him? It could be difficult, as I've never met him before. I'm afraid he might refuse me."

The green eyes narrowed and she wished he would remove that muffler that hid so much of his face. "You should have thought of that before you came."

"I didn't have a choice," she returned, her tone sharp. "It's very important."

The green eyes assessed her head to foot. Finally, he said, "Just tell him the truth . . . if you can."

"Of course I can," she said with a touch of asperity. "I'm not a storyteller, Mr. Hay. I plan on being honest, but I fear the earl will refuse me, even though my brother's welfare depends upon his kindness."

Mr. Hay crossed his arms over his broad chest, but offered no word of encouragement.

Her jaw tightened, a flash of irritation making her snap, "Fine. Thank you for your assistance in making the trip here. I suppose it's too much to expect you to offer to do more." She spun on her heel to march off.

"Hold." The softly spoken word halted her in her tracks.

She turned back to face him.

"I know one thing about the earl that might assist you."

"What?"

"He cannot stand a woman who is anything other than meek."

She curled her nose. "Meek? How archaic."

His eyes seemed to twinkle, though she was certain it was a trick of the pale light. "Erroll is from an old family. Perhaps he's merely acting as he was taught."

"That makes sense."

"Yes, it does. Now, if you'll excuse me, I must be off."

ONE NIGHT IN SCOTLAND

"Of course. Oh, wait. I almost forgot." She dug into her pocket and pulled out her purse to fish out two shillings. It was a dear sum, but a bargain was a bargain. She grasped his wrist and turned his hand palm up, ignoring the way her heart immediately began to gallop as if yearning to run straight toward him. *Such a curious reaction! Am I affected by green eyes? I've certainly never seen any that color.*

She placed the shillings in his gloved hand. "Your payment."

His long fingers curled over the coins. "Of course. I would have hated to have hunted you down and"—his gaze flickered over her in a way she was totally unused to—"demanded payment."

For some reason, the thought of being "hunted down" by this man did not raise a feeling of alarm, but of shivery pleasure. "I am not a woman to avoid paying what is due."

"I didn't think you were." He glanced over her head toward the castle, then bent low. "One more word of caution: The earl has a temper. Do not cross him."

"I have to be meek *and* watch for his temper? What a termagant!"

"You can't say you weren't warned. Now, I must be off." He turned and climbed into the coach seat beside his assistant, his cloak flapping damply in the snow.

Mary watched the coach jerk into motion and cross the courtyard toward the stables. No doubt their rescuer desired to rest his horses before he continued home.

Where was his home? Was it close by? Would *he* be

close by? An unsettling sweep of yearning swept over
her. His presence had made her feel safe, which was
utter nonsense.

"Miss? May we go in?" Abigail called. "I'm chilled to
the bone, I am."

"Of course." Embarrassed that she'd forgotten her
maid, Mary hurried to the woman's side. "Good evening," she said to the footman. "We would like to see
the earl. 'Tis a matter of grave import."

"Of course, miss. This way, please."

Mary climbed the steps, Abigail behind her.

As they stepped into the foyer, the huge oak doors,
trimmed with hammered iron plates and engraved in a
crisscross of battle heraldry, closed behind them with an
ominous thud. Mary looked around her and promptly
forgot to remove her gloves and cloak. Never had she
seen such a staggeringly grand entryway. Even her sisters'
impressive residences didn't measure up to this one.

"Gor!" Abigail's eyes couldn't be wider as her gaze
swept over the marble floor to the wide, double staircase trimmed by a sweeping carved oak railing. The tall
walls were adorned with rich red silk, and decorated
with huge colorful tapestries that swirled with bright
color, while high overhead swung a massive crystal
chandelier. The effect was one of sumptuous grandeur.

*I can only imagine how large the earl's sense of self-importance
must be, living in such a luxurious manner.* Mary's trepidation
increased as she tucked her gloves into her cloak pockets
and handed her damp cloak to a waiting footman.

As she turned to gaze at a huge gilded mirror that
hung to one side of the entryway, a very small, elflike

man approached. Dressed in the sedate clothing of a butler, he possessed a remarkable mane of reddish hair, a pug nose, and a great number of freckles.

He effortlessly took charge of the large number of footmen. With nothing more than the flick of his finger or a short nod, he had them all scurrying hither and yon to do his bidding.

Within seconds, he had Mary's and Abigail's trunks removed for storage, and their cloaks and gloves taken to a cloakroom to dry.

He bowed to Mary. "Good evening, miss. I am Hamish Muir, the butler of New Slains. The earl has asked that you await him in the library."

The earl's servants were very efficient to have already announced her presence. It was a promising sign that he was willing to meet her with so little information. Perhaps Mr. Hay had mistaken the earl, after all.

"Excellent. I would li—"

Abigail placed her hand on Mary's arm. "Miss, do ye mind if instead o' accompanyin' ye, I rest a bit? I'm banged to the knockers after that trip."

Mary took in her maid's pale face. "Yes, of course, although it will leave me with no chaperone. I shall ask that the door be left open and—"

"Miss," the butler said in a smooth tone, "you will not be seeing the earl alone. All of the proprieties will be met without the presence of your maid."

"Oh? Who else will be—"

But the butler was already instructing a footman to escort Abigail to the servants' quarters and had arranged for a warm posset to be delivered to her there.

Finally, Muir turned back to Mary. "Miss, if you'll come this way." The butler gestured toward the largest pair of doors in the hallway. Of elaborately carved wood, they were ten feet tall at the highest point, and arched to fit the graceful door frame. Two large brass knobs, polished to mirror shininess, gleamed against the dark wood like two suspicious eyes.

Steeling herself, Mary followed the butler toward the doors. She grimaced as she caught a glimpse of herself as they passed a large gilt-edged mirror. Her hair was sadly limp after her travels, her gown wrinkled, her face drawn and tired.

She hated presenting herself so and almost requested time to change into a fresh gown, but she didn't wish to delay the meeting.

As she walked behind Muir, the cold outside air seeped around the front doors. She shivered, keenly aware of her wet boots and sopping-wet hem, both leaching every bit of warmth from her body. She could no longer feel her toes, and it was all she could do not to shiver uncontrollably.

Muir knocked once, then opened both panels and stood aside. As Mary passed him, he announced in a rather pretentious voice, "Miss Mary Hurst."

Mary frowned. How had he known her name? She hadn't told him and— Her gaze met the earl's as he turned from stirring the fire.

He was tall, though not as tall as the giant who'd brought her here, and his face was infinitely more patrician. Blue, blue eyes framed by spectacles and light brown hair augmented the almost delicate, pale face of an obvious scholar. Though the man was dressed fashionably, his shoulders were stooped and rounded, as befitted a man who spent hours over his tomes.

He looked so much like the image Mary had fixed in her mind of a scholar earl that she immediately felt at ease and hurried forward, hands outstretched. "Lord Erroll, I'm so glad to finally meet you."

The man accepted her hand, sending a startled glance over Mary's shoulder. "Yes, but I'm— That is to say, I'm quite sorry that—"

"For the love of God!" came a deep, rich voice that Mary instantly recognized as Mr. Hay's.

She stiffened as the voice continued, "Neason, don't be a dithering fool. You aren't the one who owes an apology; the lady does: for lying."

Meanwhile, I continue my search for clues as to the final resting place of the Hurst Amulet. The only idea we have of the size and shape of the amulet is on a portrait of Queen Elizabeth, who received it as a gift from the laird of Clan MacLean after he stole it from the Hurst family. Family legend has it that Elizabeth became afraid of the mystical properties of the amulet and she gave it to her chief adviser, Walsingham, and asked him to dispose of it.

After that, we have no record for centuries— until ten years ago, when an antiquities dealer brought us a drawing of the amulet and claimed that it was hidden in a tomb outside of Thebes, or Luxor, as the city is now called.

I have seen no sign of it yet, but I will not rest until I do. It has become my main goal, my obsession, and I refuse to give up. It may be madness, but it is an exciting, challenging madness for all that.

THREE

$\mathcal{M}$ary slowly turned around. There, standing by the large brace of windows, arms crossed over his broad chest, stood their dark, enigmatic rescuer.

It was suddenly, and painfully, obvious that he was no mere coachman, for no servant attended earls in their private libraries or called them by their given name.

He'd removed his greatcoat; the thick muffler was gone. In its place was a silk scarf that wrapped about his neck and swathed his throat and lower jaw. Mary eyed the man's black silk cravat. Her brother Robert was something of a dandy, and she was certain he would have laughed at Mr. Hay's hurried attempt at fashion. No one tied their cravat so that it covered their lower jaw and a portion of their chin. Even the dandies with their high shirt collars allowed their faces to show.

The entire effect was secretive and disturbing, the black silk making the man's golden skin seem even more exotic, his green eyes even more compelling.

His eyes glinted at her as he lifted a brow, his mouth quirked in an amused half-grin. "Surprised?"

"Very," she answered truthfully. "I thought to never see you again." Two minutes ago, she would have been glad for his presence, for at least she would have known one person in the room. But to see him so unexpectedly, and conveying such a smug superiority, was something of a shock.

"Erroll, you haven't introduced me," he said now, the smile on his face gently mocking her.

Mary turned an inquiring gaze toward the earl, who managed an apologetic smile. "Forgive me. This is my cousin, Err—Er, Angus Hay."

She eyed Mr. Hay with a narrowed gaze. "*You* are the earl's cousin?"

He bowed, his green eyes glinting darkly.

"You should have told me."

"When? While you were demanding a guide to the castle? Or while you were thrusting pennies into my hands?"

Her face burned. "How did you get here before me? You went to the stables."

"Where I left my coach, and came in through the rear door." He nodded to the far end of the room, where a small, narrow door paneled exactly like the wall could barely be seen, one probably used by the servants. He shrugged. "I frequently enter the house from the kitchens, don't I, Neason?"

The earl grimaced. "Angus is quite an informal sort of man."

His given name fit him well, she decided. Angus meant "one choice," and if ever there was a man who stood solid and strong, surely this was he. "Lord Erroll, your cousin played a trick upon me and pretended to be a coachman."

Erroll had the grace to look embarrassed, but Cousin Angus was not so easily shamed. "I played no tricks. You assumed and I didn't correct; that is not a trick."

The earl cleared his throat. "Angus, how did you come to meet this young lady?"

"I was at the Thorn and Thistle, having a taste of their superior brandy, when this young lady entered and said she needed a ride to the castle."

"Which you were reluctant to do," she added sharply. It was galling to think of how "Cousin Angus" must have been laughing at her. And to think that she'd asked him his thoughts on the earl! What a fool she'd been. *Consider it a lesson learned,* she told herself, straightening her shoulders.

Hay shrugged, his broad shoulders moving with the grace of a born athlete. "I had no wish to leave my place beside the fire."

The earl didn't look pleased. "Miss Hurst, please forgive my cousin. His sense of humor isn't what it should be."

"It isn't his sense of humor I worry about, it's his sense of honor."

Mr. Hay's gaze narrowed on her. Mary's cheeks heated, but she refused to look away. *Blast him for mocking me!* No simple quirk of humor would make a man like this pretend to be a mere coachman. No, he'd wished to embarrass her; she was certain that had been his intent. If only she knew why.

Mary shifted from one tired foot to the other, suddenly aware of how weary she was from her adventures. She turned to the earl. "My lord, enough of this. I came to request your help."

The earl blinked. "My help? But I'm—" He gulped. "I mean, yes, of course. Anything I can do—"

"Bloody hell," Hay muttered. "At least find out what she wants before you agree."

"I was going to ask," the earl said stiffly.

Hay's expression clearly said he thought otherwise.

Mary clenched her fists. Until she'd entered this room she'd thought of Mr. Hay as her rescuer, as someone who was on her side. Now she was discovering that he was anything but.

Feeling misused, she locked her tormenter with a haughty glare. "Sir, this conversation doesn't concern you."

"I think it does."

"Well, I think it doesn't. So if you'll kindly stop being so rude, we would *all* appreciate it."

Mr. Hay's gaze narrowed. "Careful, Miss Hurst. I warned you about the earl's temper."

"And I should warn *you* that I'm not going to stand by while you—"

"Please!" The earl looked from one to the other, his exasperation clear. "Angus, please allow Miss Hurst to speak."

Unlike his dark and inscrutable cousin, the earl's expression was harried, but kind. Mary almost felt sorry for the poor man.

He turned to her now and offered her a conciliatory smile. "Perhaps we should all take a moment and calm down a bit and— I know! We should have a drink. Miss Hurst, you must be cold. Pray come and stand by the fire and I'll pour you a glass of ratafia."

"I'll do it," Hay stated.

Surprised, Mary raised her brows at him, but he paid her no heed. Frustrated of even this little nibble of acknowledgment, she scowled at his broad back as she went to a nearby sideboard, where a decanter sat.

The earl indicated a chair, but she shook her head. "I'd rather stand, thank you. I've been sitting all evening."

"In the cold." Mr. Hay added, "You need something to warm you."

"Thank you, but I don't need a drink," she said.

"I do," Hay said bluntly. "'Tis bloody freezing outside and I need something to thaw out my bones. It was quite cold on top of that damned carriage."

Erroll gawked. "You . . . you rode on *top*?"

"Like a coachman."

The earl shook his head. "There's no telling what you'll do next."

"I couldn't very well ride inside. Not with such a prim, correct passenger."

Mary stiffened, then turned to the earl. "My lord, may I suggest that we continue this conversation *without* your cousin? There's really no need for him to be here."

The earl flushed, glancing at Mr. Hay. "I—I—"

"Miss Hurst has come to talk to you about your friend Michael Hurst. She says she is his sister."

"I *am* his sister."

Hay opened a door on the sideboard and set out three glasses. "Of course." He poured a generous splash of amber liquid into two of the glasses, hesitated, then poured half the amount into the third glass. This one he brought to Mary.

The earl eyed the glass with obvious trepidation. "Angus, do you think Miss Hurst should have brandy? It's much too strong for a woman."

"Nonsense. Our guest is made of stronger stuff than most women, aren't you, Miss Hurst?"

The mocking voice stiffened Mary's spine as nothing else could have. She took the glass and said with as much sangfroid as she could muster, "I've had brandy before."

She'd had a sip at her brother-in-law's house. He'd dared her to take a drink and she had, coughing the entire time, much to his delight.

As soon as Mr. Hay had his back to her, she regarded her glass. She took a cautious sniff, curling her nose.

Mr. Hay had just turned, a glass in his hand, his gaze narrowing as he observed her. "Just drink the damn stuff, will you? I'm not trying to poison you. It's good brandy."

He handed the earl the other glass, then returned to the table to claim the last for himself.

Mary took a cautious sip; the liquid sent smooth warmth down her throat and calmed her shivers. *Oh, this is* much *better than Hugh's brandy.* She'd have to tease him about it when she returned home. The thought of her brother-in-law's mock distress at such a claim made Mary smile.

Her two older sisters were twins, both of them staggeringly beautiful and happily married to brothers from Clan MacLean. The younger of the twins, Triona, and her husband, Hugh MacLean, and Hugh's three lively daughters were frequent visitors at the vicarage.

Mary loved it when Triona and her family came to visit. For days the rickety vicarage would be alive with laughter and giggles, reminding them all of younger days.

Still, as happy as Hugh and Triona were, Mary knew the couple had faced their own difficulties. For years, they'd wished for a child of their own, but fate and Higher Powers had not seen fit to grace them . . . so far.

Mary wasn't worried about it, though. Their grandmother, known affectionately as "Mam," was a healer and she'd said that all could be made right. Mam hadn't said how such a miracle would happen, but Mary had faith in her grandmother's expertise. If Mam said all would be right, then it would. If only Triona would believe it, too.

Mr. Hay finished his glass and poured himself another before he crossed to the largest chair by the fireplace and dropped into it.

"Angus!" the earl said softly. "You didn't invite Miss Hurst to sit first."

"If this particular lady wished to sit, she would, whether you invited her or not." He stretched his long legs before the fire and crossed them at the ankle before turning his dark gaze her way. "Very well, Miss *Hurst.* You demanded to be brought to Slains and here you stand. Now tell us what you want so we may send you back to your carriage with all due haste."

The earl sent Mary a self-conscious glance. "I'm sorry for my cousin's rudeness. He doesn't enjoy the pleasantries of society."

"Nuisances, more like," the deep voice rumbled.

The earl ignored his cousin and gestured to a chair a safe distance from his cousin, and yet still warmed by the fire. "Pray have a seat, Miss Hurst."

"Thank you." This time she took the chair he offered, more to make a point to Angus, though he didn't seem to notice. She arranged her skirts so that the hem might dry faster while she addressed the earl. "My lord, I came here at the behest of my brother, Michael Hurst. He is in danger and in dire need of your assistance."

Mr. Hay lowered his glass, his gaze pinned on Mary. "*What* danger?"

She wished the earl would ask the questions and not Mr. Hay, but one glance told her that such an occurrence was highly unlikely. The earl was entirely satisfied with his cousin being in charge. "Michael has been captured by a sufi in the Holy Lands. Here, read it for yourself." She reached into her reticule and pulled out Michael's last letter and held it out to the earl.

Erroll glanced at his cousin, who nodded once. The earl reached for the missive.

Mary noted the exchange with exasperation. *The earl is entirely under his cousin's power! What a pity, for I've never met such a shockingly untamed male.*

Erroll looked up from the letter. "Who is William?"

"Our brother. He is a sea captain for the East India Company."

The earl nodded and turned his attention to the letter.

"Well?" Mr. Hay said impatiently.

Erroll finished the letter and then gave it to his cousin. "It's as she said—Hurst is held prisoner. The letter appears to be real, for as you'll see, the hand-writing is very similar to Hurst's." The earl shook his head. "Such a pity. Hurst was a fine collector, one of the best."

"I beg your pardon," Mary said frostily. "Michael *is* a fine collector, not *was*. As you can see from that letter, he is not dead, but is being held for ransom."

Erroll had the grace to look chagrined. "I'm sorry. I didn't mean to imply— It's just that—" He sent a quick glance at his cousin who gave an almost imperceptible shake of his head.

The earl paused an awkward moment and then said, "Of course your brother is still alive. It's just that when we last heard from Hurst, he was in an especially dangerous area, and then this letter—"

"He is not dead," the giant by the fire said bluntly. "They have nothing to gain from such an act, and every-thing to gain from his being alive. However, if too much time passes . . ."

Mary's stomach roiled at the thought. *Please God, let Michael be alive and healthy when we find him.*

Erroll frowned. "Angus, perhaps we shouldn't speak of this any longer. It's distressing our guest."

Hay's eyes gleamed. "I would be concerned . . . *if* I thought she was really Hurst's sister. We've known Michael for seven years. He's a regular visitor here and he writes at least once a month, if not more."

The earl nodded. "And when he finds what he thinks is an important find, he—"

"—sends it here *with* his own analysis," Mary said impatiently. "He also often includes a complete set of drawings of the item in question. I know, because I handle most of Michael's correspondence when he's in England." She did his drawings, too, but that was neither here nor there.

The earl appeared impressed. Cousin Angus merely looked impatient.

Mary continued, "Michael's letter asks for the immediate return of an item he sent you. I *must* have that item, or as you say, he could be—" The word wouldn't come from her lips, try as she might.

The earl shifted uneasily. "There's the rub, though. When Michael sent us the—"

"Don't say another word." Cousin Angus's dark expression brokered no argument. "Not until we know for certain she is who she says she is."

Mary realized she was clenching the glass in her hand so hard that her fingers ached. She forced herself to relax. She'd thought the hardest part of her trip had been traveling to this forsaken castle. Apparently her travails were just beginning. She sighed heavily at the thought, wishing she wasn't so exhausted. The weeks of travel had been wearying and her body ached even more after the rough rocking of the carriage on the narrow road to the castle. She felt as if she'd been pummeled head to toe with a sack of flour.

She took another sip of her drink, allowing the flash of warmth to bolster her flagging spirits. She'd naively thought that her biggest challenge after finally arriving at New Slains Castle would be making the earl understand the importance of her quest. Instead, her very identity was now in question.

The entire ordeal seemed momentarily overwhelming.

She turned to the earl. "Erroll, you've known Michael for years. He must have mentioned me at some point."

"I've never heard him mention his family."

"Because he never did," Hay said bluntly, his green gaze as hard as the emeralds that adorned the gold cat Michael had once recovered from a pharaoh's tomb.

Mary frowned. "He didn't mention our two sisters, who married into the MacLean family?"

"No."

"Or our two brothers? Our father, the vicar? Our mother, who has failing eyesight? He never mentioned *any* of us?"

The earl shook his head regretfully. "Hurst made some reference to growing up in a vicarage once or twice, but you could have easily gotten that from the serial he writes for the *Post*."

Mary frowned. "He *had* to mention me. I wrote all of his correspondence, cataloged his finds, illustrated his research and— You cannot mean it! He never mentioned me *once*?"

The earl spread his pale hands. "I'm sorry."

"That ingrate! When I see him, I'll—" Mary almost stomped her foot. "I can't believe I have to prove myself to you! I traveled for *days* to get here, through the most horrid weather, sleeping in inns in lumpy beds, and once in the carriage when the mud had washed away part of the road and we could not get by. In addition, I spent hours and hours jolting about in that-that- *damned* coach—" She caught Mr. Hay's amused gaze and her cheeks heated. "I'm sorry, that wasn't very ladylike. I am just so frustrated. I made it all of the way here, and you don't even believe I'm Michael's sister! I—I just don't know what to say."

Hay quirked a brow. "Did you really think you could just show up, announce you're a relative of a missing man, wave a supposed letter from the man in our faces, and we'd just release a valuable item into your care?"

When he put it that way, it *did* sound a bit unbelievable.

Good heavens. What am I to do now?

No answer came to her usually fertile mind. She was warmer now because of the brandy, but her mind was fuzzier and less direct.

All of the trials of the past two weeks pressed in upon her. She was hungry, tired, and on the verge of tears, which was very unlike her. She wasn't usually a weepy sort, a fact Michael told her showed that she would make a great adventurer, but right now she wanted nothing more than to burst into tears.

But Michael wouldn't have been so weak, and neither would she. *This is good practice,* she told herself as she tamped down her tears. *One day, I will be an Egyptologist, too.*

After her sisters had wed, Mary had been the only female in the household other than Mother. Somehow, in assisting with the household duties, and watching her brothers grow and leave for their own exciting careers, time had passed and she'd been left at home, the last chick to leave the nest.

The last, but the most eager to do so.

There simply hadn't been any opportunities for her. Though she was well educated, that meant little to a female unless one wished to be a governess, which she most expressly did not. To be paid so little for so much work seemed only slightly less restrictive than a prison.

She could have married and set up her own household; she'd had her fair share of offers. But she hadn't fallen in love with any of her suitors, worthy though a few of them had been.

Maybe she'd waited too long. Over the years, her interest had been sparked by one thing and one thing only: writing Michael's articles for the paper.

That was her secret life. The one thing only she and Michael and no one else knew. She'd received a pretty penny for the tales, and it had given her something to do to pass the time between darning the linens, attending the few country soirees that occurred in town, and escorting Mother to church and on her visits.

But even more, writing the articles had allowed her imagination to fly. Though she wrote of Michael's adventures, in her imagination it had been she who'd sailed ships into storms, and forced open the door to a lost tomb to see the glitter of gold through the thick dust, and ridden across the hot desert on a lumpy camel.

Somewhere along the way, it had dawned on her that she, too, could be an adventurer. And now, here was her first chance to prove herself worthy of that title.

"Miss . . . Hurst," the earl said. "We—at least I—would like to be fair in this. My cousin and I aren't saying you're an impostor or anything so impolite. We—"

"Actually, that is exactly what I was saying," Hay said bluntly, watching her over the rim of his glass. "But whoever you are, we won't give you the item."

"But Michael's letter said—"

"We have a letter from Michael Hurst, too." Hay nodded to Erroll. "Show it to her."

Erroll crossed to the huge desk that sat to one side, pulled a key from his pocket, unlocked the drawer, and pulled out a number of letters. He rifled through them, found one in particular, and brought it to Mary.

She recognized the handwriting right away. No one had a worse spider's scrawl than her brother. She read the letter, aware that both the earl and his cousin were watching her.

Erroll,

I'm sending you this item to hold for me, as someone is trying to steal it. Trust no one. If someone should request it—even someone we know well—refuse them. I cannot say more now, but it's imperative that you keep this safe, for it's a vital key to discovering the Hurst Amulet.

I will write more soon,
Michael

Mary refolded the letter, stunned. *Heavens! What do I do now?*

The earl sighed. "I'm sorry." He took the letter from her nerveless fingers and returned it to the desk, where he locked it away.

"Well?" Hay said, his voice velvet soft.

Well, indeed. "It is most unlike Michael to write such a brief letter, so we must assume he was in a hurry." She pursed her lips. "However, I now know why you don't trust me; he warned you someone would come for the box."

Hay's gaze narrowed. "No one said it was a box."

She sent him an impatient glance. "I catalog Michael's finds, so I know what he's sent and to whom. An onyx box was the only item of real interest in the last invoice."

Angus and the earl exchanged a look. "Angus, perhaps she *is*—"

"Nonsense," Hay scoffed. "Whoever comes after the artifact would know exactly what it is, too."

Mary sipped her brandy and considered this. "That's true, I suppose. I wonder who he thought would come for the artifact. Your letter is dated two weeks after the one he sent us. I can only assume he forgot to mention he'd asked you to guard it so closely when he sent William to fetch it." She tapped a finger against her glass, struggling to make her tired, fuzzy mind grasp some elusive fact. "I didn't realize the onyx box had something to do with the Hurst Amulet. That's a new development."

"It was to Angus, too."

At Mary's surprised look, the earl flushed. "Your brother is much closer to Angus."

Mary looked at Hay with surprise. "He never mentioned you at all—just the earl."

"And he never mentioned you at all, either, so perhaps 'tis a pattern." Angus shrugged. "It doesn't matter. What matters is that I will not give you the onyx box, so there is really no more to be said."

"What can I do to prove myself?"

His green gaze, framed by thick black lashes, flicked across her, and Mary was painfully aware of how travelworn she must appear. Her hair was mashed and curly from the damp snow, her nose had to be red from the cold weather, her hands red and chapped, her gown creased—she couldn't look worse than she did at this moment.

She attempted to smooth her gown. "I realize I don't appear to advantage right now, but I have been traveling for some days and—"

"Don't be foolish," Angus said gruffly. "I only looked at you because Mr. Hurst is neither blond, nor does he possess any features even vaguely resembling your own."

"Oh! Michael takes after Father, while I look like Mother."

Mary thought she heard Erroll murmur, "How convenient."

Mary sent him a surprised glance. Up until now, the earl had seemed almost sympathetic. He colored when she caught his gaze, but didn't offer an explanation. *Cousin Angus's disbelief is catching. I shall have to persuade them both of my identity now.*

The thought was almost more than she could bear.

She brushed a damp curl from her cheek and realized that her hands were now shaking slightly.

Unaware of her precarious hold on her emotions, Mr. Hay continued, "Your coloring is not only different, but there's not a single physical attribute that is the same: your eyes, your nose, your—"

"Michael broke his nose five years ago in a riding accident, so that explains that. Also, he has always been on the thin side, while I . . ." Her cheeks heated and she shrugged. "Like all siblings, we have some differences. But I *do* know about his nose."

"Which you could have read about in his writing for the *Post*." Erroll spread his white hands in a deprecating manner. "I'm sorry, but I am quite fond of Mr. Hurst's newspaper serial and have read every installment. I remember that he mentioned his broken nose and how he received it. Anyone who's read those stories would know that."

Mary set her glass on a small side table with a decided *thunk*. "I'm done with this silliness. My brother's life hangs in the balance, and I have only three weeks to deliver his artifact to the port at Whitby. I cannot, *will not*, leave without it."

Angus watched his guest over the rim of his glass. She was certainly determined; no one could doubt that. But it was laughable that she should show up pretending to be Hurst's sister. Why bother with such a far-fetched pretense?

The letter she'd brought was convincing—certainly the handwriting was similar to Hurst's—but she'd offered no other proof. That, added to the fact that Hurst had never mentioned a sister of any kind, confirmed the truth for Angus. Here was the impostor that Hurst had warned would come to steal the onyx box. *Thank goodness Hurst warned me that such a thing might happen, or I might have been fooled by "Mary Hurst" and her innocent air.*

Whoever she was, she was a taking thing, small and plumply curved, her face heart-shaped, her hair a rich golden blond that complemented her creamy skin, which was pinkened by the wind. She was a riotous mass of soft color; even her gray-and-pink pelisse and gown seemed to bring lightness into the winter of his study.

He was being fanciful, but there was something about her that made him wary.

To be honest, he knew exactly what that something was. His gaze flickered past her to the large portrait over the desk where a slender, graceful blond woman stood, her hand proudly upon the blond curly head of a small child who leaned against her knee. If Angus looked at the portrait in a certain way and imagined his guest a bit thinner, her hair blonder, he could see a clear resemblance between the two.

Having the woman here, in his study, brightening the air just by breathing, exactly the way Kiera used to do, was an exquisite pain . . . and a deep, resounding pleasure. The combination was heady and toxic. Still, he shouldn't reopen old wounds, especially ones as deep as these.

As if she knew his thoughts, his guest tilted her head to one side and gave a calm, considering look that was all too familiar to his ravaged heart. "You are determined not to believe me," she said. "There must be *something* I can do to prove myself. Some evidence that will satisfy you."

Though her voice didn't have Kiera's Scottish lilt, it possessed the same husky undertones that made Angus's chest tighten. "There might be something," he heard himself reply.

This was why he'd agreed to escort this woman to the castle. The instant she'd stepped into the common room at the inn, he'd seen the resemblance. For a wild, unthinking minute, he'd thought it *was* Kiera . . . beautiful, sweet, innocent Kiera, who had died in a fire so many years ago, a fire he saw every night when he closed his eyes—

Damn it, stop this. Do not rethink what only pains you. Discover this woman's secrets and then send her away.

Angus's fingers lifted to the scarf that covered his neck and lower jaw. Beneath the smooth material, he could feel the hard ridges of the scars he'd earned that night. Though horrible, they were nothing to the scars on his soul. They'd only been married a year, and Kiera had been his one true love. He would never love like that again, and it was that thought that desolated him and left him aching and alone.

He kept thinking he'd overcome that time in his life, yet here he was with this stranger. Someone he had great cause to distrust, and yet he'd brought to his house because of nothing more than a passing resemblance.

Damn it, this is wrong. I should send her away now, before I make a fool of myself.

Yet the woman's face drew him, soothed him at the same time it tormented him. The flicker of the fire made her hair gleam with golden softness until his hands ached to touch it. Unbound, would it come to her hips, as Kiera's had done? Or would it—

He stood so abruptly that his chair recoiled, slamming back against a small table and knocking it over.

The action startled both Neason and their unwanted guest, and Angus found himself looking directly into her velvet brown eyes . . . and was instantly lost.

Who sent this woman? Who knows my weakness? Did they think they'd shock me so much that I'd give her the artifact without verifying her story?

A slow anger simmered through him. If that was the plan, then the villain had grossly misread the situation. He was now more determined than ever to find out who was behind this and make them pay.

Who was trying to play him for a fool? Who wanted the artifact that badly? What was it about the onyx box Michael Hurst had sent to New Slains Castle?

"Angus?" Neason's voice was cautious, like a person trying to gently waken someone from a deep slumber.

He heard the concern in his cousin's voice and realized that he was staring at the woman with unabashed fury. She'd pulled back, uncertainty in her gaze.

Uncertainty, but no fear.

Suddenly, with a clarity that almost unnerved him, he knew what he had to do. How to thwart this plan and discover who was at the heart of it.

He crossed to the gold-tasseled bellpull and tugged. Deep in the castle, a low gong sounded.

Within seconds, Muir stood in the doorway. He bowed to Angus. "You called, my lord?"

"My lord?" the woman repeated. Her gaze flew to him, her eyes wide. "*You* are the Earl of Erroll?"

Letter from Michael to his sister Mary, from a camp on an oasis in the Sahara Desert:

So there I was, prone upon the ground. I was furious with the brute who'd put me there. Hands fisted, I raised up to pounce upon the blackguard and give him the beating he deserved when I found myself face-to-face with a cobra.

I cannot tell you whether the animal slithered up to me while I was gathering myself, or if I merely landed near it and it made its presence known as I lifted myself. All I know is that one moment my only thought was blood and vengeance, and the next my blood ran cold as ice as I stared the snake in the eyes.

I wish I could tell you that I leapt to my feet anyway, snake be damned. Or that I wrestled the snake and then fought my opponent. But I saw the icy-cold disdain in the snake's eyes and did the only prudent thing I could—I froze in place. After a long few moments, the snake grew bored and slithered away, as had my opponent. Yet I felt that I had won, for I lived to fight another day.

*F*OUR

*A*ngus bowed to his "guest." Her brown eyes were wide, her lips parted.

She shook her head in confusion. "I don't understand. If you're the earl, then who is—" She gestured toward his cousin.

Neason flushed. "I am Neason Hay, Lord Erroll's cousin. I'm sorry to trick you, but Angus—*we* thought it might be more prudent to discover your purpose here without revealing our hand."

"The deception was no fault of his," Angus said shortly. "I only wanted to discover what trick you might be up to."

"Trick? What sort of trick could I possibly play upon you?"

"Oh, I don't know," he said silkily. "Like someone

showing up with false claims on a priceless artifact? You aren't the first, you know."

She frowned. "I'm not making a false claim."

Neason cleared his throat and Angus realized the butler was still in the room, staring stoically ahead. "Muir, prepare the turret room for our guest."

The butler's gaze flickered. "The *turret* room, my lord?"

"Yes. That will be the best one, I think. Our guest will stay with us for a while. A *very* short while."

Mary didn't like the dismissive tone, but at this moment, the idea of a soft bed appealed strongly. Even this latest unwelcome surprise—that the rude Mr. Hay was actually the earl—didn't register completely. Her mind was simply too exhausted to take it all in, and she realized she was in no condition to carry on a discussion of any kind. She was so tired that her legs trembled, and she wasn't even standing. "Yes, you are right. A good night's rest will bring us all a much clearer vision of how to deal with our situation. Tomorrow I shall think of a way to identify myself to you, and you will—"

"Oh, you'll be staying for more than one night."

She blinked, unable to ignore the threat in that silky growl. "I don't think so."

The earl's green gaze narrowed, his hard mouth barely visible over his scarf. "You will stay here as our guest until we've found a way to identify you."

Mary supposed she should be shocked, but her numb mind could only think with longing about the bed that awaited her. Surely it would be soft, the sheets fresh, the room warm—all of the things she'd missed since she'd left Wythburn Vicarage.

"Do you understand me?" the earl asked impatiently.

"Of course. You wish me to stay longer." She tried to wrap her uncooperative mind about this. "Why?"

"I wish confirmation that you are indeed Michael Hurst's sister. You will stay here until I get it."

"Very well." She turned to the butler. "I must admit I am a bit famished. Would it be possible to—"

"Miss Hurst," the earl interrupted impatiently, "you are not a guest here, but a *prisoner*."

The word sank its talons into her numbed consciousness. As she frowned at Erroll, she wondered at the scarf wrapped about his neck and covering his lower jaw. He was by the fire now and the room was quite warm. If he wore the scarf for effect, he was wasting his time; she had no patience with such fakery and—

"Angus, that's— No, you cannot." Mr. Hay appeared shocked. "You cannot just *tell* the young lady she must stay here."

"Yes, I can. I just did."

Neason shook his head. "But . . . why?"

Angus crossed his arms over his broad chest and locked his gaze on Mary. "Because if she is not who she says she is, then someone sent her—and I will know who."

Mary made a disgusted noise. "I came at Michael's behest. I showed you the letter—"

"It never mentioned you. And Hurst never mentioned you, either. You will stay here until I am certain of your identity. Until then, you may consider yourself a forced guest—or a prisoner—I don't much care which. I only care that you do not leave until we know for certain who you are."

An uncomfortable silence fell, which Mary knew she should break, but couldn't find the energy to do so. She was exhausted, and at the moment, the force of the earl's anger was too heavy for her to throw off.

Mr. Hay asked in a tentative voice, "And if she *is* Hurst's sister?"

"Then she will be free to leave."

She turned her gaze back to the earl. "*With* the box?"

He was silent a second, but then he nodded. "Aye, with the box."

Mary tried to think of the million and one objections she should have had to this plan, but her mind kept returning to the fact that upstairs, inside this grand castle, was a bed—*her* bed.

What would Michael do? He'd take the lemons and make lemonade.

She stood. "Very well, then. I agree to be your prisoner, at least for this one night."

"You will be my prisoner for longer than that."

"We'll discuss that tomorrow." She turned to the butler. "Muir, I believe I am to be remanded into your custody. I hope there is a tray of food involved, for I'm so hungry I could eat a feather pillow."

Muir's blue eyes gleamed appreciatively as he bowed. "I had prepared a tray to be brought here, but I can easily divert it to your chambers, miss."

"Excellent." She turned to her "host." "I'm not certain how a prisoner would bid their captor good night.

'Good night' seems a bit too cheerful and 'sleep well' a false sentiment. I'll settle for a terse and very French *au revoir*."

Mr. Hay uttered an uncertain laugh. "Miss Hurst, you are taking this far more calmly than I would be if I were in your situation."

"You would be calm if you'd grown up with three brothers who were forever locking you in this shed and trapping you in that tack room. The worst part is if they forget you and supper comes and goes. I trust Muir won't allow that to happen."

The butler inclined his head. "Miss, I can promise you that in this house you will not starve."

Mr. Hay stepped forward. "Angus, really! Rethink this. Though she's not showing it, you must be frightening Miss Hurst—"

"*If* that's her name. You are too trusting, Neason. Michael Hurst warned us someone would come for the artifact. This cannot be a coincidence."

Mr. Hay looked uncertain. "I know, and it's certainly damning circumstances, but—" He rubbed his neck. "I just don't know. We're in such a coil."

Mary had to agree.

The butler cleared his throat. "My lord, having never held a young lady *prisoner* before, I must ask how I am to proceed. Shall I send the footmen to the stables to gather some hobbles? Or will a simple lock and key be enough?"

Mary expected the dark earl to snap at such sarcasm, but instead, the fine lips twitched. "Muir, you've been with my family since we were both in short pants.

Forget the hobbles; you know I would never ask you to do anything irredeemable."

"Such as keeping a young lady prisoner?"

"That may be disreputable, but hopefully not irredeemable."

"Och, my lord, 'tis a fine line you walk."

"As ever," the earl agreed. "For now, put Miss Hurst in the turret guest room. Make sure she has everything she needs—her maid, fresh linens, a tray of food, some hot tea—"

"Thank you," she said fervently, her stomach growling.

His calm expression stuttered a bit. "Pardon me?"

"That sounds heavenly. Pray continue."

His gaze narrowed but he turned back to the butler. "Once our guest has been seen to, lock the door on her and her maid and have the footmen stand guard. They are not to allow her to leave her room."

Muir merely bowed. "Very well, my lord."

Right now she'd be happy with a stack of hay in the stable, providing it offered some warmth from the weather.

Mary folded her hands together. "Now that that's settled, I must ask how you propose to ascertain who I am? I hope it doesn't take long for my brother William is to meet me in three weeks' time at the dock in Whitby to take the box to Egypt and arrange an exchange for Michael's freedom."

"I will be glad to tell you. The adventurer Mr. Young frequently stayed with Hurst at his home at Wythram Vicarage. I know, for Hurst complained of Mr. Young's propensity to snore. If that's so, then Young should know you as well."

"I know Mr. Young quite well. Pray write to him immediately. How far away does he live?"

"Three days' ride from here, no more." Angus expected a blistering riposte to this, but all he received was a very tired shrug.

"Fine. I'll be your prisoner—for now." She looked past Angus to the waiting butler. "Let us go, Muir. I am so fatigued that in another ten minutes you will have to assign one of the footmen to carry me."

The butler bowed. "Of course, miss."

Mary made a blind curtsy toward the room. "Good night, then."

Mr. Hay bowed gracefully. "Pray do not fear. We—" He glanced at his cousin. "*We* are not uncivilized."

"Speak for yourself," the earl said, his expression grim. "Sleep if you can, Miss Hurst. It might be a velvet prison, but make no mistake, a prison it is, and will be until we hear from Mr. Young."

Mary gave him a tired smile. "We shall see about that, my lord." With a quick curtsy, she followed the butler from the room.

As soon as her footsteps faded, Neason turned to his cousin. "You cannot keep her under lock and key."

"I know. There could be a fire." Angus shot a hard look at his cousin. "Of course I thought of that, fool."

Neason's face reddened. "I'm sorry. I should have known you would have realized the potential danger."

Angus's shoulders tightened. There would never again be a fire in New Slains Castle; he'd ensured that wouldn't happen. Only the best lamps were used, and those were carefully monitored and numbered, so none were left in a forgotten location where they might unwittingly cause a problem.

Moreover, the chimneys were kept in perfect repair and cleaned every month without fail. He'd also installed an advanced water collection system that allowed rainwater to be stored in a cistern on the roof and released into various parts of the castle at the turn of a nozzle. *If I'd made those additions before, Kiera would still be here.* But going back was not an option; therein lay only madness and despair. He *had* to go forward; life had given him no choice.

Angus turned toward the door.

"Where are you going?" Neason asked.

"The turret holds two guest rooms: the turret room and the overlook suite. I will sleep in the latter."

"But you said you'd never again enter the overlook suite since it was Kiera's favorite."

That was true: Kiera had used the room frequently, claiming the light was perfect for her paintings. But now was not the time to be tied to the past.

Angus paused by the door. "The two rooms adjoin. I will have Muir move my things to the overlook suite. If there is a fire, I will be the first to know."

"Angus, is that wise? As you've pointed out, we don't know this woman. If you move into the adjoining room, she might cry foul of another sort. You'll be separated by only a single door and—"

Angus waved an impatient hand. "She will never know I'm there. I don't spend many hours in my bed chamber as it is." Sleep hadn't come easily to him since the fire. "There's no reason to be concerned. I'm well able to take care of myself."

Neason folded his lips as if to hold back another comment, but then sighed and shook his head. "I have other objections to this arrangement, but I can see they'd only fall on deaf ears."

"Not deaf. Just decided."

Neason chuckled weakly. "I suppose you're hungry after your turn as coachman?"

"Starving. Will you order dinner while I talk to Muir about my sleeping arrangements?"

"Of course. I'll send a footman to the kitchen at once."

"Excellent. I will return shortly."

Angus left. Neason worried far too much. The only risk he was taking was in allowing that woman to remain while he looked into her story. "Keep your friends close, and your enemies closer," he muttered under his breath.

Once he disproved her story, woe betide her. There would be no mercy then.

Letter from Michael to his sister Mary, from the banks of the Cairo River in Egypt:

It's funny how many little things you get used to—attached to, even—and never realize it until you travel abroad and those things are not available.

For example, a nice down pillow. Ah, how I have longed for the one on my bed at Wythburn. And while I get used to the hard pallets we sleep on while we travel, whenever I find myself someplace with a comfortable down pillow, I find myself smiling like a fool and dreaming of life at the vicarage.

One of the beauties of traveling is that you learn what you truly value when you are home. And little things that you might take for granted are sweeter, softer, larger, and infinitely better for the experience of not having them.

$\mathcal{F}$IVE

$\mathcal{I}$t's a very nice bedchamber," Mary said as she looked about their room in the bright morning light.

"Aye," Abigail said. "Fer a prison."

"It could be worse."

"If ye say so, miss."

Despite the maid's sour looks, Mary had to appreciate the fine room's thick rugs and rich furnishings. This morning a maid had arrived with a breakfast tray, followed shortly by a large brass tub that had been placed in front of the fireplace and filled with steaming, scented water.

Though she knew she should immediately plan her escape, Mary couldn't refuse such a luxury. She dipped her fingers into the warm water as she looked about the room, her appreciation deepening. "I was too tired to

notice last night, but I am impressed with the furnishings, too."

Abigail sniffed. "I don't like bein' locked away like a
criminal."

"Neither do I, but at least they've seen to our
comfort."

"I suppose ye could say that," Abigail said with a
disapproving sniff.

"Was the trundle bed uncomfortable?"

"Not at all, miss. It was much better than most of
the beds we've slept in along the road. It was just the
thought of bein' locked in. I felt as if I couldn't *breathe*!
You're a mite more chipper about this than I am, miss."

"I'm not chipper, I'm hopeful. Last night I spent
almost an hour in conversation with our host and I realized the futility of arguing. If we want to get out of this
fix, we're going to have to find a way other than reasoning with a complete barbarian."

Abigail unfolded a large towel and placed it beside
the tub. "We should have known 'twasn't a good idea to
come to New Slains Castle. All those men in the tavern
said so. It's a pity that one offered to drive us here."

"Actually, *that* was the earl."

Abigail's eyes widened. "*No!* That scarred, wrapped-
up man was an *earl?*"

Mary frowned. "Scarred?"

"Aye, didn't ye see where his scarf met his jaw?"

"I didn't see anything beyond the scarf. His eyes
drew most of my attention."

"La, he do have the devil's own eyes." Abigail shivered, her breasts quivering as if made of aspic.

Mary decided she should speak with the maid about her low-cut gowns. The footmen guarding their door had fallen all over themselves when Abigail assisted the housekeeper, Mrs. MacFarren, with the breakfast tray.

Abigail shook her head. "Ever' time that man looked at me, I felt the touch of the devil, I did."

"You think the devil has eyes the color of a new leaf? It seems far too pretty of a color."

"I don't know, miss, all I know is that he has eyes as can make yer knees shake if he gets angry wit' ye."

Mary couldn't argue with that. The man was a mystery, dressed in such a way, and that scarf.

She remembered the burned wing of the castle and her heart stuttered. "His scars . . . were they from a burn?"

"I hadn't thought of it, miss, but . . . yes, I'd think so. They was angry ridged scars all rippled and—" She curled her nose. "I wonder how much of 'im is scarred up beneath his clothes?"

"I don't know, but it's a pity that it happened. No one deserves such pain."

"Indeed, miss. Don't think on it any longer. Come, get into the bath." Abigail assisted Mary out of her robe and helped her into the tub.

Mary gave a blissful sigh as she sank beneath the water.

"I never knew a woman so given to bathin', miss."

"The tub at Wythburn Vicarage is much smaller, and we've never had so much hot water. Tepid was the usual temperature, so this is a gift."

"I suppose so," Abigail said, looking doubtful.

Mary submerged up to her chin in the wonderfully warm, lilac-scented water. "Ah, this is wondrous. It didn't take the footmen long to fill it, either."

"That's because the household has hot water at their beck and call. I seen last night how they prepared it. There's a cistern located directly behind the kitchen's cookstove, which is never let to go out during the entire winter, but burns all night and day, so there's always hot water at the ready."

"That's quite a modern convenience." Mary thought of the burned and hollow wing of New Slains Castle that she'd seen on first arriving. "It seems the exterior of New Slains Castle is very different from its interior." She wondered if that was true of the owner as well.

"Indeed, miss, the kitchens are bang up to the knocker, they are. One o' the maids tol' me that the servants had heated water fer their own baths as well." Abigail pulled one of Mary's trunks forward. "*And* they each have their own room, and all have a window and their own beds and wardrobes." Abigail shook her head. "I never would have thought such, when we first drove up to this charred pile o' rocks."

Mary doused her hair and reached for the soap. "It is a forbidding structure." She pulled her hair to one side and lathered it. "I wonder when that portion of the castle burned?"

"Seven years ago, miss." Abigail glanced at the closed door, then said in a lowered voice, "Muiren—she's the upstairs maid fer the east wing—says the earl lost his wife in that fire."

"Oh, dear. How . . . how horrible." Mary tried to

picture the dark and forbidding man with a wife, and couldn't quite make the image form.

"Aye," Abigail continued. "I heard tell they was wildly happy, too. Or was until the fire broke out. She didn't escape and the entire place was almost lost. It took every man in the village to keep the fire from spreading to the rest o' the castle. By morning, the entire wing had burned down."

"How did they save the rest of the castle? The roofs are timber, there are staircases and walls and—goodness, a lot of wood and plaster."

"They say everyone from the village came and helped, carrying seawater in barrels by cart up and down the cliff road. The rest o' the place was damaged, but not as much."

Mary shook her head. "That's so sad. No wonder the earl is so unsmiling."

"Aye, 'twas a dreadful thing. Muiren said the fire was so fierce that no trace was found of the countess afterward. The earl almost died as well, tryin' to save his ladylove. It's a romantic story, even though the man's scars ruin him fer any other woman."

"Abigail, that's not true! Scars or no, he's *very* attractive."

"Miss, there's no need to yell."

Mary's cheeks heated. "I didn't yell; I was just surprised you thought the earl was 'ruined.'"

"Hm." Abigail removed a silver-backed brush and comb from inside the small trunk and placed them on the dresser. "They said he almost lost his mind after he realized his wife was gone, callin' fer her from his sleep fer weeks afterward. They feared he'd die from a broken heart."

Mary dipped her hair underwater, mainly so she could shut her eyes and let a lone tear pass unnoticed. It was such a sad, tragic story, though it explained the earl's dark bitterness.

She sat back up and soaped her hair, wondering how he'd been before the accident. She couldn't imagine Erroll as a laughing, deeply-in-love youth, though it was obvious that the man was capable of true, deep feelings.

Perhaps it was because his darkness sat on him with long-term familiarity. *That must be it. He's still in mourning.* Her heart ached at the thought.

How horrible for a life to end so quickly. And to be left with such scars, both inside and out . . .

She wondered if the earl kept the scarf on even in warmer weather, and what other parts of him carried the same damage? Had there been scars on his hands? She'd have to pay closer attention when she saw him next.

She held her breath and dipped beneath the water once more, her soapy hair spreading about her. She ran her hands through it until the soap was gone, and then emerged from the water.

"Abigail, would you hand me a towel? I wish I could stay in the water longer, but I've work to do. I must convince the earl to release Michael's artifact into my care as quickly as possible."

Abigail handed Mary a towel for her hair, then helped her from the tub. Mary wrapped another towel about her. As she dried herself before the crackling fire, she considered their position. "I must request an audience with the earl. Ask the footman to send my request."

Abigail bobbed a curtsy, then crossed to the door. She opened it softly, then went outside. Mary heard the low murmur of voices. After a few moments Abigail returned, shutting the door sharply behind her.

"Well?"

"No."

"No? They won't even ask?"

"Apparently the earl already informed them that ye'd be askin' such a thing, fer I hadn't so much as begun to speak when one o' the footmen said all smart-like, 'Ye cannot see his lordship. Ye and yer missus are to stay in yer room unless the earl sends fer ye.'"

Despite her disappointment, Mary had to laugh at Abigail's pert imitation of the broad accent. "You do that very well."

"Me grandfather was Scottish, so I've heard enough o' it." Abigail scooted a chair close to the fire. "Lean back and I'll brush yer hair 'til it's dry."

"Of course." Mary obligingly leaned back.

Abigail carefully pulled the brush through Mary's blond hair. "I've never seen such long hair. It's all the way to yer waist."

"It's quite unfashionable, but I'm not exactly a fashionable sort." Mary looked down ruefully. "I wish I could be, but I'm a bit too . . . rounded."

Abigail *tsked.* "Law, miss, ye look as fine as a penny."

"Thank you, but you should see my sisters. The sad

truth is that current fashion does very little for someone of my size."

"Ye've a womanly figure, miss, and ye don't need to worry about reducing. Now, Miss Fonteroy, the baker's daughter, *she* needs to reduce. If you can't see yer own feet, 'tis time."

"I'm sure I shall get there if we are forced to eat here much longer. The food is beyond delicious. I had *two* bowls of that wondrous beef stew last night and I don't know how many pieces of fresh, warm bread, and the eggs and ham that were served this morning—" Mary sighed.

"Aye, I had some o' the meat pie in the kitchen and 'twas the best I ever ate. They also had kippers and—" Abigail continued to expound on the various dishes she'd seen in the kitchen below.

Mary's mind wandered to Michael. Was he hale and hearty? Was he hungry or cold or— *No. I can't think about that. He's always been fortunate; I will just pray that his fortune continues.* She closed her eyes and said a quick prayer, then sent her thoughts to her brother. *Hold on, Michael. I will be in port with that artifact the second William arrives.*

Of course, if she didn't find a way to even speak to the earl, that might not be true. Michael's letter had hardened the man's heart against them all. Why had he written that missive? Had something happened after he'd sent his letter home? Had he discovered that he was about to be double-crossed in some fashion?

What a difficult task this had become. She'd thought it would be simple enough to fetch the artifact to William; she'd even welcomed embarking on a true life adventure. But being locked away in a castle by a dark earl was much more than she'd bargained for.

If only she could unlock the way to their host's heart and his generosity. He was the key to everything.

Michael would have been able to do that, for no one was more charming when he tried. In his quest to obtain antiquities of value and not be cheated by the locals who specialized in such things, Michael had become adept in reading his fellow man. He'd often explained to Mary how he'd found a variety of clues that told him about a man's moral turpitude and, as a result, he'd been cheated less than most other explorers.

Abigail moved on from talking about the delicious food in the kitchens of Slains Castle to the amounts and qualities of fine linens in the linen room. The maid's even brush strokes, combined with the wonderful bath and meal, and the comforting crackle of the fire, almost made Mary forget that she was a prisoner.

But she was. And her first duty was to escape her prison cell and win her freedom. The next time the maid paused for breath, Mary said, "As soon as I'm dressed, we'll begin our revolt."

The brush faltered. "A *revolt,* miss?"

"Do you wish to get out of here or not?" Mary asked, surprised at her maid's hesitation.

"Aye, but I don't wish to make the earl angry. Ye just have to look at him to see he's a dangerous man."

"Nonsense. Just because he's scarred—"

"And has locked us in this room!"

"He thinks I'm a thief, so of course he was forced to

act. I would have done the same if I'd been in his shoes. There's no reason to think he's dangerous."

"But . . . how do ye *know,* miss?"

"For one thing, he lives with his cousin, who seems very nice."

Abigail bit her lip. "Well . . . I did hear one o' the servants say last night that Mr. Hay was a quiet gent, and was the countess's playmate from a young age. When she died, he stuck beside the earl even durin' the worst o' times."

"There you go, then. Would Mr. Hay stay here if the earl were an evil man?"

"I can't imagine it, no."

"Me, neither. Furthermore, you've spent some time with the servants; are *they* afraid of him?"

"They scamper whenever he calls, miss, but no, I don't think they are."

"Exactly. Finally, would an evil man make sure his servants had hot running water and excellent fare on their tables? Or a prisoner, for that matter? Just look at our room and the fare we were served. I, for one, have never had such a perfect bath."

"I suppose yer right, then, miss."

"I think I am. Despite his rude ways, his actions show signs of decency. Plus, Michael liked and trusted this man. That's enough of a recommendation for me. I daresay that if we'd ridden up like normal people and had been introduced to his lordship, he would treat us very differently."

Abigail nodded. "Ye make sense, miss. But if the earl's not dangerous, then why are you plannin' an escape?"

"Not an escape; a revolt. However decent the earl may be under other circumstances, we must get that artifact soon. I've only three weeks to collect it and make my way to Whitby. Necessity must rule us in this instance, Abigail. Pure necessity."

"Yes, miss."

Mary smiled. "We are agreed, then. Now pin up my hair. We've work to do."

"But we've no weapons!"

"We don't need weapons. All we need is a little effort and this furniture."

Abigail blinked. "Ye ain't going to throw it, are ye? Fer there are few pieces I can lift."

"We don't have to lift them far; just a few inches off the floor. Do you think you can do that?"

Abigail considered it and nodded. "Except the bed and the great wardrobe over there, and per'aps the desk, I think I can lift most o' it."

"Excellent. So bring me my blue morning gown and a matching ribbon. We've a battle to wage."

Letter from Michael to his sister Mary, from a caravan crossing the Sahara Desert:

Mary, how I wish you could see this great desert. It is an endless rolling mountain of golden sand, and to the unknowing, there seems to be very little else. It is impossible to imagine a single person, much less a whole tribe, surviving in such a place.

And yet they do.

Those who live here know how to avoid the sun, find food, and even water in this barrenest of lands. Mary, no matter where you are or what you do, remember to actively look for opportunities to mold your surroundings to your benefit. Knowledge and action combined can win over any adversity known to man.

$\mathcal{S}$IX

"No, *slam* it down. Like this." Mary, dressed in her good blue morning gown, held on to the back of a chair—a solid, sturdy chair with nice thick legs. She tilted the chair forward so that the back legs were a good foot from the floor and then she slammed down the chair with a satisfyingly loud *thump*!

Abigail nodded and did the same to the chair she held, the sound reverberating.

"Excellent," Mary said approvingly. "Now do it until the earl arrives." She gave her chair another *thump*. "It will probably take a good ten minutes or longer, because the library's on the first floor and we're on the third."

"Are ye sure he will come?" Abigail asked over their noise.

"I'm positive," Mary said, raising her voice to be heard. "These old round turrets are like a drum; they carry noise horribly. My brother-in-law Alexander MacLean owns a castle and it has the same issues. Caitlyn is forever complaining that she cannot even sneeze without her husband hearing her and coming to see if she needs a shawl."

"Yer sisters married well, they did."

Yes, they had. One day, Mary wished for the same. But not until she'd found a way to do her fair share of adventuring.

"Ye think his lordship won't like the noise? Mayhap he'll just ignore it."

"He'll hate it; he's a scholar. I had the impression the library was his favorite room, too, not only because the doors are the largest in the grand hall, but because his papers were locked in a desk there. He wouldn't have those far from his own research, regardless of the—"

The door slowly opened.

Mary's heart began to pound uncomfortably, but settled back to normal when a very young footman stuck his head around the corner. "Och, miss!" he said over the noise, his eyes wide as he noted their actions. He said something else, but his voice didn't carry over the thumping, though his gaze managed to find Abigail's décolletage.

Mary nodded to the maid and they paused, the silence as sudden as it was deafening.

The footman smiled, looking relieved. "Och, thank ye, miss! I couldna hear me own voice in me own head."

"It will not last, so you had best speak quickly," Mary kindly told the footman.

His smile faded, his gaze flickering between her and

Abigail. "I—I was goin' to see if ye needed anything, miss. Ye only have to ask if ye'd like some tea or hot wash water or more logs fer the fire. Ye dinna have to make a din to—"

"We want our freedom."

"That's right," Abigail chimed in. "Our freedom!"

"You can see that we don't have a choice," Mary said. "Until someone allows us out of this room, we shall continue making noise."

The footman looked uncomfortable. "That's a problem, miss. The earl dinna like noise. He will be angry."

"Excellent," Mary replied cheerfully. "I was just telling Abigail that I wouldn't be surprised to discover he needs perfect quiet when he's researching, doesn't he?"

The footman nodded. "Aye, miss! We've strict orders not to clatter about and to hold our tongues when he's workin'."

"See, Abigail? Though our captor looks like a surly giant, he's really a simple scholar. If there's one thing I know, it's scholars. All three of my brothers are scholarly. Michael the most, but even William, the sea captain, is in the process of writing a tome about the history of sailing, while Robert has undertaken selling Michael's antiquities and has become quite knowledgeable in that area."

Abigail nodded. "Ye would know scholars, then."

"And so I know that the earl is most likely very rigid in his expectations of silence, especially when he is researching."

The footman looked impressed. "Och, miss! That's the right o' it."

"Which is why, Abigail, you and I will continue making noise."

The footman's face fell. "Miss, fer yer own sakes, I wouldn't advise tha'. The earl is a quiet man, but he has a quick temper. Ye dinna wish to stir his blood."

"That is where you're wrong." Mary nodded to Abigail and they began thumping once again.

The footman sighed heavily before bowing and leaving, looking as if he expected to be chastised at any moment.

As the door closed behind him, Mary glanced at the clock. If she were a wagering sort, she'd say the earl would burst into their room in approximately five more minutes.

She tilted the chair higher the next time, then slammed it down with all of her might. *Yes, that's quite a bit more—*

The door slammed open, causing Abigail to drop her chair and squeak while Mary froze in place.

The earl was framed by the doorway, his broad shoulders almost filling the space, his head barely clearing the door frame. His dark hair was mussed about his stern visage, his lips pressed in fury, a neck cloth knotted about his throat.

He stalked into the room, a man the size of a great black bear, yet with a firm jaw and flashing pale green eyes.

A delicious shiver ran down Mary's spine. *He arrives like the hero in a play, ready to fight a villain.*

Only, *he* was the villain. Still, she had to admit that the man possessed an unconscious theatrical flair. No one could be immune to the way he moved, all athletic grace and restrained power; the second he walked into a room, he dominated the space and the people without even trying. Added to that was his penchant to dress all in black, and the scarf that covered his jaw and hid a rumored scar . . . Who could blame her for shivering whenever he was near?

His icy gaze locked on her now.

She dipped a quick curtsy. "My lord, how kind of you to join us."

"I will not have this racket in my house."

"And I will not be locked in a room like a mad dog."

His mouth thinned, his hands fisted at his side. The tension in the room grew so thick that Mary thought that she could walk upon it. She stood behind her chair, ready to resume her noise warfare at a second's notice.

But Abigail was not so sternly made. She swallowed noisily, looking from her mistress to the earl and back, her eyes wide, her breath swift.

Erroll turned suddenly, his gaze now locked upon the maid. "*You.*"

Abigail let the chair she was holding drop back and dipped a jerky curtsy, her face pale. "Y-y-yes, m-m-me lord?"

"*Out.*" The earl didn't even glance at Abigail's heaving chest before turning back to Mary.

He wasn't an easily distracted man, she'd give him that, for the maid was difficult to ignore.

"Aye, m-m-my lord, but I—I—" Abigail gulped and shot an uncertain glance at Mary.

"It's quite all right," Mary said despite her own

racing heart. "I wish to have a word with his lordship and this will be the perfect opportunity."

Abigail needed no more encouragement and she scuttled toward the door.

"Close it," the earl ordered, his gaze locked on Mary.

With a final, worried backward glance at Mary, Abigail closed the door behind her.

The earl crossed his arms over his broad chest and scowled. "I don't appreciate being awakened in such a fashion."

Mary realized that the earl must have dressed in extreme haste, for his waistcoat was hanging open and his shirt was half tucked. His coat, too, was slightly askew, as if he'd pulled it on while walking.

That was odd. One of the servants must have rushed to his apartments and awoken him with a complaint about the noise, which had obviously made him furiously toss on his clothes and race here. But how had he gotten here so fast? His bedchamber was in the opposite wing; Muir had let that fact slip as he escorted her here last night.

Well, however it happened, her ploy had worked, for here he was.

She folded her hands primly before her and smiled. "I can see that we awakened you and it's put you in an ill mood. I'm not being unreasonable, for I *did* ask to be allowed out, but we were refused."

"On my orders."

"Exactly. Therefore, I was forced to more extreme measures. If you'll unlock the door and leave it unlocked, I promise the noise won't happen again."

"No."

Her calm smile slipped. No explanation, no appreciation of her logic, just "no" in a deadly cold voice. She lifted her chin. "Fine. Then I'll continue with my concert." She grasped the chair, rocked it forward on its front legs, then slammed it down onto the floor.

"Stop that."

"Not until you release me from this room."

A low rumble remarkably like a growl emanated from the earl. "Do not push me in this manner. You will regret it."

"Do not push *me,* my lord. I won't accept such rude treatment."

His lips were almost white as he attempted to hold back God only knew what sort of improper retort.

Mary's heart thudded rapidly and she had to quell a childish desire to hike her skirts and run. She'd wanted to ignite him to action, and she had his attention now. *Don't get rattled. Face your enemy and do not flinch.*

She cleared her throat. "This is an intolerable situation. I'm not happy being locked away."

"I'm not happy that you're making so much noise that I cannot even think in peace."

"Then allow me out. I promise to behave myself. I shall be a perfect guest while we wait to hear from Mr. Young."

"No. I won't have you traipsing around, looking for that damned artifact every time my back is turned."

She frowned, tapping one foot in impatience.

He lifted a brow. "I don't hear you offering to refrain from such a search."

"I suppose I could, but it wouldn't be honest," she

replied regretfully. "However much I wish for my freedom, it would be useless to pretend I'm not desperate to
place my hands on that artifact."

"You are doing your purpose a grave disservice with
that announcement."

"It's the truth." She gripped the back of the chair
tighter and leaned forward. "Erroll, my brother's life
hangs in the balance. I *must* have that artifact."

His gaze narrowed. "You are almost convincing. . . ."

She closed her eyes and counted to ten. "You will
see how mistaken you are when Mr. Young confirms my
identity."

"*If* that happens, then the artifact is yours. But until
then, you will remain in this room and cease this noise."

"Erroll, I cannot—"

"No. That's my final word. There is no more to be
said." He turned and strode back toward the door.

"No."

He paused, one hand on the knob before he shot her
a dark look over his shoulder. "*What?*"

"I said no. It's not in my nature to sit tamely by and
acquiesce to such barbaric behavior."

His green gaze flickered over her. "You will do as you
are told and that's that." He reached for the knob and
turned it.

Meanwhile, she gripped the chair again, lifted it, and
dropped it to the ground. *THUNK!*

She did it again. And again. And—

The earl spun on his heel, curses snapping from his
lips as he strode across the room toward her, his green
gaze furious.

Mary instinctively stepped away, which was fortu-itous, as the earl snatched up her chair and strode to the window. To Mary's shock, he threw open the window, glanced down to the courtyard, and then tossed the chair over the ledge.

With a splintering crash, the chair smashed on the cobblestones below.

Mary blinked.

Erroll turned away from the window, a faint smile touching his mouth. "There."

"That was—" She couldn't find the words, couldn't believe he'd done such a thing.

"Now, you will behave yourself and remain quietly in your room as you've been told. I shall see to it that some books are brought for your amusement. Hopefully we'll hear from Mr. Young in a week or so—"

"A *week?*"

The earl frowned. "I asked Mr. Young to return here and identify you in person, just so there can be no misunderstanding. So it will be a week, at least."

A *week?* A *whole* week?

Mary clenched her fists at her sides. She was so angry she could have stomped her foot, but she refused to give him the satisfaction. "My lord, I don't think you understand. I must deliver that artifact to my—"

"To your brother William. You informed me of that fact last night. As far as I'm concerned, your brother can wait; I will not release the artifact until I am completely certain you are who you say you are. I owe Michael Hurst my caution, if nothing else."

She lifted her chin. "He doesn't need your caution; he

needs your *help*, which you could grant if you'd just give me that artifact and release me so that I can deliver it!"

He scowled, his hands opening and closing at his sides. "You will not be reasonable."

"If you mean will I accept your bullying, then the answer is *no*."

"Fine." He crossed to another chair, swooped it up, and tossed it out the window as well. He did it again, and yet again. The cool outside air began to wash over the room as it emptied, stirring the curtains and making Mary shiver as wood splintered upon the courtyard below.

As Erroll reached for the final chair, this one a lovely cushioned one covered with embroidered tapestry, she could bear no more. "Oh, stop! It's a horrid waste. Those are beautiful chairs."

He shrugged. "If I wish to replace them, I'll order more." And with that, that last chair joined its fellows on the cobblestones below.

Mary rubbed her forehead. When she was growing up in the vicarage, a chair—especially one as finely made as these—was a treasure to be enjoyed and savored, not something to be tossed away like a broken dish. The wastefulness banished her fear as nothing else could have.

Had Erroll been one of her brothers, she'd have set him to rights with a few well-chosen words. But he was her enemy sworn, so she held her anger like a shield, using her scorn as her bolster in the coming confrontation.

Mary didn't know what Michael would do in this

situation, and suddenly she didn't care. She'd handle this her own way. *If the furnishings mean so little to him, then let him toss all of them.*

She eyed the remaining furniture, then pointed to a small stool. "I could make noise with that."

His brows snapped down. "You challenge me, woman."

"Someone needs to."

Scowling as blackly as a pirate, he strode to the stool, snatched it up, and tossed it out the window.

She waited until she heard the crash from the courtyard before she pointed to the tapestry-covered seat to the dressing table. "And that."

Seconds later, it joined the others.

She pointed to the fire poker set. "And those, of course. You wouldn't believe the noise I could make with iron."

Without a second's delay, they joined the tumbled, splintered pile in the courtyard.

"Anything else?" he asked grimly.

"Oh, I'm sure I'll find something." She gave him a brilliantly smug smile, her anger hidden behind her teeth. "I don't cry quit simply because someone else cannot keep their temper."

For one second, she feared she'd gone too far, for his mouth thinned in a most ominous way. Instead, he turned on his heel and emptied out the remainder of movable furniture, tossing each item one at a time out the window. When he was done, nothing was left in the room other than a large wardrobe, the massive bed, and the heavy, marble-topped dressing table.

Mary looked about the nearly empty room. "That was certainly dramatic."

His gaze narrowed, as she shrugged. "It may be a bit late to mention this, but I suppose you couldn't have had the furniture removed and stored, rather than destroying it?"

"I could, but it wouldn't have made my point."

"Your point being that you've a horrid temper and can act like a complete and utter ass? Yes, I'd say you've made your point quite well."

He was across the room so quickly that she didn't have time to do more than suck in her breath. He glared down at her, his broad shoulders blocking all of the light from the windows, and she was once again astounded at his size.

His deep voice roiled across her like the hot lick of flames. "Listen to me well: I will not brook insolence. You *will* do as you're told. Until Mr. Young confirms your identity, you will remain here, in this room, and behave yourself. If you don't, then you won't have even the luxuries you have now. Am I understood?"

She straightened her shoulders and tilted her head back to stare up into his haughty face. "Even if you take *all* of the furnishings *and* toss them out the window *and* remove me from this room *and* lock me away in the—the—the stables, I will do what I must to make certain you are every bit as miserable as I. Am *I* understood?"

Angus had never been so furious in his entire life. This woman, this impostor, who'd dared come to *his* home to steal an object entrusted to him by one of the few men he deemed a friend, did not deserve even the kindnesses he had bestowed upon her—a luxurious bed-chamber with her maid in attendance. Why, he'd even left his own comfortable bedchamber for the smaller one adjacent to this to make certain she was safe!

Yet the chit showed no gratitude and actively at-tempted to irk him. Well, she'd succeeded.

He knew some of his anger had to do with being awakened from a rare, deep sleep, but more of it was be-cause she refused to be bent to his will. He wasn't used to that, and he'd be damned if he'd start now.

Even now she glared up at him as if unafraid and unmoved by his fury. Yet she lied, and he knew it. Her modestly covered chest—temptingly generous—rose and fell quickly, straining at her pale blue gown. Her sherry-colored eyes were slightly dilated, her lips parted, her creamy skin flushed.

Every word she uttered was a deliberate challenge. Well, the chit was about to get what she so desperately desired: an answer for her impertinence.

He grasped her to him, lifted her off her feet, and pulled her curvaceous figure against him. He had in-tended to simply hold her there until she begged to be released, but once he felt her warm skin beneath his hands, the pressure of her generous breasts upon his chest, the excited gasp from her parted lips, suddenly holding her wasn't nearly enough.

He bent his head and kissed her, pouring all of his discontent, fury, and heated desire into it.

The instant his mouth closed over hers, he realized his mistake. His anger fled before an onslaught of pure, red-hot lust. He forgot why he was mad, why she was locked here in this room, forgot everything but the blinding sensuality of her soft curves pressed against him while her lavender scent engulfed him like a velvet prison.

She froze for a second, then she, too, was lost in the heat that flared between them. He could feel the thunder of her heart as it merged with his, the desperation of her hands as they grasped his coat.

He cupped her to him, lifting her higher until her arms wrapped about his neck. She moaned against his mouth, opening her lips beneath his, desperately seeking.

He was vaguely surprised at her boldness, yet her response answered his own passion so clearly that he didn't question it, but welcomed and encouraged it. He teased her lips farther apart and deepened the kiss, holding her firmly to him, no longer thinking—just feeling, enjoying, tasting and touching and stroking. His hands never stilled, but molded her to him, cupping her rounded ass, sliding up her sides to find her generous breasts and—

A shout rose through the open window as a servant found the pile of broken furniture. Recalled to his senses, Angus reluctantly broke the kiss and slid Mary to the floor.

Her eyes were still closed, her lips still parted as she panted, her hands bunched about his lapels as if she might fall if she released them.

The sight relaxed him. He might be flushed with passion, but she was utterly overcome.

The thought soothed his irritation as nothing else had, and he felt a sense of self-satisfaction as he gently released his hold.

Her eyes fluttered open and she gazed up at him in bemused amazement, her mouth temptingly swollen from his kiss. For a wild, impulsive moment he considered kissing her again, but reason returned.

He stepped away and her hands fell from his lapels. "There." He had to clear his throat from the husky passion that still gripped him. "Let that be a lesson to you not to try my temper."

She blinked and opened her mouth as if to say something, but no words tumbled from her parted lips.

Ha! He might have a husky voice, but she was rendered speechless by a mere kiss.

Smirking, he went to the window and closed it. Then he strode to the door, pausing to look back.

She still stood in the center of the almost-empty room. As he watched, she pressed a hand to her lips as if they still tingled from his kiss. Even more interesting, she made no move to argue with him—not a single word or look turned his way.

That was more like it. Though the kiss had affected him more than he'd wished, he was no slave to it as she was. He, therefore, was stronger than she.

Now I know how to stop her. He gave her a mocking bow. "Good day, Miss Hurst. I shall send your maid to you. If you maintain your decorum for the rest of the day, I shall send in a chair with your dinner so that you may have some comfort, though it will be removed once you finish. In the meantime, I believe I shall go for my morning ride."

Satisfied and feeling magnanimous, he left, closing the door behind him.

Letter from Michael Hurst to Angus Hay, the Earl of Erroll, from Cairo, the house of a trusted guide:

Erroll,

Enclosed you will find the artifact I mentioned when I last visited. It's every bit as glorious as I expected, but I am stymied in my attempts to read the inscription, which could reveal so much. Is the vessel that of a lost pharaoh? Did it hold kohl to outline the seductive eyes of a queen? Or did it have a more mundane use—an ink pot for a merchant, perhaps? We may never know.

As ever, I'm frustrated by our lack of comprehension of hieroglyphs. I wish to heaven that Young would hurry and finish his studies. When last I spoke to him, he mentioned a stone found by Napoleon's forces during the Egyptian campaign that might now be in the British Museum archives. If he can gain access to that, our fondest desires might be answered.

It's a pity that he'll probably spend more time negotiating with the curators of our nation's museum than he would tracking down and procuring the stone from an antiquities dealer from a foreign land, but so it goes.

$\mathcal{S}$EVEN

The next morning, Muir assisted Angus from his mud-spattered greatcoat, then handed it to a waiting footman. "I trust your ride was beneficial, my lord."

"Beneficial? To my health? Or my temperament?"

"Yes, my lord."

Angus grinned. "The answer is yes. To both."

"Excellent, my lord. I believe Mr. Hay awaits you in the breakfast room."

"Wonderful, for I'm starving. Let him know I shall join him as soon as I wash and change."

Muir bowed and took the muffler Angus had just unwrapped from his neck, careful to leave the silk scarf in place. The butler murmured instructions to an underling before returning to Angus's side. "I shall have some hot water sent to your room."

"Thank you." Angus tilted his head to one side and listened. The house was silent, he noted with satisfaction. Despite their epic battle yesterday, he didn't think he'd heard the last of Miss Outraged.

The thought made him grin. The grin was followed by a chuckle, a sound so unfamiliar that the footman standing outside the breakfast room door stared incredulously.

The butler's cold glare recalled the footman to his senses and, blushing, he returned to his usual stoic stance.

"My lord, you seem to be in a very good mood."

"Yes. 'Tis the peace and quiet."

Muir folded his gloved hands neatly before him. "I can only suppose you're speaking about the young lady's attempt to gain your attention yesterday."

"Precisely. She was a pain, but I believe I've found a way to solve that problem." His kiss had worked wonders.

"Excellent news, my lord. I can only hope that means that there's no need to keep Miss Hurst locked away like a prisoner."

"No, it doesn't mean that at all."

Muir's expression never changed, yet his disapproval was palpable. "That's quite unfortunate, my lord," he said in a repressive voice.

Angus's good humor dampened. He knew that Muir thought it was a disgrace to the Hay family name to hold a lady prisoner. "Muir, I cannot be held to the traditional rules of behavior in this case. There is far too much at stake."

Muir didn't look convinced, but he wisely bowed and didn't repeat his objections.

"Thank you." Angus turned and made his way upstairs to the hallway leading to the top two rooms in the turret.

The overlook suite had been Kiera's favorite for the way the sun poured into the huge windows every afternoon. She'd loved to paint and this had been her workroom. If he closed his eyes, he could almost hear her low, lilting voice as she talked about her paintings and those of other artists she admired. Though he'd attempted to listen, his thoughts had been elsewhere, usually on his own studies.

Now he wished he'd listened more. He wished he'd done *many* things more.

He paused on the landing, pained by the memory. She'd been so passionate about her art, yet so hesitant in other areas of her life—namely him.

He shoved the thought away irritably. That was in the past, and it didn't lessen the truth of this day—which was that she was gone and he was left to carry on.

He turned down the corridor, surprising the footmen who stood guard beside his guest's door. At the sight of him, they jumped to attention.

Angus frowned, realizing they'd been lounging against the wall. "I will have chairs sent to you."

"Thank you, me lord," said the closest one, his young voice breaking in the middle of his sentence.

"Any trouble this morning?"

The other footman, a lanky youth named Thomas, shook his head. "Nay, me lord. Nary a peep."

The even younger footman, whose blond hair and romantic good looks would soon make him unemployable in any household with an unwed female of marriageable age, nodded enthusiastically. "Quiet as a mouse, she's been."

"Good, Dougal. Keep your eye on that door. She's not to leave." Angus moved on to his own door, fourteen feet down the corridor. Once inside, he sat on a plush chair by the fireplace and removed his boots, setting the muddied footwear on the hearth.

As he reached for his shoes, he heard through the adjoining door the sound of someone pacing the length of the room. No doubt she'd been pacing since she'd risen, attempting to work her way out of her dilemma. There was no "work" to be done. She'd just have to wait for Mr. Young's response.

The steps continued, firm and quick, back and forth, back and forth.

Angus stood to collect a fresh shirt from his wardrobe but instead found himself standing at the connecting door, his head bent to catch every crisp step. Was she thinking of escape? Or of their kiss yesterday? Whatever thoughts she might have, she was obviously ill at ease, which was exactly how he wanted her.

She had to be thinking of the kiss, for it had almost rattled him, too. Fortunately, he understood the intricacies of attraction; how it occurred when one least expected it, and rarely lasted past a proper introduction. She'd been completely overwhelmed; he'd seen it on her face and still felt a bit of pride about that.

But it wouldn't do to pretend that the situation

wasn't fraught with dangers. Angus had meant the kiss to be a quick you-will-do-as-I-say kiss, but it had changed quickly into a genuine, passion-hot, blinded-by-lust kiss that still made him tingle in all of the right places.

He'd be foolish to deny his attraction to her. It was obvious that she felt it, too, which posed an interesting question. Could he use that attraction to his advantage? Could he fan the flames of her passion and gain a confession from her without losing control of his own?

He suddenly realized he was pressing his hand against the connecting door, as if attempting to reach through it. He frowned and stepped away as if it had burned his fingers.

There was a price to keeping "Mary Hurst" under his roof, which was that he had to keep tight control over himself. It was a price he would willingly pay in order to discover her secrets.

Angus absently rubbed his cheek, his fingers tracing over the scars. At first they had been an angry red but now they were pale, almost the color of his own skin, although melted into hard ridges like the waves of a choppy ocean. The scars ran along the lower line of his jaw, neck, and shoulder. One arm was partially damaged, though over the years he'd won back the use of it.

He'd done so with agony and pain, going to the stables twice a day and lifting hay bales, though his tightened, scarred muscles and skin had screamed at the agony. He'd refused to allow the pain to win, and eventually the constant stretching had done the trick. That and Muir, who'd discovered some miraculous unguent.

He never said where he'd found the stuff, or what was in it, but it smelled of camphor, mint, and—oddly—iron. Whatever was in it, Angus didn't think he'd have ever returned to his normal strength without it. The unguent softened the hard ridges of the scar, allowed it to become more pliable, and relieved him from the agony of just moving.

Because of the unguent and the hours he'd spent in the stables, he could now shave himself, pull himself onto his own horse, stretch his arms well over his head—and throw an entire room of furniture out a window into the courtyard. It had also allowed him to hold his fiery opponent and deliver a well-deserved kiss.

The thought instantly made his blood heat, and he had to force himself to finish dressing. He washed quickly and then tugged on clean boots, and knotted his cravat about his throat in a way he was certain would make Neason wince. It had been Neason's fondest hope that Angus might one day hire a valet, but Angus had refused. After spending so many months in bed recovering from his burns, he savored the ability to do things for himself.

Finished dressing, he started to leave, but paused once again by the connecting door. No more footsteps filled the silence. *She must be standing at the window, or sitting on her bed. One thing was for certain: She wasn't reclining in a chair.*

He smiled, remembering her face as he'd tossed her furniture from her window. She'd been shocked and angered, but not a bit afraid. He had to respect her for that.

He left his room and headed downstairs, where he

requested that two chairs be taken up to the footmen outside the turret bedchamber.

Angus then went on to the breakfast room, where he found Neason pacing the carpet, a worried expression on his face. "You're the second person I've met today who is determined to wear a hole through my carpets," Angus said.

Neason grinned sheepishly. "I'm sorry. I was waiting to speak with you."

"I was out riding."

"I know; Muir informed me when I came to breakfast. You were gone a long time."

"Was I?" Angus took the chair at the head of the table and pulled forward a coffeepot that had been kept warm over a flame.

"Yes. He said you left shortly after nine and it's almost eleven now." Neason dropped into the seat nearest Angus. "I was worried about you. You don't normally ride for that long."

"I had a lot to think about." Like how warm and spicy a certain unwanted guest had tasted yesterday, and also in last night's dreams. Warm, wanton, sensual dreams.

I shouldn't have had that glass of whiskey after midnight. He didn't usually drink that late, but he hadn't been able to get to sleep.

"I had a lot to think about, too," Neason said darkly. "Did you write the letter to Young?"

Angus nodded. "I sent it yesterday with a groom. We should have our reply within the week."

"God, I hope so." Neason dropped his forehead

into his hand. "I can't believe we've taken a woman *prisoner.*"

Angus shrugged. Holding Mary prisoner hadn't disturbed his sleep. What *had* kept him awake was the shape of her very fine brown eyes. There was something about them—their tilt, or the unusual sherry color, or the curve of her lashes, or—

Bloody hell, what difference does that *make?* Who cared about her eyes? He certainly didn't. He was simply challenged by her. Once he'd solved the mystery of who she was and who had sent her to steal from him, he'd cease thinking of her.

He poured himself some coffee and mixed cream into the fragrant brew. He had to admit that she was attractive. Not his usual style, but he saw her differently since that damned kiss.

It was a good thing she was locked away out of sight.

He glanced at his cousin. "You look tired, Neason. Perhaps you should take a nap."

"No, no. We're to begin work on the papyrus scroll the British Museum wishes analyzed."

"Did you transcribe my notes?"

"What I could. Your handwriting is as bad as a set of hieroglyphs."

Angus helped himself to some eggs from a flowered dish. "Nonsense. It's not that bad."

Neason sighed. "Angus, we must speak about Miss Hurst."

"So speak."

"I've been thinking of it all night, and we can't hold a woman prisoner."

Angus took a piece of richly crusted bread, broke it in half, and spread butter over it. "I'm not fond of the idea myself, and I'm more than willing to listen to alternative ideas. Do you have any?"

Neason was silent for a long moment. "No."

"Do *you* believe her story?"

Neason fiddled absently with the coffeepot. "I wish I could."

Angus ate his bread, wondering if he should check on his prisoner. She'd spent all of yesterday in a nearly empty room with nothing to do; she might be more malleable now.

"Angus?" Neason had leaned forward, his blue gaze intent. "I keep thinking about the artifact Hurst sent us. When we examined it, it didn't strike me as being particularly valuable."

"No. I've seen a number of similar boxes, although none in such excellent condition."

"So why is someone so desperate to take it?"

"I don't know." Angus pushed his plate away, his mind racing ahead. "If I could only decipher the hieroglyphics. I know Young and several others are working on the riddle, but we must find a way to break the code." He poured himself more coffee. "We'll study the box further this afternoon. Perhaps we missed something."

Neason gave a wry smile. "You mean that *you* will examine it further. When I have an artifact to study, I always run into blank walls and already-found facts. You and Hurst seem to have a knack for finding the truly valuable items and recognizing them at a glance."

"You'd develop that knack, too, if you'd study more."

Neason sighed. "I've studied, and it hasn't helped. But that isn't important now; this woman is. If she's here to steal the artifact as Hurst's letter to us suggested, then he might indeed be in trouble."

"He might. But he's more than capable of saving himself, whatever fix he might be in." Angus wiped his mouth and leaned back in his chair. "Still, I will be glad to hear from him and know he's well."

Neason nodded. "As will I." He drummed his fingers upon the table. "Angus, what will you do if Miss Hurst *is* who she says?"

"That's not likely to happen."

"How do you know?"

"There are clues. Take her hands, for instance. While not as rough as a washmaid's, they are not those of a lady of quality's." Angus smiled darkly. "Whatever her reason for coming here, I'll discover it. There's nothing I love more than a good mystery."

"Just be cautious, Angus. She reminds me of . . . someone."

Angus didn't answer.

"I was struck by the resemblance as soon as she entered the library. You can't tell me you didn't notice it, too."

"There is something similar about the eyes, but that is all," Angus said shortly.

"It's more than that. Her coloring is almost the same, and her mouth is—" Neason spread his hands wide. "Angus, I don't want you to lose sight of where you are now." He hesitated but then added softly, "Kiera was so beautiful, so—" His voice broke. "Sometimes it is as if she never left. I can almost hear her laughter. It echoes for me. And late at night, I dream of the fire. The flames. I can still see it all—"

"*Stop,*" Angus said hoarsely. He realized he was gripping his coffee cup so tightly that it quivered, as if ready to shatter. He forced his fingers to loosen. "I've asked you not to speak of that night."

"I—I just—I'm sorry. I didn't mean to bring up such a painful subject. I just didn't want you to suffer as you once did, and the resemblance of this woman to Kiera is—" Neason wiped his eyes as if brushing away a cobweb. "That woman shouldn't be here. When you see her, you will remember— And that won't help any of us."

"She is locked in her room. It's highly unlikely I'll see her at all."

"But you intend on questioning her further at some point, don't you?"

Angus didn't answer.

Neason leaned closer. "Angus, let *me* be the one to speak with her. I can protect you from that."

"I don't need protection," Angus snapped. Though he owed Neason for his support during the dark days after Kiera's death, there was no reason for such smothering. "I am not afraid of this Hurst woman."

Neason reddened. "Perhaps you should be."

"Nonsense. She's *not* Kiera. I am not likely to forget that." He tossed his napkin on the table and stood. "Come. Let's retire to my study and examine Hurst's artifact to see what we may have missed."

Neason sighed. "Very well."

Thirty minutes later, Angus leaned back in his chair. "Interesting."

Neason scowled. "I just don't see it. It's a simple long, narrow onyx box, lightly chased in gold. It isn't that unusual." He frowned at the box for a moment. "Perhaps 'tis the gold?"

"At one time, perhaps, but not now. There's not enough of it left."

"Perhaps 'tis amazingly ancient?"

"It's old enough, but . . . no. That can't be it. I venture to say it's from the time of Ramesses II, but I need to do more research."

Neason leaned forward to look at the box, placed upon a large white ink blotter in the middle of Angus's desk, the curtains parted to allow the daylight in. "Why is it such an odd shape, so narrow and long?"

"Most likely it was built to hold a papyrus of some sort."

"Just a scroll?" Neason looked disappointed. "So it wasn't even made to hold a treasure."

"Neason, a clean, undamaged papyrus *is* a treasure. We have few of those in decent enough shape to read."

"I know, I just—" Neason shrugged, grimacing a bit. "I do not have your love of scholarship for scholarship's sake."

"There are plenty of people who claim to be Egyptologists, who look only for gold. They have no respect for the items they find, and frequently abandon or damage them." Angus couldn't begin to express his disdain for those people. "Hurst seemed to think this artifact was of huge importance; if he believed it, then so do I. I just have to find out what he saw in it."

"Have you opened it?"

"Yes. There is a latch on the end."

Neason examined it, then reached forward and touched his finger to a notch. The box opened without a sound. Neason looked inside. "As you said, nothing."

Angus leaned back and rubbed his chin, trying to imagine all of the uses for such a box other than as a papyrus holder. It was almost seven inches in length, only two inches high, and two inches in width. Each side was covered with a line of hieroglyphs.

Neason pointed to the writing. "There are so many characters."

"I've been attempting to decipher the hieroglyphs but they are too advanced." Angus used a small piece of velvet to lift the box. He squinted at the sides and then handed it to Neason, who handled it reverently.

"Whatever it is, it's beautiful." Neason reluctantly handed it back. "I'm certain the British Museum would pay a pretty price for it." There was no disguising the excitement in Neason's voice. "I should write—"

"No." Angus replaced the box on the cloth. "It's not for sale." Angus opened a drawer, pulled out a magnifying glass, and peered at the inscription. "This piece is somehow special. Hurst didn't reveal where he procured it, but I had the impression that was part of his excitement. I wonder if our guest knows where the purchase took place. That might be useful information."

"So you are going to speak to her again."

"How else will I discover her secrets?"

Neason bit his lip. "Angus, don't get distracted. You've made so many discoveries these last few months, and you don't want to waste time on this woman, whoever she is."

Angus looked up from his magnifying glass. "When you're done clucking like a mother hen, feel free to find some paper and a wax pencil. If we can make a tracing of these hieroglyphs, I know several people who could help us decipher them—at least partially."

Neason's face reddened, but he collected the requested supplies while Angus contemplated his next move. He would send a copy of the hieroglyphs to his fellow scholar Jean-Francois Champollion. Perhaps the Frenchman could make sense of them. In the meantime, Angus would attack this mystery through his only means available. *What secrets do you hold, Mistress Mary? And how many can I win from you?*

Angus wasn't certain, but he knew he would enjoy trying. In fact, he'd—

CLANG.

The noise echoed hollowly through the room.

Neason looked up from collecting the supplies from the desk. "Angus, did you—"

CLANG. CLANG. CLANG.

The chandelier overhead swayed and a book fell over on a shelf.

CLANG. CLANG. CLANGCLANGCLANGCLANG!

A small cloud of ash puffed out of the chimney with each thump. The noise was even louder than the chair banging. *Much* louder.

So I didn't tame her, after all. A grin flickered to life. *By God, she has spirit.*

"What is *that*?" Neason asked.

"That, my dear cousin, is our guest making her displeasure known. I disarmed her noisy ways yesterday, but it appears she has re-armed herself."

"Yesterday?"

"Yes. Didn't you hear her and her maid thumping about?"

"That was *her*? I heard some noise but it was swiftly halted, so I assumed the servants had been moving something."

"That was our guest banging chairs on the floor in an effort to irritate me into releasing her. So—"

CLANGCLANGCLANG!

He lifted a brow but continued, "So I relieved her of them."

"You you relieved her of the *chairs*?"

"Every one, along with every stool, every small table—anything that could be banged about. Her room is empty except for her bed, a wardrobe, and a desk, all too heavy to lift."

"Then . . ." Neason glanced at the ceiling again. "What is she thumping on the floor now? I—"

CLANGCLANGCLANGCLANGCLANGCLANG!

Angus headed for the door. "Stay here and make a copy of the hieroglyphs. I'll take care of our guest."

He closed the door behind him, went past the startled footmen, and ran lightly up the grand staircase. The clanging continued, even louder now. She was enjoying herself, of course.

You little termagant. Wait until I get my hands on you this time.

Letter from Michael to his sister Mary, from the consulate's house in Cairo:

As soon as the sarcophagus was delivered, I knew I'd been cheated. It was a very good forgery, but I knew what to look for. When I realized what had happened, I was furious. I went to confront the seller, but he—obviously knowing I wouldn't accept being cheated—had packed up shop and disappeared. It took me almost two years to find the scoundrel and force him to return my funds, but I eventually did.

Still, I learned something from that episode—now, when I purchase an artifact, I won't allow it out of my sight until it's safely delivered. I have never been tricked thusly since.

Mary, we are all wont to make mistakes, but if we learn from each trick, each error, and refuse to allow it to happen again, then the experience is not a loss, but a lifelong gain. Our pride may sting for the moment, but our future will be the better for it.

EIGHT

*M*ary slammed her silver-backed brush against the iron grate, the clang satisfyingly deep. Thankfully, the fire was almost out. She would have smiled except the belching ash made her sneeze.

Each strike resonated through the chimney like a gong, which pleased her no end. That would show Erroll that she was not to be kept down.

She swung again and again, then paused to rub her shoulder, which was beginning to ache. Worse than the ache, her eyes burned from the ash in the air. It was also far from comfortable kneeling on the hard hearth, so close to the fire, but she continued on.

Mary rolled her shoulders and then began clanging again. If she were being truthful with herself, she'd have to acknowledge that her real frustration wasn't about being locked in her room: She was certain she would eventually win her way free. No, her frustration was because try as she would, she couldn't forget the earl's kiss yesterday.

Her experience with kisses was very limited. The few single men of marriageable age who lived near Wythburn were sober and quiet and not the sort to steal kisses, especially from their vicar's daughter. It was one thing to flout the strictures of society, and quite another to do so under the shocked eyes of one's clergyman.

She felt fortunate that she'd managed to experience the two quick and entirely unsatisfactory kisses she had, prior to arriving in Scotland, though she didn't recall either one with any real clarity.

But Mary was certain she'd never forget the kiss from the earl. It had been passionate and sensual, powerful and— She couldn't even find the words to describe how it had made her feel. Even now, a day later, her lips still tingled.

She was relatively sure that wasn't how a true adventurer should react to a mere kiss. A true adventurer took things in stride, calmly and logically. They didn't imagine a moment over and over and over until the feel, smell, and memory were indelibly etched in their mind.

No, a real adventurer would be inured to such distractions as kisses and aching shoulders.

Steeling herself, she slammed the brush even harder, her aim slightly off. Instead of hitting the edge of the grate, the tip of her brush came down on a smoldering log. Sparks rained through the air and the log broke in two, half of it dropping to the floor and rolling to the edge of the hearth, just inches from her gown.

She gasped and jumped back just as the door slammed open.

The earl's cold green gaze took in the situation in a second and he cursed. In a moment he'd crossed to the fireplace, yanked the brush from her nerveless hand, and shoved the smoldering log back into the fireplace with his booted foot.

When he was done, he turned to face her. His mouth was white, his green gaze glittering with anger. "What in *hell* were you doing?"

Mary could only open and shut her mouth, still reeling from how close the fiery log had come to her skirts.

"Damn it, answer me! Do you know what could have happened?"

The harsh voice snapped her to attention. "Of course I know," she said in a voice that shook only slightly. "I was being careful, but then I became distracted and—" She shook her head, looking toward the grate, where the logs now burned merrily as if nothing untoward had ever happened. "I accidentally hit one of the logs and it came out."

Erroll sent her a dark glare. "This castle burned once already; I won't have it happen again."

Guilt washed over Mary. *Oh, no. I didn't even think of that. No wonder he looks so pale.*

"Erroll, I didn't mean to put you or anyone else at risk. I just wanted to make noise, and you left me very few options otherwise."

He sent her a look that let her know how little he thought of her reasoning before he carried her brush to the two gawking footmen in the doorway. "This is to stay outside with you."

The footmen nodded and disappeared.

Angus turned back to Mary. "There. We're done."

Somehow Mary had the feeling she'd disappointed him. The thought bothered her far more than it should have. "I'm sorry if I disrupted your day, but I must speak with you."

"If you'd wanted something, you could have told one of the footmen."

"Oh? Would they have brought me a chair? That would be far easier to bang on the floor than my brush."

"I'm surprised you didn't bang the brush upon the floor."

"It would have damaged the wood. Besides, I used the echo from the chimney to amplify the sound." She said the last with a bit of pride. "I thought that was rather intelligent of me."

His lips twitched and some of the anger in his gaze lightened.

So our dark earl has a sense of humor, does he? That's good to know. That one small fact helped, for it reminded her that he was human and just as capable of making mistakes as she was. All she had to do was find those mistakes, and use them to her advantage.

He glanced about her empty room. "I suppose I should thank you for not decimating my floors."

"You should, but I doubt you will." Mary glanced down at her gown, grimacing when she saw the ash smudges. "I fear I've ruined my gown."

"It serves you right," he said heartlessly.

She frowned. "It's no wonder I ruined my gown, seeing as how I have no chairs to sit upon. I had to sit upon the edge of my bed to comb my hair, which was most uncomfortable."

He shrugged, unmoved. "It's your fault you have no chairs, just as it's your fault that you now won't have a brush for your hair."

The man was impossible. Through her irritation, she still couldn't help but note the startling contrast between his black hair and his pale green eyes, highlighted by the sunlight streaming through the windows. The long golden beams burnished his skin and traced the hard contours of his mouth until he looked like a Greek god of vengeance.

When she'd first met him, she'd believed that a strong dose of sunlight would strip him of some of the dark mystery he exuded, but their meeting this morning had dispelled that. If anything, the sunlight made him all the more compelling, for it made his wonderful eyes seem all the more green, the shade of a new leaf. Framed by thick black lashes, they were incredibly beautiful and made her plain brown eyes seem woefully unamazing.

She caught his cool gaze and said quickly, "I'm surprised you didn't toss my brush out of the window as you did the chairs."

"I have been informed by my butler, whose opinion I value, that tossing things out in such a fashion causes considerable damage to the rosebushes."

Was that a gleam of sardonic humor in his eyes? Intrigued, she said, "You can't convince me that you care about what happens to the rosebushes after you were so cavalier in your treatment of your furnishings."

"I don't care about either of them. What I *do* care

about is the fact that my gardener's family has been with New Slains Castle for over four generations. I'd be loathe to lose him because I'd unwittingly crushed his shrubbery."

She had to admit that made sense. "I wish you felt as much concern for my well-being. If you'd just allow me out of this room, I'd—"

"—do what you could to find, and then take, the object you've so brazenly demanded."

She couldn't deny that.

He smiled, his face relaxed. "At least you're honest."

"For all the good it's done me." She plopped her fists on her hips. "Erroll, you can't keep me in here! If you do, I warn you, I shall find another way of making noise."

Angus didn't doubt that one bit. He'd thought being locked in her room would have lowered her spirits, but it seemed to have merely inflamed them. For some reason, he found himself fascinated by the conundrum she presented. Though she was nearly as dusty as a chimney sweep, she somehow glowed. Her fine eyes flashed with spirit while her creamy skin was flushed. One cheek had been smudged by ash, and a fine coating of it clung to her arms and skirts. Her fists, which rested on her hips, were covered in soot and would no doubt leave traces of that upon her skirts.

His lips twitched and it was with difficulty that he suppressed a grin as his gaze flickered over her hair. Several thick curls had fallen from their pins and now fell in froths and waves about her. The dark gold of ripe wheat, it shone in the sunlight that streamed in from the window, sparkling as if lit from within and forming a nimbus about her heart-shaped face. One curl curved about her neck and down to cup one of her breasts as gently as a lover.

He found himself wondering her age, for all smudged and dusty, she looked quite young. Too young to have trekked all of the way here from England. "How old are you?"

Suspicion entered her expression. "Why do you wish to know?"

"If you are Hurst's sister, then every fact I gather aids me in either confirming or denying your claims."

She rubbed the tip of her nose, leaving a black smear across it. "I'm twenty and seven."

That surprised him. "I would have thought closer to seventeen."

"How old are *you*?"

"That doesn't matter."

"You asked me," she pointed out fairly.

He supposed it wouldn't hurt to tell her. "I'm thirty and five."

She looked surprised. "Really? I'd have thought you were at least—" Her cheeks heated. "I—I mean you look very . . . distinguished."

His urge to grin disappeared.

She flushed and said hastily, "That's a compliment."

"For a male under the age of fifty, no, it's not." He crossed his arms and looked about the room. "Now that your brush is gone, I can see nothing else that can be used as a weapon of torture. I believe you are completely disarmed."

"It's not very comfortable," she replied, frowning.

She brushed a strand of golden hair from her cheek and tucked it behind her ear, her soot-streaked fingers leaving a smudge.

He looked about the nearly empty room and tried to imagine himself in just such a situation. She was right; it was intolerable. He turned and went to the doorway. A footman immediately stood at attention. "Thomas, bring two chairs from the bedchamber next door. The deep-blue ones."

"Yes, me lord." The footman turned to do as he was bid.

"I'll also need a hammer and some nails."

Thomas paused, exchanging a startled glance with the other footman. "Pardon, me lord, did ye say—"

"You heard me. Bring them here at once."

"Yes, me lord!" The two footmen scurried off and Angus returned to the bedchamber. He paused at the door. Should he close it? He had no intention of allowing himself to kiss her again—that had been a one-time slip. But in privacy, perhaps he could gain some information from her.

He closed the door. Mary was still beside the fireplace, a doleful expression on her ash-streaked face.

"I've ordered two chairs for you."

She brightened.

"*But* they will be nailed to the floor, so you won't be able to use them for your nefarious plans."

He could see she was unhappy with that, but after a silent struggle, she shrugged. "Michael says one must always focus on the positive. At least I'll have chairs."

"I daresay it was inconvenient being without them."

She made a rueful face. "I didn't think I'd miss them so much, but it hasn't been pleasant. We either sat upon the floor or on my bed."

She sent him a look from under her lashes. "I suppose I must thank you for making my captivity so luxurious. Or it was before you threw the furniture from the windows."

He shrugged. "I have no wish to see you suffer."

"Thank you," she returned dryly.

He found himself fighting a grin. "So, what have you been doing since yesterday?" He glanced around the room but saw no books either upon the bed, the dresser, or the washstand. "I sent you some books from the library. Were they not to your liking?" He'd deliberately chosen books that he'd known wouldn't engage her interest. The last thing he wanted was for her to be entertained; boredom might encourage her to confess her real intentions in order to win her freedom.

He fully expected to send her on her way once he knew who'd sent her; this woman was a mere pawn. An attractive, engaging, and far-too-similar-to-Keira pawn.

"Oh yes, I received the books. I already sent them back to the library."

He heard a faint dismissal in her tone, stirring him to ask, "Why?"

"I'd already read two of them and the other was quite short. I'd finished it within the hour, so there was no reason to keep them here." She tilted her head to one side. "Michael apparently has many of the same books as you, though I suppose that's not surprising, since you specialize in the same area. The treatise on trade along the Euphrates was new to me and I daresay he'd enjoy that immensely, though it was quite short. The other two—the study of the manifest records from the ancient monastery that served to supply the Crusades, and the large tome on Xerxes—are among his favorites."

"I find it hard to believe you've read them all."

She lifted her brows, a faint smile touching her mouth. "Do you wish to quiz me?"

"I might."

Her lips quirked, her eyes gleaming with humor and a touch of challenge. "Then do so."

She hadn't flinched. *Interesting.* "Who was Xerxes's father?"

"Darius the Great."

"And he usurped whose throne to gain power?"

"Darius plotted along with six other noble Persian families to assassinate Smerdis under the pretext that Smerdis was an impostor."

Angus couldn't help but be impressed. "And was Smerdis an impostor?"

Her brow creased, her gaze darkening. "That's a good question and one that is hotly debated. What I do know is that Darius assumed power the morning after the assassination, and spent a considerable amount of time quelling rebellions in his new kingdom by those unwilling to accept him as the new king. So, if Smerdis *was* an impostor, he was quite a well-liked one."

So far, she was correct. "What do you think?"

She pursed her lips, the gesture sending an instant flood of warmth through Angus so that it was difficult for him to follow her words. "I think it's possible

Smerdis was an impostor since he'd spent a good bit of his youth abroad at various wars. Added to that, there were rumors that his own brother wished him dead and had, in fact, killed him. I think Darius was correct in saying Smerdis wasn't the son of the old king, but I don't think Darius really cared. Darius was a ruthless man and would have had Smerdis killed, anyway. The deception just gave Darius an excuse."

Angus was taken by the intensity of her expression. She'd given the topic some thought. "What did Michael think?"

She shook her head. "Michael believed Smerdis wasn't an impostor at all and that Darius made up the whole story. He wished to research it to a more solid conclusion." She sent Angus a sharp glance. "But you knew that."

He had, as did most people who knew Hurst. *She, or the person who sent her to steal the onyx box, might have known Hurst, but that doesn't prove that she is his sister.* He shrugged. "Smerdis has been a frequent topic at the Society. I'm sure many of us have wished to do the same."

"Oh!" Her hands fisted at her sides and for a second, he half expected her to stomp one of her slippered feet. Instead, she merely narrowed her gaze. "You are so stubborn!"

"I'm practical and cautious. It would behoove you to be the same."

"I'll think more cautiously when I've been released. Now is the time for action. Thus far, I've spent all of my time trying to think of a way to escape."

He leaned against the wall. "To no avail, obviously."

Her lips quirked, her eyes sparkling. "Oh, do not give up on me yet. I will think of something."

"I don't doubt it."

Her full mouth curved into a smile. "I must say, it's nice to have some company, even unwilling company." She gestured around the empty room. "It's a bit lonely here."

"You have your maid."

She offered him a droll look. "Have you spoken to my maid?"

"Not at length. Why? Is she a dullard?"

"Not at all. But she dislikes to read, is more concerned with how attractive she finds one of your stable hands than in planning an escape, and has never traveled out of the hamlet in which she was born until she came here, and she is woefully unimpressed with our venture so far."

He chuckled. "She sounds dreadful."

"Oh, no. She's a good sort of woman, just not for twelve hours a day. I sent her to iron a gown because I couldn't stand to hear another word about the men you've hired to work with your horses. According to Abigail, they're all broad-shouldered and as handsome as Greek gods—" Mary had been waving her hand as she spoke and suddenly caught sight of her black-streaked fingers. "Oh, no! My fingernails are totally black."

She crossed to the washstand and Angus found himself watching the sway of her hips beneath her soot-streaked gown. Every movement was natural and yet as graceful as a dancer's.

She dipped her hands into the water and began

scrubbing, *tsk*ing the entire time. As she reached for the soap, she caught sight of herself in the mirror over the basin. "No! I look a mess." She sent him a quick glance. "You could have told me."

"I've never met a woman who would be grateful for being informed that she looked unkempt."

She grimaced, dipped the hand towel into the basin, and scrubbed her face. When she finished she patted her skin dry and folded the hand towel and replaced it by the basin. Then she repinned her hair until it was once more contained. "There. Now I am at least presentable."

She looked far more than presentable. She looked fresh and lovely and completely delicious.

The last thought surprised Angus. He didn't usually appreciate such nonsense. But this woman was more than a mere woman: She was also a puzzle he had yet to solve.

She turned from the dressing table and caught his gaze. She lifted her brows. "Yes?"

"I was wondering why your brother never mentioned you."

"I don't know why, but I intend on having that very conversation with him the second he is home. Did he mention any of our other siblings? Our two sisters? Our brothers William and Robert?"

"No. Not a word."

"So he never told you, then, that William is a sea captain and that Robert has become an attaché to the Home Office and handles most of Michael's transactions at the auction houses in London?"

"No. But then, I don't know that I ever told your brother anything of a personal nature about myself."

"You never mentioned *anything* personal?"

Angus shrugged. "No."

"But . . . he's spent *weeks* with you! Why, just last year, he stayed at New Slains for almost a month."

"So he did. And we spoke every day on a number of important subjects."

"*What* important subjects?"

"About our work, of course."

"And nothing else?"

He shrugged. "There was no need to talk of anything else." At her astounded gaze he waved a dismissive hand. "Women feel this incessant need to burden their conversation with trivia. Men talk about what needs to be talked about and when that's done, we're quite comfortable with silence."

"It seems to me that you never talk about the *really* important things, like family and feelings and—"

"Nonsense. We discussed many topics of great importance. The ordering of the dynasties, whether or not the rumor of the female pharaoh might be true, whether we are as close to unlocking the secrets of the hieroglyphs as we've been led to believe, and all manner of things."

"So Michael is just a business acquaintance, then."

Angus frowned. "Of course not. He is a friend and a good one, too, which is why I am not about to simply hand over his artifact without making certain it's what he would really want."

"He wouldn't wish his sister to be locked away like a common criminal."

"Your safety here is not at risk, so all we're talking about is comfort." Angus narrowed his gaze. "You claim to know Michael. Do you think he would choose your comfort over the loss of one of his artifacts, one he apparently prizes greatly?" He could tell he had her with that statement, for she thought of it for a short while, and then grimaced.

"I didn't realize the onyx box had anything to do with the Hurst Amulet," she admitted with great reluctance.

"Which is Michael's greatest treasure."

"*If* he can find it. He's been looking for it since he first went overseas."

"Which you know, as it was written about in Hurst's popular newspaper serial."

She grimaced. "I wish I'd never written that blasted serial!"

Angus lifted his brows.

Her gaze narrowed. "You don't believe me about that, either."

He shrugged. "I see no proof."

"Blast it, must I prove *everything*?" She threw up a hand. "Don't answer that. I can see that you are a great skeptic, so I already know the answer."

"It has stood me in good stead thus far."

"I daresay it makes you an excellent researcher, but a horrid host." She sighed. "Yes, I wrote the serial. I still write it; one is due next week, in fact."

"Really?" he asked politely.

"Yes, *really*." She rubbed her forehead, but after a moment, she said in a grudging tone, "Fine. Don't believe me. I suppose I can understand that. It was a secret, after all, so why should I expect you to believe it just because I've told you?"

A flicker of appreciation for her calm logic made him add, "Why would Michael have you write his serial?"

"He was too busy to do so, and the editor hounded him. Eventually I wrote one just to silence the man's incessant demands. But as soon as he'd published it and realized how strong the response was, the editor just asked for another and another. Michael thought it a waste when I first began it, but it has been to his benefit. He's gotten a good bit of fame, and people will now pay him to speak, not to mention the many sponsors he's gotten from the endeavor. I think he enjoys the fame, too."

She met Angus's gaze. "Is there anything you wish to ask me about Michael? Some fact or another that he let slip with you? His favorite breakfast? How he travels? The color of his favorite portmanteau?"

"I am willing to listen to anything you wish to say."

She began ticking things off on her fingers. "Michael loves ham and eggs for breakfast. He travels with Anhur, his Egyptian servant. They have a very contentious relationship, far more than one might expect had Michael taken a British servant. Michael is an excellent rider and has more horses than necessary; it's probably his biggest weakness. As a child he was frequently ill, so now he refuses to admit when he feels ill unless absolutely forced. Michael is—"

"Hold. Michael was ill as a child? That's not in the serial."

"Neither is his preferred breakfast. Since he's been a frequent visitor here, surely that rang true."

It had, but it was a very piddly detail in the grand scheme of things. "Perhaps you've met Mr. Hurst. He's society's darling since that damned serial was printed."

"*Oh!* I am wasting my time." She crossed her arms, the gesture pressing her generous breasts upward.

Angus's mouth went dry. *God, she had deliciously plump breasts.* He tamped down a fierce flare of lust and forced himself to think of other things. *I must encourage her to continue talking about Michael. She might reveal some truth that will help me discover who she really is.*

"What else can you tell me about him?"

She waved a hand. "Ask me anything."

"Which hand does he use?"

"He likes to say he is ambidextrous, but he uses his left hand with the most ease."

That was true. "What do you know about the vicarage where he grew up?"

"It was old and leaky, the stairs crooked and the carpet threadbare . . . or it used to be."

"Used to?"

"My sisters both married well. Over the last ten years, they have been systematically fixing the vicarage. Now the steps are straight and no longer creak, the windows are all new, the fireplaces don't belch smoke, and there are new carpets and furnishings in almost every room. Whenever he returns home, Michael always declares he wouldn't know the place except for the crooked front porch; there is no fixing that."

"Your sisters married well? I believe you mentioned them before."

"They married into Clan MacLean. If Mr. Young's

house wasn't so close, I'd have asked one of my brother-in-laws to vouch for me."

"Clan MacLean? Near Stirling?"

"Yes."

"That's much farther than Mr. Young's house. However, if we don't hear from him soon, we might well send word to your brother-in-laws."

"But that would take a week out *and* back! I don't have that sort of time!" Her velvety brown gaze turned pleading. "Michael is in grave danger. I *must* get that item to him."

"And I must protect it," Angus said.

"Please! I'll answer anything you care to ask."

"Hurst warned me that someone would come for the item. Why do you think he did that?"

"I don't know, but I wish I did. I have to admit, the tone of the letter is such that I wouldn't dismiss it, either. Michael is not given to dramatics. If he said someone was going to come for the artifact, I'd believe it."

"So why should I believe you?"

"I've thought about that," she answered evenly. "The gist of his letter was that someone you *knew* might come for it. Not someone you didn't know."

"Your interpretation is questionable. He warned of someone coming for the item, and that it *might* be someone I knew, not that it would be."

"Then why didn't he just name the person if he thought you might know the traitor? He thinks you are being watched."

"By whom? Neason? There is no one else in this castle, no one with access to my records and artifacts."

"I don't know what Michael meant, but it was obvious that he didn't feel he could be forthright." She paced quickly back and forth before the fireplace. "If he was warning you about someone specific, then it had to be someone you *both* know. But who?"

"This is ridiculous. You are playing with words in an effort to distract me."

"I've tried to give you some facts about Michael's life, but you dismissed them all."

"Hurst's gossipy column has more followers than even Byron. Who doesn't know the details of his life?"

"There must be something I know about him that I didn't write in that silly series." She pursed her lips and tilted her head to one side. With her heart-shaped face, and her soft lips pursed just so, she looked like a rogue cherub.

Some of Angus's hard feelings softened, which made him frown. Damn it, he owed it to Michael to delve into her past any way he could.

She tapped her chin with a slender finger, pacing the length of the carpet. "But perhaps not. No matter what sort of personal information I might supply, it is doubtful you would know of it, since your relationship with him apparently didn't delve any deeper than your professional interests."

Angus watched, completely fascinated. He wasn't certain what it was—her calm logic, which spoke to his researcher's soul, the way her full bosom jiggled whenever she turned on her heel, or the erotic combination of both, but he was content watching her.

She turned again, her skirts flaring and showing her ankles. "You both know Mr. Young. He was a frequent visitor at Wythburn Vicarage, as you know, along with his sister Miriam."

Angus called his recalcitrant attention back to order. "Everyone knows Young travels with his sister. She serves as his secretary."

"As I do for Michael when he's home." She absently brushed a strand of blond hair from her cheek. As she'd paced, thick strands of her hair had slowly come loose from the pins. She paid them no heed, but brushed each strand away if it chanced touch her face, which made Angus think she was used to it.

She had glorious hair; thick and blond, it looped into fat curls that brushed her shoulder and would hang far down her back. He wondered how she'd look wearing nothing but her hair, and had such an instantaneous reaction that he had to look away and count prime numbers to one thousand before he could breathe normally again.

She paused in her pacing just a few feet from him. "In addition to Young, you both know Champollion, too."

"Everyone in our field knows them. They are the closest to discovering the secret to the hieroglyphs."

"Yes, but you both have *personal* knowledge, which others do not. For example, I know that Young was brought up as a Quaker, has nine brothers and sisters, is an excellent physician, knows twelve languages, and has theorized in many other fields other than hieroglyphs. He also wrote a very notable article entitled 'Egypt' for the *Encyclopaedia Britannica*.

"As for Champollion, he is a good bit younger than

Mr. Young, is a known classical scholar, orientalist, and linguist, is furthering Young's studies on the hieroglyphs, and is soon to publish a translation that Michael—and I assume you, as well—is eagerly awaiting." She turned to him. "True?"

Angus frowned. "I wasn't aware of Young's religious views or of Champollion's age for I've never met him face-to-face."

"But . . . you said you know Young and Champollion well."

"I know their work well, Young more than Champollion. I doubt Michael knows that much about them, either. Which makes me wonder how *you* know so much."

"Because I've spoken to them both when they came to visit Michael! For the love of heaven, don't you researchers talk about anything other than antiquities?"

No, they didn't. Up until now, Angus hadn't considered that a hindrance. Irritated at feeling as if he had failed a test of some sort, he shrugged. "Both Young and Champollion are famed in the scientific community. I'm sure that sort of knowledge is fairly common."

Her gaze narrowed as she considered this, and Angus found himself fighting a smile when she absently twisted a newly loosened curl about her fingers and then could not get them undone.

"Oh, fiddle!" She wiggled her fingers until the hair released them. She caught his faintly amused gaze and flushed, her creamy skin warming with a hint of pink. "I always do that. Father says I once got my hand so entangled that they were forced to cut it."

"Your hand?"

Her lips quirked. "No, my hair."

His gaze flickered to the riotous mass of curls that she'd attempted to pin up, some of which now covered her shoulder. "You must have been quite young when that happened."

"Very, for I don't even remember it." She brushed the curl over her shoulder as if it bothered her. "Anyway, as I was going to say, I can give you a description of Mr. Young if that will help. He is moderate in height, with graying hair and blue-gray eyes. His sister Miriam is taller than he by an inch, with light brown hair that she wears in a tight chignon. She also wears very sensible clothing and shoes, while Mr. Young tends toward the fashionable."

Angus shrugged. "All that proves is that you've met them. You could have seen them at a lecture or at an inn. Young will talk to a stump, so it wouldn't be difficult to meet him and come away knowing far more than a casual observer should."

"Oh, for the love of peace—if you feel that way about Young, then there was no reason to ask him to come here at all! Besides, do you really think he will drop everything he's doing and come running merely to identify me?"

"Why not?"

She could think of three or four good reasons. Finally, she said, "I hope he comes soon."

"If he's at home, he'll come. I have a few items he's been particularly interested in."

When Mr. Young identified her, that would solve

all of her problems. Erroll would be forced to admit she was who she said, and to release the onyx box into her custody. "I hope he's home," she said fervently.

She looked up to catch the earl's gaze. "My lord, whatever happens, do not forget that Michael's life is in a stranger's hands. I fear for him—and you should, too."

"I believe that Hurst is in some difficulties." The earl hesitated, then added, "Unlike you, I don't fear for him. Hurst is a man of vast personal resources. If he is in trouble, he will find a way out of it, probably well before you get this artifact to him."

"But we don't know that."

"Don't we?" The earl's dark gaze shuttered, a considering look resting on his expressive face. "I wonder if Hurst wasn't coerced into writing the letter you brought. It seemed a little forced."

Mary blinked. She hadn't considered that. *Had* Michael written it under duress? "It's possible, I suppose. But until I have reason to do otherwise, I must follow the dictates of his letter."

"Fine. Do as you wish. Michael was on his way here when he was detained, and I consider him a friend. Just know this: If Mr. Young identifies you as an impostor, you will pay for your deception."

The threat sent a shiver down her spine. "What would you do if I was an impostor?"

"You had better hope you never find out."

She fisted her hands, so frustrated she could stomp her feet. Her situation was so difficult; she was bored, and sad, and worried, and—oh, a thousand other unpleasant emotions. She'd been prepared to deal with the exciting parts of this adventure. No one had said a word about the waiting.

"Look, Erroll, we're not going to agree on anything until Young arrives, so"—she threw up her hands—"we'll wait, blast it. Meanwhile, what's the harm in allowing me access to the library or a sitting room? Can't I at least eat with the household? I'm so *bored,* and I cannot stay locked inside these four walls for another five or six *days!*"

"I won't have you wandering through the house, searching for that damned box."

She shrugged. "So have the footmen watch me."

"I feel safer with you locked here." He hesitated. "In addition to the two chairs, I'll send up a broader selection of books to tide you over until Mr. Young arrives."

"You're too kind." She almost spat the words, she was so angry.

"What I *am* is careful. It's what makes my research acceptable."

"That's not true. What makes your research respected is your ability to recognize the importance of seemingly mundane objects. Look at the presentation you did to the Royal Society on the Temple of Ptah, and why it had to be located in Memphis and not in Tigris, as many had suggested. Martinique and that fool Daniels had written that ridiculous paper saying the temple was mentioned in some papyrus scroll, and you refuted that sloppy bit of research by pointing out that the scroll listed where various objects had gone to, not where they'd come from. Michael said it set the society on its

ear for weeks, for most of them had accepted Martinique's and Daniels's interpretation without verifying a
thing. *That,* Lord Erroll, is what you are known for."

His gaze narrowed and she dared hope she'd convinced him with her knowledge. After a moment, he
said, "So you've followed my work."

"Michael said you had an eye for antiquities like
no other, and that he'd trust you over ten Daniels or
Martinques."

"I am flattered. But that will not gain you the freedom to wander about my house and steal that object at
will."

That did it. She marched up to him, her temper
barely held. "Erroll, I am not going to meekly sit in this
room and wait while our friend Young makes the trek to
this godforsaken castle!"

He crossed his arms and rocked back on his heels.
With his dark clothing and hair, the ever-present black
silk scarf swathing his lower jaw and neck, and those
green eyes, he looked nothing like a staid researcher and
every bit a pirate, ruthless and daring. "This is *my* house,
and I am lord and master here. The only laws I recognize are my own, and the sooner you realize what that
means, the better."

"Fine. Be master of your burned-down castle. *I* am
the mistress of my own life, and I say which laws I follow and which I won't, including *yours,* Lord Erroll. I
will make this imprisonment unpleasant for everyone,
especially *you.* You've already seen that I can do that,
and I won't stop now."

His eyes darkened a second before he moved. She

whirled in a desperate effort to dart out of reach, her heel catching on the hem of her gown.

He grabbed her about the waist and spun her around and lifted her until they were chest to chest. She knew he was angry and was attempting to show her who was in charge of her fate, and for the veriest second, she was truly afraid.

But then reason returned. Michael thought the world of this man, and she trusted her brother's instincts. Her own instincts told her that the earl was a complex individual, formed by a tragedy and by the isolation of his home. In a way, she could almost feel sympathy for his position and—

"Now you will listen to me," he stated, his voice low and threatening, banishing any sympathy she might have felt. "I will have no more talk of who will do what to whom. You came willingly to my castle, and you'll stay until I say you can leave."

How had this man gotten to be so *bossy*? "If you want me to be more accepting of your rules, you'll have to negotiate far more than you've done so far."

"You'd best have a care, Miss Hurst, or whatever your name is. I am not trifling here. I say you will remain here, and here you will remain."

She sniffed. "Humph."

Angus couldn't believe it. She'd *sniffed* at him, dismissing him completely with one gesture. How dare she? By God, he would show her what he would and would not stand for. He lifted her higher and considered kissing her. *You swore you wouldn't kiss her again,* his logical side whispered in his ear. *Have a care.*

But the lusty side of him fought to overrule it. His body was achingly aware of the softness of her curves, of the full press of her breasts against his chest.

Somehow, some way, he would conquer this woman, bend her to his will. He already knew there was only one way to silence her infuriating speech.

But he'd vowed not to lose control again, and if he kissed her, he didn't know if he'd have the strength to step away.

While Angus wrestled with that thought, his captive grasped his collar, her eyes flashing daggers, and planted a kiss upon his surprised lips.

A ferocious mixture of pleasure and fury dissolved Angus's self-control with one fell blow. Giving in to the passion, he tightened his arms about her and deepened the kiss.

Letter from Michael to his sister Mary, from Old Alexandria:

I have been sitting in this hot, smell-plagued port for two weeks now, waiting for the local officials to approve our cargo so we may set sail. Such is the art of the negotiation: If you appear to be in a hurry, you lose. By the same token, if you hesitate too long, you lose. I do not like to lose.

If I do not hear from the port master today, we intend on setting sail under dark of night, regulations and gun ships be damned. If we do not, our stores will be depleted ere we get to sea, which may be what they're hoping for. It costs a fortune to stock the ship from the port master's stores; this is how he makes his real money.

There comes a time in every endeavor when one must take fate by the lapels and explain the need for urgency. Now may be that time.

$\mathcal{N}$INE

Whatever had propelled Mary into this deep, endless kiss held her there, powerless to stop it. Kisses were better when seasoned with passion, and her passion *exploded* for the infuriating earl. It was always there, simmering under the surface, coloring every word he said, every move he made with a sensual connotation.

The earl shifted his hold on her, sliding one of his large hands over her bottom and lifting her higher, holding her against him as easily as if she'd weighed no more than two stone.

It was shocking to think of a man's hand placed in such an intimate manner, so Mary decided not to think of it. Instead, she'd enjoy the feel of his warm body against hers.

As he cupped her to him she shivered with growing

need. She slipped her arms about his neck and clung like a torn sail in a raging storm, hanging on with both hands as passion buffeted her and sent her senses reeling until she could no more think than stand. All she could do was *feel.*

The earl devoured her, kissing her with ruthless intent, with power and domination blended with pure lust. And Mary was lost before it all.

Angus, for his part, had never been so stirred. This woman fit him like no other, her lavender scent stirring his senses until he could barely think. In some ways she seemed an innocent, so it had been a shock when he'd felt her hands clutching his lapels and her mouth had opened so eagerly under his. With the ferocity of a storm, she demanded an embrace and deepened it, then turned it into something else. Something hotter. Something more passionate. More everything.

Suddenly he was awash in her clean fragrance, in the silken feel of her hair as it brushed his hands, the softness of her curves as they melded to his. Passion roared to life, and just like that, Angus was no longer in control.

She moaned against his mouth and he ground his hips to hers, demanding more. She gasped, shivering erotically.

And then they were no longer standing by the fireplace, but beside the bed. Angus pressed her back, her knees bending as he bent over her and pressed her into the mattress. She clutched him and pulled him forward, her mouth desperate against his own.

Angus slipped a hand up her hip to her breast. He

savored the full mound that filled his hand, kneading it gently, his thumb finding her nipple through the thin material. He flicked it once, twice . . . She moaned against his mouth, rocking her hips back and forth. Angus pressed his knee between her legs and she parted as sweetly as a flower.

Her hands never stopped, never stilled. She tugged at his shirt, pulling him forward, arching against him.

His hand cupped her calf and he slowly slid it up, across the smoothness of her knee to the delicate warmth of her thigh. She was a plush woman, rounded and fulfilling. It was impossible not to be fully aware of her femininity.

She moaned as his hand slid up her thigh, not touching and yet so close . . . he paused there to tease her yet more, enjoying the feel of her warm breast and peaked nipple.

He'd never been entranced by a plentiful bosom before and he now wondered why. His cock was as hard as a stone with yearning. He placed a string of kisses down her cheek to the sweetness of her neck, and then on to her breast. Through the material of her gown, he laved her hardened nipple.

She gasped and arched, her eyes flying open to meet his. Chocolate brown with flecks of gold and green, her eyes shone, her soft mouth parted, her breath ragged and pleading, so spontaneous and natural that his cock reared as if to meet her. Angus moaned and pressed his hips to hers, opening her thighs even more so that his cock ground into her.

For an exquisite moment their hips pressed tightly

together, their hands and mouths teasing and pleasing, their breath ragged and out of control as he slowly slid his hand to her chemise and—

A noise in the hallway halted him as surely as a bucket of ice water. *The footmen and the chairs.*

With a muffled curse, he forced himself to release her and straighten, tugging her skirt down as he stepped away, his heart thudding sickly against his chest. His mouth tingled where she'd pressed hers, his entire body yearning for more. God, he was so ready that he ached with it.

Mary stood, adjusting her gown, her hair mussed and falling about her flushed face. She looked up at him, her lips swollen from his embrace, her eyes smoky and mysterious. Her chest rose and fell against her disheveled gown.

Angus raked his hair with a hand that was not quite steady as he collected his wits. "I should not have allowed that to happen. I—I'm sorry. That was an error on my part."

She glanced at the door where the scraping continued, then walked as calm as cold water to her dresser, where she began to put up her hair using pins from a small glass dish.

"There is no apology necessary," Mary said. "If you remember, I began it. I fear my temper got the best of me."

He noted that she was careful not to meet his gaze and that her hands shook a bit. But he bowed his head. "I am older, though, and you are a guest in my house. This was . . . it won't happen again."

He couldn't believe he'd allowed his passions to

enflame him to the point where he'd lost control. *Yet again,* he reminded himself harshly. *What is it about this woman that I cannot keep my hands from her?*

"It won't happen again?" she repeated. "That's a pity, for I enjoyed it very much."

He frowned. "You . . . you enjoyed it?"

Her gaze met his in her dressing table mirror and he could see that she wasn't as calm as her words belied. "Of course I did."

"But enjoying something doesn't mean it should happen," he said gruffly.

"That's true." She finished pinning her hair and began to smooth her gown. "And you're right; it's most improper. I had no idea a kiss could be so . . ." She shook her head as to clear it and then gave a shaky laugh. "I hardly know what to say."

"There is nothing to say," he said bleakly, guilt washing over him. *What if this really is Hurst's little sister? He will not be amused that I allowed my passions to push me in such a direction. Of course, she was most enthusiastic . . .* He looked at her with narrowed eyes. *Perhaps that is part of her plan, to seduce me and gain my trust. Whatever her purpose, the outcome cannot be good.* "I will endeavor not to visit again."

He opened the door and looked down the hall, where the two footmen were dragging two chairs.

"I thought I told you to fetch the chairs from my bedchamber?"

The footmen paused in their endeavors, looking at each other uncertainly. Before either could speak, Muir appeared from where he'd been following behind. "Your pardon, my lord. The young men came to request assistance in removing the chairs from your bedchamber for they were quite heavy."

"Aye, me lord," the younger one said, wiping his brow. "We couldna get either o' them out the door. They are very good chairs, they are."

"Too good to be thrown out the window," Muir continued smoothly, handing the closest footman a hammer and a bag of nails. "Therefore, I suggested the footmen take the chairs from the front parlor instead. They're more suited to a lady, as they're a bit smaller, and they're slipcovered, in case you decide to toss them from the window, as well."

"Thank you, Muir. I'm sure these chairs will do quite well." Angus turned to the footmen. "I'll leave you two to nail the chairs to the floor."

Muir closed his eyes in obvious pain and the footmen exchanged astonished looks. The tallest footman cleared his throat. "Ah, pardon me, my lord, but *where* in the room shall we nail them?"

"I'll leave that up to the lady. If you'll give me one moment to say farewell, then you may enter and begin your duties." Satisfied all would be taken care of, he turned back into the room.

Mary stood by the window, looking out onto the courtyard, sunlight streaming over her. She'd pinned up her hair so that it frothed down one side of her face in thick curls. Her gown was straightened, her expression, serene. Anyone looking at her would never known he'd just kissed her passionately.

How can she look as if nothing has happened? And yet even as he had the thought, she rubbed her arms as if cold. *Ah, she can't hide her reaction completely.* But seeing her there, bathed in the golden light, did nothing to reduce his own reaction. He knew he had to limit his contact with her beginning immediately, so he did nothing to engage her in further conversation, but merely said in a short tone, "Two chairs are being brought for you now. If you wish for anything other than your freedom, merely let the footmen know."

Then he left, nodding to Muir and the footmen as he walked by.

Inside the room there was a moment of silence, and then a frustrated noise and the stamp of a foot, followed by a thud. A shoe, perhaps?

Angus left for the library. Whoever she was, she knew his desire far too well. Had whoever sent her known his weaknesses? But how could they, when Angus was just now discovering them himself?

It made no sense. None of it did—least of all his reaction to a short, plump, mocking fluff of a girl who he was almost certain was a liar and a thief.

Angus entered the library, briskly ordering his cousin to bring the wax rubbing of the hieroglyphs for further study. He would immerse himself in his work and forget the woman upstairs.

"Here you are," Neason said. "We might be better off sending these to Champollion rather than Young. They say he's even closer to breaking the hieroglyphic code than Young is."

"I trust Young more," Angus told him. "If he cannot do it, then we'll send it on to Champollion." He sat in his desk chair, noting a smudge of ash across the back of his fingers. He must have gotten that from Mary's skirt when he'd kissed her and— Memories made his traitorous body react as he realized her lavender scent lingered about him.

I cannot allow this fascination to hold me. In the back of his mind whispered another voice. *What if she is who she says she is? You've already gone over the line, if she's an innocent. What will you do then?*

He whipped out a handkerchief and scrubbed the ash from his hand. She couldn't be Hurst's sister, for she wasn't a true innocent. She was far too passionate and eager.

He pushed the uncomfortable thoughts aside and pulled his magnifying glass from his desk. "Come, Neason. Bring a pen and paper and let's see what more we can deduce from Hurst's antiquity."

Neason covered his ears. "I've never heard such a horrible voice!"

It was the next morning and Angus sat at his desk holding his head in his hands. "Voice? I've never heard such a horrible *noise.*"

Neason grimaced as the noise rose again, a shrill caterwauling mew that echoed down the hallways and invaded every inch of New Slains Castle. "Is that . . . Good God, I believe she's singing 'Greensleeves.'"

Despite his irritation, Angus's lips twitched. He had to give her credit; the lass had a sense of humor.

The singing stopped, the sudden silence even more deafening.

Neason gave a sigh of relief. "Finally! I didn't think she'd ever quit. I've never—"

The singing began again with renewed vigor.

Neason looked so insulted that Angus chuckled. "She can't keep it up forever. She will soon be hoarse and there will be an end to it."

Neason sighed. "She's certainly determined."

"Yes, she is." Angus sent an appreciative glance at the ceiling, noting that the chandelier was actually vibrating a bit.

She was definitely shaking the castle walls. If he hadn't placed her in a turret room, the sound would have dissipated, but the turret's older fireplace served as a funnel and channeled the noise directly into the rest of the castle.

Acoustically speaking, she had them all over a barrel, and he suspected she knew it.

He hid a faint smile and bent to examine the onyx box again. Whatever he did to still Miss Hurst's attempts to annoy them all into submission, he would make sure he only visited her with the door to her bedchamber left open.

The singing changed.

Neason blinked. "What's she singing now?"

"Apparently our guest is an opera lover."

"If she loved it, she wouldn't be doing *that* to it," Neason replied fervently. "I'm surprised to hear such a voice from such a feminine woman."

She was that, Angus agreed, remembering her from yesterday, beating a rousing staccato upon the grate with a hair brush, soot clinging to her gown and face. She'd looked like an Amazon on the warpath.

A knock sounded on the door, barely audible over the opera screeching down the chimney. Upon being bid to enter, Muir came to Angus's desk and lowered a silver salver. A folded sheet of paper rested upon it.

Angus eyed it with interest. "From our guest, I assume?"

The butler nodded just as the singing halted, and gave a relieved sigh. "Miss Hurst asked that I deliver this to you, my lord. *Please* read it."

Angus reached for the letter and opened it.

Lord Erroll,

As you may have noticed, I have found a new and improved way to gain your attention. Pray release me from my room and I promise to sit very quietly in whatever room you choose.

Sincerely yours,
Miss Mary Hurst

"Well?" Neason asked impatiently.

Angus shrugged. "She wants out of her room—a fact you may have noticed." He reread the missive, then drew a clean sheet of paper over and picked up his pen.

Miss—

He paused, the pen hovering over the paper. What could he call her? He'd be damned if he'd call her Miss Hurst unless he knew for certain that was her name.

He put the pen to paper.

Miss Fortune,
　　You may caterwaul until you have no voice. I find it quite a pleasant distraction from the usual silence of my library. I do love a good opera.
　　　　　　　　　　　　　　　　Sincerely,
　　　　　　　　　　　　　　　　Erroll

　　Angus waved the paper in the air to dry the ink, and then folded it and handed it to Muir. "Please take this to Miss Fortune."

　　Muir, who'd reached for the letter, paused. "Miss Fortune, my lord?"

　　"That's what we'll call our guest from now on."

　　Muir sighed. "I take that to mean that you did not agree to the young lady's request?"

　　"You would be right in that assumption, Muir. I'm not going to be threatened by—" The horrible singing began again.

　　Angus lifted a brow at the butler. "Pray take her my answer before she cracks the stone in the fireplace."

　　The butler bowed and left.

　　Neason came to stand beside the desk. "I keep thinking about that box. Could it be the quality of the gold chasing that makes it so valuable?"

　　"No, it's too light." Angus held the box in one hand. "It's attractive enough and would sell to a curiosity collector easily, but you wouldn't get full value. Something tells me this holds some secret. I just don't know what it is. I wonder if it's—"

　　The singing stopped abruptly.

Neason and Angus both glanced at the ceiling. "Finally!" Neason breathed. He sent Angus a side-glance. "I hope you weren't rude to Miss H— I beg your pardon, to Miss *Fortune.*"

"What would it matter if I was?"

"Because I will go mad if she continues her assault on our peace!"

"Neason, the only way to silence Miss Fortune is if we tied her to a stake in the middle of her bedchamber, out of reach of every piece of furniture, every chimney, and every potential noisemaker. I already took away most of her furnishings, and I went through the room and removed every bangable object I could find. Until this morning, I thought she was again disarmed, but I see I erred."

"Are you certain keeping her locked up is wise?"

"I won't have her roaming about the household looking for this." Angus peered back at the box. As he did so, the sun sent a slender beam down one side. He frowned. The box wasn't straight on all sides. The difference was slight, but he'd spent so much time examining it that he wondered why he hadn't seen it before. He bent forward to peer more closely and—

The caterwauling began again, this time a hymn. Off key and boisterous, it belted through the castle like a rowdy tavern verse. At least he'd induced her to forgo opera.

He sighed and pushed the box away, tossing his magnifying glass upon the desk. "I cannot think with that howling." He rubbed his temples, where a headache was beginning to build. She wasn't going to quit;

that much was obvious. After all, what else did she have to do other than plan ways to annoy the living hell out of him?

A soft knock preceded Muir, who carried the salver directly to Angus. "Your answer, my lord."

Angus took the missive and unfolded it.

Lord Annoyance,
I know for a fact that a researcher values silence, so do not attempt to pull the wool over my eyes. I hope you enjoy classical hymn music. As a vicar's daughter, I know an unending number of them.
                              Yours,
                                Miss Fortune

Angus stood. "That does it."

Neason stood as well. "Are you going to let her out of her room, then? I must admit she's been very shrewd, and I wouldn't blame you for giving in and—"

"I'm not giving in. What I *am* going to do is defang this particular annoyance."

Neason sighed. "Angus, perhaps *I* should speak with her. I know she bothers you."

Muir bowed. "It's quite noticeable, my lord. You have been scowling an unusual amount of late."

The wench did bother him, though not in the way Neason or Muir imagined. "I'm going to allow our guest out of her chambers, but only with an escort. It's a pain and I shall have to keep that box locked away, but it must be done."

Neason looked relieved. "That's for the best. Besides,

I've been thinking that if we keep her locked in her room, we'll never discover anything about her."

Angus turned to Muir. "I will allow her out of her bedchamber for three hours a day, between ten and one. She is to eat in her room, for I won't have her disrupting my meals with her chatter."

"Very well, my lord."

"She's not to enter this room, ever. Set the sitting room aside for her private use. She may also walk in the gardens if the weather permits, but I will *not* have her left unattended, not even for a moment."

"Yes, my lord. I shall set two footmen to watch her at all times."

"Very good. Tell the rest of the staff that she's to be watched like the thief she is. If she does anything suspicious, I will know of it."

"Yes, my lord. I shall inform the staff immediately. Will there be anything else?"

"That will do for now. I will inform our guest of the new rules."

The butler bowed and left the room.

"That's an excellent move," Neason said. "With the entire staff at watch, she won't be able to charm a few footmen into doing her bidding."

"Charm? That woman has no charm."

"I'm sure she can display it when it's necessary. She's actually very pretty, in her way. Rather like a milkmaid." Neason sent a curious glance at Angus. "Don't you think so?"

"I suppose she's well enough." If she were a milkmaid, then she was the queen of them all. "Lock that box in my drawer." He gave Neason the key. "Meanwhile, I'll inform our lively caterwauling poltergeist that beginning tomorrow, she may come downstairs for a daily visit." Angus flicked a glance at Neason. "Perhaps you can charm her into revealing something."

Neason colored. "I doubt that. I never had your way with women."

"And I never had your way with a pistol, so we are even."

"I think you got the good end of that bargain." Neason grinned and began to gather items off the desk. "I'll put the tracings away, too."

"Thank you." Angus left and made his way up the stairs, aware of a stir at the realization that in a moment he would be in her room. *But I will not touch her. Not even once.* Though he repeated the stricture several times, his body refused to stop simmering in excitement.

He came to her room and nodded to the footmen. "Have you spoken with Muir?"

The youngest one nodded. "Aye, me lord."

"Good. Beginning tomorrow, Miss Fortune may leave her chambers from ten to one. Watch her like a hawk. It wouldn't surprise me if she attempted to flee."

"Yes, me lord."

Angus nodded. "Open the door and leave it open." He waited until the footmen had done so and then entered the room.

Mary was sitting in one of her two chairs, this one nailed to the floor beside the fireplace. She was bent at the waist, her elbows on her knees, ready to belt out another hymn when she caught sight of him and jumped to her feet. "My lord! I didn't hear you knock."

"That's because I didn't."

Her frown was swift. "That's rude."

"So is screeching."

"I was singing."

"I can assure you that you were screeching." He crossed his arms. "Surely you can sing better than that."

Mary had to grin at the sardonic question. "You'll never know, my lord, unless you allow me out of this room."

The earl regarded her through half-closed eyes. "Fine."

She almost fell over. "Did . . . did you say 'fine'?"

He shrugged. "I came to tell you that I've changed my mind. You may visit downstairs—"

"Thank you!"

"—but only for a few hours each day."

"Why only a few hours?"

"You should thank me for those. I am giving somewhat; you have to give, too."

"But I'm so bored in here," she said, wincing at the petulant sound of her own voice.

"I'm certain you'll be bored once you come downstairs, too, for I don't intend on amusing you. You are still a prisoner here, and you may not leave the castle proper. I will have footmen watching you at all times."

Mary had expected no less, and she nodded. "May I go into the gardens?"

"It's still cold but it is expected to get warmer, so

yes, you may walk the gardens if you wish to exercise. However, you are not to go past the garden gate."

That was acceptable. She longed to get out of doors. "And may I have access to the library?"

"No. I will select a book or two for you, provided they are not my research tomes."

"No! I was especially hoping to read some of those." He quirked a brow and she hurried to add, "But of course I'll be grateful for a book of any kind."

He nodded and then turned on his heel. She hurried to step forward. "My lord?"

He paused on the threshold and sent her a hard glance. "Yes?"

She dipped a curtsy. "Thank you." When she rose, she found his gaze locked on her décolletage, his mouth white and tense.

The air had changed palpably; she could almost feel the heavy attraction. Her body instantly reacted, her nipples hardening, her skin prickling, her breathing growing shallow and rapid. In that instant, she yearned for his touch in a way she'd never yearned before.

The earl's brows snapped down and he gave her a jerky bow. "Good day. You may begin your visitation tomorrow morning."

"In the morning? But I want—"

"In the morning or not at all."

She noted how close he stayed to the door, almost as if he were about to fly out.

She took a step forward and he straightened, his jaw set.

Ah ha! she thought, relief flooding through her. *He*

is uneasy near me. Our kiss discombobulated him as much as it did me. Heaven knows I've relived that kiss over and over, especially his reaction to it. That one aspect had kept her from feeling foolish—he'd been just as involved in their embrace as she'd been.

Mary took another step forward, moving more quickly this time so that Erroll didn't have time to move out of the way.

Then she placed her palm flat on his chest, right at the bottom of his cravat. For a long moment they looked at one another; Mary's entire body tingled from head to toe. Even her hair seemed to crackle with the attraction that flew between them. Beneath her fingertips, his heart drummed an extra beat.

She couldn't help herself. Eyes locked, she slowly rose onto her tippy-toes and leaned in to press her lips to his.

He muttered a curse and spun away.

Her body ached with instant disappointment. Mary dropped back to her heels and bit back a sigh.

The earl stopped by the door and glanced back. "There will be no more of that."

"That's a great deal too bad," Mary said truthfully.

His gaze narrowed, a harsh look to the line of his mouth. "If you think to offer your body in order to gain Hurst's artifact, then think again. I will not be lured by you or anyone else to give up what has been left under my protection."

Mary's good humor fled, her face warming until she feared it might burst into flames. "How dare you suggest such a thing! I merely wished to kiss you because . . ." She'd liked it. But suddenly, the idea of saying such a thing out loud seemed brash and wrong. *What's happened to me? Every time I'm with this man, I forget who I am,* what *I am.*

He glared at her. "I was going to offer to replace your furnishings, but I can see you don't wish for them."

"Oh, no! *Please* replace the furnishings! I didn't mean to upset you, I just—"

But he'd already stalked from the room as if he couldn't leave fast enough, slamming the door behind him.

Letter from Michael to Angus Hay, Earl of Erroll, from a caravan heading for the Sahara Desert:

One day, my old friend, I shall bring you to see the land of the antiquities we both love so much. Until I'd traveled here myself and seen the wonders with my own eyes, the objects didn't have the relevance that they now have.

In order to understand something really and truly well, you must know where it came from. There is no other way to appreciate its value.

$\mathcal{T}$EN

$\mathcal{A}$ half hour later, a knock sounded on her door and Abigail entered followed by a Mrs. MacFadden, the housekeeper.

Almost as broad as she was high, the little woman was a bustle of energy. Her round face was wreathed with smiles and instantly everything seemed a bit more cheerful.

Mary held out her hand. "It's very nice to meet you."

Mrs. MacFadden pumped Mary's hand up and down. "And 'tis good to meet ye, too, missy. I would ha' been here sooner, but we were tol' not to visit ye whilst ye were a prisoner. But now I'm to oversee the replacement o' yer furnishings, I am."

Mary sent an amazed look at Abigail, who nodded as hard as she could.

"Oh, yes, miss! We're to get a roomful of furniture, and the two chairs by the fireplace are to have the nails removed, and all *sorts* of things!"

So the earl had changed his mind after all. That was something, at least. Still, she couldn't help but feel a little irritated that he hadn't told her himself.

Two footmen staggered into the room carrying a large, low table.

The housekeeper pointed to the rug before the fireplace. "Put it there and dinna be rippin' up the rug when ye set it down, neither."

They did as they were told as two more young men entered, each carrying a chair. The housekeeper issued orders right and left as more and more furnishings arrived. In a remarkably short time, Mary's room looked inhabitable yet again.

As the final footman left, the housekeeper looked about with satisfaction. "There. Tha's much better, is it no', lassie?"

"It's wonderful. Where did all of this furniture come from?"

"Och, now, I wasn't told where to fetch the furnishings, so I took some from each bedchamber. A chair from this one, a table from tha'. They dinna match exactly, but I can have them covered one by one and we'll be good as new before ye know it."

"Won't these things be missed?"

"If they are, 'twill be his lordship's fault and no one else's." The housekeeper blew out her breath in irritation. "Tha's wha' he gets fer tossin' all yer nice furnishin' oot the window."

"I understand I'm to be allowed out of my room tomorrow?" Mary said.

"From ten to one every day."

Abigail frowned at this. "Ten to one? But that's only three hours!"

"I know," Mrs. MacFadden said. "And so I tol' his lordship." The housekeeper sent Mary a pitying look. "We all love the earl and he's good to us, he is. But there comes a time when ye have to stand up and be heard, and so I told Muir."

"The butler?"

"Aye. He's the only one his lordship'll listen to. 'Tis because o' Muir that ye have yer furnishings back."

"Ah. He requested it, did he?"

"Indeed he did, miss. And offered to come and nail it all down hisself, if need be, but there's no need fer tha', is there, miss?" Mrs. MacFadden regarded Mary with an anxious air.

"Of course not. Since I'm allowed out, even if it's just for a few hours a day, I've no reason to cause such a racket."

Mrs. MacFadden clapped her hands together. "And so Muir promised his lordship!"

"One thing at a time, hmm?" Mary suggested.

Mrs. MacFadden beamed. "There ye be, lassie! Och, 'tis about time ye were let out of yer room. If I tol' Mr. Muir once't, I tol' him a thousand times that 'tisn't right fer a wee thing to be locked away no matter if she stole something from his lordship or no—"

"I didn't steal anything; I came to ask for an artifact that belongs to my brother. But I didn't realize the earl would ask for proof of my relationship, so we're at an impasse until Mr. Young arrives and verifies I am who I say I am."

"Och, is tha' how 'tis? I dinna know! I'm certain tha' once Mr. Young arrives, his lordship will treat ye nicer. He's a good mon, but he's not been the same since the tragedy."

"His wife's death?"

"Aye, miss. After tha', he took to his bed and we'd given up all hope he might ever arise. If it weren't fer Mr. Hay, I dinna think his lordship would ha' recovered."

"They seem close."

"Like brothers, they are, although—" She shook her head and chuckled, her girth shaking like a bowl of marmalade. "Och, listen to me goin' on and on! How I do talk!"

"No, no, it's very interesting! I don't feel that I've gotten to know the earl under the best of circumstances. Once he realizes I'm who I say I am, I'm sure things will change." She really believed that, too, although she wasn't certain how. Would he feel guilty for treating her so horribly? Would he even care?

She simply didn't know. "I'm still shocked that Erroll tossed all of the furniture from the window."

"Och, 'tis no matter, fer the earl has more than enough gold. He's a right talented trader in antiquities, ye know, and brings in so much coin tha' I dinna know how he'll spend it all!"

The housekeeper whisked a cloth from a pocket and began to walk about the room, dusting the furnishings. "I'm verrah lucky to be here at New Slains. Whilst other castles have gone to wrack and ruin because there's no more gold in the coffers, my lord's managed to keep this one bang up t' the knocker."

"Except the damaged wing," Abigail said.

Mrs. MacFadden nodded, her chins quivering. "Aye, a pity tha', fer it was the most beautiful part o' the castle, and the oldest, too. But such are old buildings. Even with improvements, they are ne'er as safe as the new ones." She tucked away her dust rag and shook her head sadly. "The earl's ne'er been the same since tha' night, puir mon. It near breaks my heart when I think of how ill he was, and how burned. Och, 'twas horrid."

"I'd heard that he tried to save his wife."

"He was near crazed to find her, runnin' into the burnin' part o' the castle before anyone could stop him. Even Mr. Hay couldna hold him back and—"

"Mr. Hay was there?"

"Aye. He grabbed on to the earl's arm, but his lordship is much stronger. He knocked Mr. Hay right into two footmen as were about to hold his lordship in place."

"He would have been furious if they'd stopped him."

"Aye, but he would have been uninjured and we all knew 'twas too late fer her ladyship." Mrs. MacFadden pulled a lace handkerchief from her pocket and wiped her eyes. "Och, enough o' that! Will there be anything else, miss? I'm sendin' up a tray of tea right now."

Mary longed to ask more questions, but couldn't think of a way to do it without seeming intrusive. "No, I think that will be all. I look forward to my freedom tomorrow. Do you think it will be warm enough to sit outside?"

"'Twill be a bit chilly, miss. 'Tis a typical Scottish spring, wit' snow one day and sunshine the next."

The housekeeper looked around with satisfaction, then waddled to the door. "Yer tea will arrive any time now, miss. If ye need anythin' else, ye've but to send one o' the footmen and they'll fetch me triple haste."

"Thank you, Mrs. MacFadden. I'm sure I'll be much more comfortable now. I can't thank you enough."

"There, now, all I did was scavenge ye a few chairs. 'Twas nothing." Dipping a curtsy, the housekeeper left.

As the door closed, Mary looked at Abigail. "Is she always so talkative?"

"Yes, miss. I tried to arrive ahead o' her to warn ye, but once the earl lifted the ban, nothin' would do but she'd come herself."

"That's quite all right. Mrs. MacFadden seems like a fount of useful information. Michael always said that the key to overcoming seemingly insurmountable odds lies in the collecting of as much information as possible. Frequently, things are seen as 'insurmountable' merely from a lack of know-how.

"Meanwhile, we must continue to progress our own cause. We've won the right to leave our room for three hours per day. Now we must find a way to expand that time." She began to pace, her arms crossed, tapping one finger against her chin. "But how?"

"Miss, surely ye should enjoy yer new right fer a day or two afore ye go pressin' fer more?"

"It will never do to stop pressing. We must remember our ultimate goal; we are fighting for our freedom. *All* of it, not a paltry three hours."

Abigail sighed. "Very well, miss. What do we do?"

So far, she'd used annoyance to wear the earl down, so she couldn't use that approach again. His reaction might be the opposite of her intentions. She needed a way to make him *want* her nearby. But how?

She frowned, her mind flickering through their conversations. Of course, her mind wished to linger at the most importunate of those times—times when she'd lost complete sight of her goal. She attempted to banish her memories, but her mind lingered on one in particular, of Erroll gazing at her décolletage with that dark, almost hungry look. She knew he planned on avoiding her; that was painfully obvious from his actions during this last visit. But she needed his attention, for he held the key to the onyx box.

She looked down to where her full breasts were contained by her chemise and covered by her modest gown.

Her gaze then went to Abigail, who was, as usual, on display. She wore a round-necked gown with her breasts pressed up into the opening until she appeared as if with one good sneeze she might overflow her gown.

Men didn't ignore Abigail. Ever.

A smile curved Mary's lips even as her cheeks heated. Did she dare?

Yes, she did. "Abigail, fetch me that blue gown, the one with the lace inset in the décolletage."

The maid brightened. "That's a lovely gown, miss. Do you wish to wear that tomorrow?"

"Yes, but *without* the lace inset."

Abigail gawked. "But miss, that'll be—it'll look a mite—ye canno' be serious. Ye never dress revealin'."

"I suspect the earl means to ignore me entirely when I'm free. I need his attention if I'm to find that artifact and free Michael. So I'm taking a page from your book."

Abigail looked down at her own low-cut gown, a slow smile spreading across her face. "Ohhhh! It does help one get things, miss. The footmen rarely let me carry a tray up the stairs, though they never offer to help the third floor maid." Abigail paused as if to imagine all of the trays she'd avoided carrying, a smile upon her face. After a moment, though, her brow lowered and her smile had disappeared. "Miss? I wonder . . . what if Lord Erroll thinks ye're trying to seduce him?"

Mary's cheeks heated. "He already thinks that, so I hardly believe this will make any difference."

Abigail's eyes widened. "What on earth could make him think such a thing, miss? Why, ye're the most lady-like miss I ever worked fer!"

"Lord Erroll wouldn't agree with that sentiment, and I don't know that I care." Which was a blatant lie, but Mary wasn't about to begin exchanging confidences with her maid. "It's a risk, but necessary. If I do things right, he won't be able to ignore me."

"*Are* ye plannin' on seducin' him, miss? Fer I don't think that's a wise plan, ye bein' an innocent an' all." The maid added, "If ye wish, I would be willin' to seduce him to gain the key—"

"*No.*" Mary was surprised at the force of her own voice, but the concept was simply untenable. "It won't come to that."

"So ye're not tryin' to seduce him?"

"No. I'm trying to gain his attention, that's all."

"Ah," the maid said, her voice indicating disbelief.

"Believe me, it won't need to go that far." Mary thought of how Erroll had left so abruptly this morning.

"Very well, miss. And once ye have his attention?"

"I shall convince him to give us our freedom. I cannot plead our case unless he's willing to engage in a conversation."

"That makes sense."

"So I plan to be the world's most *noticeable* guest."

"That's a good plan, miss—so long as ye don't annoy the earl and he locks us both away again."

"Oh, he won't dare do that. Not if he doesn't wish me to start singing again." She smiled as Abigail chuckled.

"He didn't like that, did he, miss?"

"Not at all. Unless I've read our host wrong, he already regrets bringing us to New Slains and would gladly send us away if he was able. By the time Mr. Young arrives, the earl will be *eager* to give us the artifact and send us on our way."

Abigail looked impressed. "Ye've thought of everything, haven't ye, miss?"

"I've tried, Abigail. I've really tried."

"And I think ye've done it, miss. Sit here while I fetch that gown, and we'll make certain no man in the entire castle can ignore ye." With a wink and a grin, Abigail hurried to the wardrobe.

And soon they were busily snipping threads, talking and chuckling the entire time.

"Law, miss! I canno' pin yer hair when ye keep shiftin' like that."

"I'm sorry. I just cannot seem to sit still this morning." Mary looked at her reflection in the mirror, noting how good the new neckline looked. It wasn't *too* low—Abigail's was much lower—but it was low enough to command attention. She shifted to one side to get a different look and Abigail sighed.

"Aye, ye're as restless as a hunk of bacon fat in a hot pan."

Mary wrinkled her nose. "Where *do* you get your sayings?"

"From me grammer, miss."

"Your grammer?"

"Aye, me mother's mother."

"Ah, your grandmother. We call our grandmother 'Mam.' They say she's a witch." At Abigail's alarmed look, Mary added hastily, "She's not, although our family history is filled with stories of white witches. My brother's especially fond of one story, that of an amber amulet. It's rumored to be magical in some way and—"

Abigail squeaked. "*Magical,* miss?"

Mary chuckled at the maid's excitement. "It's *rumored* to be magical, Abigail. Pay attention!"

The maid's face fell. "Ye don't believe it?"

"Oh, no. It's family lore; you know how that is."

Oddly, Mary had dreamed of the amber amulet last night. She'd slept restlessly, nervous and excited about the coming day, and yet her dream had been so vivid. In it, after years of searching distant lands, Michael had returned home with the amulet. She'd been coming down the stairs of the vicarage and he'd grinned up at her, so much like the last time she'd seen him that her heart ached, even in her sleep. He'd then held up the amulet. "Mary, I found it!"

The amulet had gleamed, catching the bright rays of the morning sun, and she hadn't been able to take her eyes off of it. Suddenly she was no longer at the top of the stairs, but at the bottom, the amulet in her hands. Michael was talking to Father and Mother, his deep voice excited as he told how he'd found it. Mary didn't hear most of it, for her attention was on the amulet in her hands. Framed in heavy silver, deeply etched, the amulet was warm to the touch. As she'd stared deeply into the amber, the voices had faded and she saw swirls of mists rising through the gem. In the mist, she'd seen Erroll standing before a washbasin with no shirt, carefully shaving around the scars on his jaw and neck. She'd peered closer, noting the ridges of scars that ran from his jaw down his neck, over his shoulder and halfway down one arm; then her gaze had moved on to his muscular chest and his powerful arms. He was beautiful. In her sleep, she'd murmured that and he'd turned as if he could hear her, his gaze searching the room.

Suddenly fearful that she'd been seen, she'd dropped the amulet . . . and had woken up, her heart beating a thousand times a minute.

Thank goodness it was only a dream. Yet I wonder about the earl's scars more than ever now.

It had been an odd dream, especially since it had

been that ancient family heirloom—an amber amulet—
that had drawn Michael into Egypt.

"Miss, I do wish ye'd tell me more about yer family
and the magical amulet."

"There's not much to tell. We had the amulet for
centuries, though there's no record of it really being
magical, only rumor. Someone stole it—a member of
Clan MacLean—and gave it to Queen Elizabeth, who
grew fearful of it. According to one of the letters written in her own hand, she gave it away to someone traveling to a distant land, but she never said to whom or
where they were going."

Abigail fixed a pin in Mary's hair. "A magical amulet
and white witches! Now, that's a family history, miss.
Mine isn't so colorful, though they do say me great-
great-grandfather was a smuggler. I used t' think that
was excitin', but now it just seems a good way to end up
hangin' off the ropes at Tyburn."

"Oh, I've always wanted to do something exciting
like smuggling or being carried off by a prince on a white
horse," Mary said, "so I can see why you once thought
that. Of course, if you'd asked me six months ago what
I'd think of being locked up in a half-burned-down but
very luxurious castle by a mysterious, handsome earl,
I would have thought it the most romantic thing ever.
Now I realize that romance has very little to do with
adventure. My mam would tell me that, for she's had a
very colorful life." Mary pursed her lips. "I should write
to her, if I'm allowed. She's a bundle of good advice."

Abigail finished placing the last pin in Mary's hair.
"I must say, miss, that if I had to be locked in a castle,

I couldn't ask fer a more resourceful mistress. At least now we don't have to stay in the room all of the time."

"Why, thank you." Mary eyed her hair in the mirror. It was simply pinned back, with two small braids wrapped around the crown and holding the many pins that kept it in place. "And if I had to be locked away, I can't think of a better companion who would bear our circumstances with such fortitude *or* create such a lovely coiffure."

Abigail flushed with pleasure. "Thank 'ee, miss! 'Tis a pleasure to serve ye. Ye've the longest hair I've ever had the pleasure to pin up, and 'tis a challenge."

Mary sighed. "I really should have it cut, but I worry it will look so different, and what if I don't like it?"

"'Tis so beautiful, I'd keep it just the way 'tis." Abigail straightened the dresser top. "Where are you off to now, miss?"

"I shall go downstairs and do what I can to gain an audience with his lordship. What are you going to do to fill your day?"

"I've two of yer gowns to wash, then there's a footman who wishes me to go on a picnic."

"It's a bit cold for a picnic."

Abigail grinned. "So I'm hopin', miss. 'Tis nice to have a man warm ye on a blustery day."

Mary laughed as they went to the door. Whatever challenges that came her way, she was ready to face them.

Letter from Michael to his sister Mary, written on a ship rounding the Cape of Good Hope:

Mary, I think I found a mention of the amulet in the records of a traveler to Elizabeth's court in 1568! He was an ambassador who brought her many gifts from his own country. In return, she gave him the amulet . . . or I think it is the amulet, for his description is vague. But I cannot ignore the year and the fact that within two months he declared the amulet "cursed" and sold it the second he set foot upon his homeland, never taking it to his superiors.

My curiosity is even stronger than before. Was our family amulet really cursed? It made several of its owners uncomfortable enough that they wished to be rid of it, despite its value.

Perhaps I should go further back in history and trace the amulet to its origin, before it was delivered into our family's hands.

ELEVEN

$\mathcal{M}$ary made her way down the grand stairs, her footmen guards following her. The sun streamed in the mullioned window and made the castle seem bright and airy, a direct contrast to its owner.

Her confinement had given her a new appreciation for all that she saw—the warm red of the rugs upon the landings, the bright colors of the tapestries on the walls, the smell of beeswax used to polish the wood floors until they shone.

The entire castle looked fresh and ready to be enjoyed. As she went down the stairs, she paused to examine the portraits that lined the wall.

"Who is in this portrait?"

One of the footmen following her peered at the large portrait. Over ten feet tall, it dominated the wall supporting the grand staircase. It was of a woman dressed in the height of fashion thirty or forty years ago.

"Sorry, miss." He shook his head. "There are more than a hundred portraits in the castle and I dinna know them all. This one looks to be someone grand. That's a nice gown, isn't it?" he asked naively.

"Very nice." Mary frowned at the picture. The woman looked about her own age but had a haughty, sneering look. Indeed, though the woman was beautiful, there was an almost feral expression. "Whoever she is, I'm glad I never had to face her in a ballroom. I get the feeling she might have been somewhat overbearing."

From behind her came a quiet voice. "She was not *quite* as cold-natured as she appears in that portrait."

Mary whirled to find Mr. Hay standing in the foyer below them, his head tilted back as he eyed the portrait with a thoughtful expression.

"You know her, then?" Mary asked.

"I knew her better than most. She was my aunt, Lord Erroll's mother."

Mary's cheeks heated. "Oh, dear! I shouldn't have said anything disparaging."

Mr. Hay's solemn blue eyes began to twinkle. "It's a wretched portrait and she hated it, which is why my uncle—Angus's father—hung it here to begin with."

"They didn't get along, then." Mary headed down the stairs toward Mr. Hay.

"They fought over everything from the placement of the sugar on the dining-room table to whether they should allow their newly orphaned nephew to live with them here."

Mary reached the bottom of the stairs. "That had to have been difficult for you."

He shrugged. "Fortunately, I had Angus. He told me the way things were, and encouraged me not to take anything to heart that was said by either."

How terrible that the earl had grown up with such bitterness around him. "It sounds as if they disliked one another quite a bit."

Mr. Hay shot her an amused look. "'Dislike' is too mild a word. They actively hated one another and did everything they could to disrupt each other's life, at the expense of their own child. I've often wondered if that's why Erroll is so unwilling to listen to ideas other than his own. The best way to avoid arguments is to always be in the right, which would—" Hay clamped his mouth closed and looked at the hovering footmen before turning a bright red. He sent Mary an apologetic glance. "As I was saying, that's a portrait of my late aunt, may she rest in peace."

Mary hid a smile at such an abrupt about-face, though she thought Mr. Hay's confidences quite interesting. In fact, while he'd been speaking, it had dawned on her that although Erroll had clearly decided to avoid her, his cousin had not. She'd be a fool not to encourage Mr. Hay's confidences if they could help her understand her gaoler.

With that in mind, she joined him where he stood to one side of the stairs. "If you've a few moments, perhaps you could tell me about these family portraits in the stairway? Some of them are quite lovely."

He flushed and looked absurdly pleased. "I would be delighted!"

His eagerness was appealing, though the way his glance encompassed her low décolletage was not. *I planned to capture the earl's attention, not anyone else's. The fortunate thing is that Mr. Hay seems quite mild mannered and will follow the proprieties.*

With that reassuring thought, she took his arm, careful to maintain a good distance between them. As her fingers brushed over the fine cloth of his coat, she thought her brother Robert would have approved of Mr. Hay's fashionable attire, which would have been admired in the best drawing rooms in England.

She smiled. Much to his father's eternal concern and his brothers' and sisters' vast amusement, since moving to London and being introduced to the ton, Robert had become a notable expert in all things worldly. It was rumored that he was frequently called upon to advise the Duchess of Devonshire—a known leader of the fashionable set—on her couture.

Mary noted the square-cut ruby pinned in the folds of Mr. Hay's exquisite cravat and realized that her brother would be quite green with envy if he ever chanced to see it.

Mr. Hay turned to the footmen. "I shall escort Miss Hurst from here."

The footmen bowed and retreated, staying in sight, but not so close as to overhear the conversation.

Mary couldn't help but give a faint sigh of relief. "Though I know they are only doing their duty, it is onerous to be escorted everywhere one goes."

"I can only imagine," he said fervently.

"I appreciate that you have called off the footmen, at least while we are talking. In return, I promise not to attempt an escape while you are nearby."

"An— I beg your pardon?"

"If I did escape, I'm almost certain Lord Erroll might accuse you of assisting me, and that would never do."

Mr. Hay blinked. "You . . . you would actually attempt an escape?"

"I would if I thought I could find a conveyance—a horse or a cart, I'd even take a donkey if one could be found. However, try as I might, I can't think of a way to remove an animal of any sort from the stables without it being noticed."

Mr. Hay's look of astonishment melted into a laugh. "Miss Hurst, I begin to think you resemble your brother far more than my cousin has realized."

She regarded him evenly. "Then *you* believe me?"

His laughter died a bit. "Perhaps. I can't quite decide."

"That's fair, I suppose. At least you're giving me a chance."

"I am afraid not to; you might have a knife hidden in your pocket."

She chuckled. "I assure you that my bravado does not extend to violence."

"For that, I can only be thankful." Mr. Hay patted her hand as he led her up the stairs to the first portrait. "Angus so rarely has visitors, other than his cronies from the society, that it's nice to speak to a nonscholarly person for a change."

"Thank you. I'll try to remember not to bore you by listing the final rulers of the Ptolemaic dynasty."

"I can't tell you how relieved I am to hear that." He wrinkled his nose, looking like a rueful boy. "I try to appreciate my cousin's academic bent, but I fear I lack the patience to absorb it. I'd rather confine myself to the few areas he allows me—serving as the man of business for the estate, and buying and selling the small items from his research that he deems too unimportant to keep."

"You serve as his man of business?"

"Someone must see to the running of the estate, and New Slains sits upon extensive grounds. Some of it's cultivated, though the rents are quite small. At one time I'd thought to expand that, but Angus has no interest in such."

"A castle this size can't be very easy to maintain. But I suppose it's a normal domicile to you, since it's where you grew up."

He looked around the grand foyer with fondness. "Actually, I was raised in much more modest circumstances, and when I first saw the castle, I was intimidated. But that was years ago, and now New Slains is home. I cannot imagine living anywhere else."

She heard the pride in his voice. "You love the castle."

"Yes. It's amazingly sound. Even after the fire, we were able to—" He stopped suddenly. "But you didn't wish to hear about the castle, but the paintings."

He indicated the first portrait, which was of an astonishingly handsome man dressed in the Elizabethan style, complete with a ruff about this neck and, lower, an embarrassingly prominent codpiece. Mr. Hay, filled with obvious admiration for this particular ancestor, launched into a lengthy speech about the origins of the earldom and the fortunes of the Hay family. He did the same for each portrait on display.

As he did so, he divulged a delicious amount of family gossip. Mary listened carefully when her tour guide began to speak about the more recent portraits, noting that until Mr. Hay had arrived, the earl had been raised alone in the castle. She tried to imagine being raised in such a cavernous household without other playmates, and almost shivered at the thought.

Her life had been so different; the creaky old vicarage had been filled with voices and laughter, shared chores and practical jokes. In contrast, the castle seemed a cold place for a lone child.

They stopped in front of smallish portrait of a rather gray-faced man who stared sullenly from the canvas. "This was the old earl, Angus's father and my uncle."

"He looks rather bitter."

Mr. Hay hesitated, and then bent down to say in a low voice, "He had a horrid temper, as did my aunt. I heard some incredibly colorful and theatrical arguments in this very hall. In fact, I once watched the countess toss two priceless vases over that balustrade." Mr. Hay pointed to the landing above them. "One of them almost hit the old earl, who had just come from his study for the express purpose of yelling at her for some bill that had arrived."

"They fought over money, then?"

"And what to serve for dinner, the placement of a set-tee in the sitting room, the color of the new china—" He shook his head. "There was no peace in this household."

"Goodness." Mary looked at the balustrade. "You could have witnessed a murder! That's a horrible memory."

"I have dozens like it." His brows lowered. "The only thing they truly agreed upon was that Angus should take his education as far as possible. Which suited him fine, for it kept him away at school and out of the house during chaotic times."

"He went away to school, then."

"Oh, yes. To the finest."

"And you? Did you go, too?"

His smile took on a faintly bitter twist. "I went, but it seemed I was always called back here to help with this and that. Eventually I took over the running of the estate, and— Well, here I am."

"I know how that can happen. One day you agree to accept this or that responsibility and suddenly, it's six years later and you're still doing it, only now it's expected."

He appeared much struck. "Yes! That's exactly how it happens. How did you know?"

"Because I am the last child living at home, and the care of my parents came onto my shoulders. I love them dearly, but I sometimes wish it hadn't been I who'd been named caretaker."

"I understand," he said fervently.

"Yes, but . . . Mr. Hay, forgive me if I'm being for-ward, but there is one significant difference in our cases.

My parents are getting older and need someone to assist them, but your cousin is quite capable of running his own estate."

"When would he do his research if he was constantly tied up in the management of New Slains? As he will tell you, he is a very busy man."

"I think less of your cousin every time you open your mouth."

"Miss Hurst, my cousin is not an easy person to live with, but he always does things *right*. There is no halfway with Angus. Surely that's worth something."

"I've already noticed Erroll's inflexible character. It dawned on me every time I tried to open the door of my bedchamber."

"I fear you've seen the worst of him."

Had she seen the worst of the dark earl? Somehow, she didn't think so.

Mr. Hay sighed. "If you knew him better, you'd see him more clearly. He is considered to be a brilliant man by many of the highest-ranking members of the society. In fact, he receives all sorts of offers from people who wish him to speak here and there, or to take over their projects in all sorts of foreign lands. He is in great demand."

"But he refuses to travel, being self-conscious of his scars."

Mr. Hay looked surprised. "How do you know that?"

"Because he keeps them covered."

"Ah. You are right; he never leaves the castle except to visit the village, or on his morning rides."

"He rides?"

"Yes. He rides every day for hours for exercise. And sometimes, for variation, he goes to the barn and stacks bales of hay."

That must be how the man kept so fit, for he fairly rippled with muscles.

Angus Hay took life on his own terms, regardless of what was expected or wanted by others. He was a formidable opponent; one who dealt with arguments by simply declaring himself the victor. Meanwhile, his cousin had grown up in the shadow of the earl's overwhelming personality, stunted in growth like a tree trying to find purchase on a castle wall. The roots had taken between the stones, but the tree would never grow to its full potential.

The poor man. I must wonder, though: Am I like that, too? She put her hand on his arm. "Thank you for showing me the picture gallery."

"I'll accept your thanks once I've finished with my task." With a self-deprecating smile, he gestured to the wall before them. "We should conclude with the portrait that started it all: that of my aunt, the late countess." He looked up at the portrait with a wistful expression. "In the Hay family, passion is always rewarded, regardless of what form it takes."

"I'm certainly glad she wasn't *my* mother."

"As am I," came a deeper male voice from directly behind her.

Mary started and turned to find Erroll standing just outside the library door. His cool green gaze flickered over her, resting briefly on her lower-than-usual neckline.

Instantly, Mary's blood heated. She frowned. *I mustn't react to him in such a way. I wanted his attention, and now I must use it to find out what I can about him—his strengths and his weaknesses.* "Lord Erroll," she said. "I'm sorry if I said anything untoward about your mother."

"No you're not."

"Well, she *does* look a bit testy."

He shrugged, apparently unmoved by her observation. "We are all testy at times."

"That's very true," she said. "Still, I think she appears as if she might have been a bit *more* testy than the rest of us."

His lips twitched and she had the deep satisfaction of seeing his eyes flicker with amusement. "I am surprised no one has yet attempted to throttle you."

"Angus!" Mr. Hay's face reddened. "There's no need to be rude."

"Actually," Mary said fairly, "my comment about Erroll's mother was far ruder than anything he has said. Besides, my brothers have mentioned the desire to throttle me hundreds of times. I'm used to such a reaction."

"I am not surprised," the earl said dryly.

Mr. Hay bowed. "Miss Hurst—"

"Miss Fortune," the earl corrected smoothly.

Mary waved a hand. "Miss Fortune is fine—provided you don't mind if I call you Lord Hawk."

The earl frowned. "Hawk?"

"Yes. You have the look of a hawk. I've frequently noticed it, but hadn't said anything. Trying to be polite, you know. But since you prefer to dispense with such silliness, Miss Fortune and Lord Hawk it is."

Mr. Hay looked amused. "Angus, I believe she has you with that one."

"We shall see about that," the earl said, eyeing Mary with unfeigned interest. "Perhaps I'll call you Trouble instead, for so far you've been nothing but."

Mr. Hay sent her an apologetic look as if to atone for his cousin's rudeness, then said, "Now that you've been released from your prison walls, if it warms up, perhaps you'd like to walk the garden and stretch your legs."

Under normal circumstances, Mary would have agreed with alacrity. She was used to taking long tramps through the woods at the vicarage, often walking all the way to the village if the weather was pleasant. After such a long confinement, a stroll sounded blissful. But she had no desire to spend more time with Mr. Hay, though he'd been a valuable source of information. The earl held the key to this puzzle. Though she knew she'd have possession of the artifact once Mr. Young arrived, it was possible that Lord Erroll had discovered how the box was tied to Michael's search for the Hurst Amulet.

"Mr. Hay, thank you, but I'd rather sit for a while and just enjoy being out of that bedchamber. Perhaps we could take a walk later?"

He looked disappointed, but bowed. "Of course. I believe the sitting room has been reserved for your use."

Her smile slipped. "The sitting room."

"Yes," the earl said, a sardonic glint in his eyes. "Surely you didn't think you'd be allowed to roam about the house unsupervised."

"No, but I did want to select a book to read." She

pointed over the earl's shoulder. "I believe that's the library?"

"No. The library is off-limits."

"I know you suggested that—"

"It wasn't a suggestion."

"—but the library is the room I'd enjoy the most. Far more than the sitting room."

Mr. Hay cleared his throat. "Angus, perhaps we could simply allow Miss Hurst to select one or two books."

The earl faced his cousin. "Neason, I told you that I didn't wish—"

Mary took the opportunity to slip past the earl and enter the library, unsurprised when her two footmen immediately established themselves at each side of the door.

She hadn't been in the library since the first night, and it was pleasant to see it in the light of day. It was a large, long room with glorious windows. There were shelves and shelves of books, and she folded her hands together to keep from reaching for them. How she loved to read—biographies, plays, books about the flora and fauna of a region, historical tomes, and of course, novels; she loved them all. She also loved the heavy oak paneling that lined the room, and the ornate carvings that decorated the large fireplace mantel and the corners of the shelves.

But best of all was the bank of windows down one side of the room that opened onto a garden, which was blooming with fresh spring green. No doubt it would be riotous with color once the earth warmed.

"I believe I'll just stay here," she announced to herself, pleased with the room.

"Like hell," came a growl from behind her. "You are welcome to make your home in the sitting room, but not here. Never here."

The earl's gaze flickered across the room, resting briefly on his desk before it locked on her, once again reminding her of a bird of prey.

Aha. That's where he locked Michael's letter. Could it also be where he's keeping the onyx box?

She caught his narrowed gaze and offered a smile. "It's a lovely room."

"Compliment it all you wish; you are not staying here."

His attitude irked her, so she found a chair and reclined upon it, adjusting her blue muslin gown over the tips of her slippers. "I do love a room with books."

Like someone who had too many books and didn't know the true value of them, he glanced indifferently at the walls of shelves.

Mr. Hay, who'd followed the earl in, smiled. "Are you a great reader, Miss Hurst?"

"I'd rather read than eat."

Mr. Hay looked surprised. "So you're a bluestocking, then?"

"I enjoy a good book. I hardly think I deserve any other name than that of 'reader.' "

Mr. Hay turned red. "I didn't mean anything derogatory."

She smiled. "Of course not."

His strained expression relaxed. "Thank you. I'm

just not used to women who are bookish, and you don't appear to be the type to spend time reading and such."

Mary's smile faded.

The earl chuckled, catching Mary unaware. *He's beautiful when he laughs.*

When he scowled, one was only aware of his mocking eyes, which made one feel smaller than a worm. A *small* worm. But when he smiled, the tension left his face, his eyes warmed, and he appeared years younger. But even more, he looked approachable.

He shook his head, still chuckling. "Neason, perhaps now would be a good time to excuse yourself. A crate arrived this morning and the items need to be cataloged."

Mr. Hay brightened. "A crate? Who sent it?"

"A sea captain just returned from Greece. He wishes us to identify the items and set a price."

"They're all for sale?"

"They will be once we prepare them. He's offered us first crack at bidding on them, too."

"Excellent!"

"If there are any items of interest, I would like to write about them and present it to the science association."

"I'll go now!" He bowed to Mary. "Miss Hurst, if you'll forgive me—"

He reminded her so much of Michael in his eagerness that she smiled kindly and waved him on. "Of course!"

"Thank you!" He headed out the door.

"My," Mary said, "he is certainly enthusiastic."

"If only his enthusiasm over opening a crate of unknown items matched his interest in researching the ones we've already unwrapped."

She chuckled. "Impatient, is he?"

"A bit."

"I enjoy the research aspect myself. In fact, I do all of Michael's drawings."

He sent her a disbelieving look.

She added, "I'm very good, too. Perhaps I can do some of your drawings while we're awaiting Mr. Young. In the few papers of yours that I've seen when Michael returned from his Science Academy lectures, I've noticed that your drawings could use more finesse."

His eyes flashed. "There is nothing wrong with the drawings."

"They seem a little crude."

His gaze narrowed.

"Don't shoot the messenger! I am merely telling you what I—and others—have noticed."

"By 'others,' I assume you're talking about Hurst."

"My brother, yes."

The earl's gaze flickered over her, lingering just a half second too long on her décolletage.

A rush of excitement ran through her and she deliberately bent over as if to untangle her heel from her hem. Through her lashes, she noted that the earl froze in place, his gaze glued to her.

Hiding her smile, Mary straightened and looked directly at the earl. She raised her brows. "I'm sorry . . . did you say something?"

His lips thinned and he abruptly crossed his arms

over his chest. "Miss Fortune, find a damn book and leave. I've work to do."

"Oh yes. You need to correct your drawings. They really do reflect poorly on your research—"

"I don't care about finesse. The drawings represent the object, and that is all that matters."

"Lord Hawk, your research is impeccable, and you have a gift with words. But your poorly executed drawings detract from your articles."

He tilted his head to one side, his gaze narrowing. He looked very much like a hawk then, with his intent green gaze, the hard line of his nose. Even more hawkish was the way he looked at her, as if she were a plump rabbit and he a very, very hungry bird of prey.

Mary wet her lips, suddenly nervous. She'd wanted his interest; she just hadn't been ready for the feeling of being pursued. She felt cold and hot at the same time and extremely uncomfortable. She only wished she had a shawl to tug over her chest.

From where he stood, Angus saw the uncertainty in Mary's expression even as he felt the tension in the room subtly change. Amusement dawned as he realized she was nervous and it didn't take him long to realize why—as she shifted in her seat she crossed her arms, then uncrossed them, then crossed them again.

Angus rubbed his mouth to hide a grin. *Ah! So the display was intentional, but not necessarily comfortable.* He had to applaud her for using her considerable charms to her advantage. He didn't blame her; he'd been known to use his height when the situation warranted it. Why shouldn't a woman use her physical charms when the opportunity arose?

He allowed his gaze to linger on her breasts now. *Damn, but she's an armful. Perhaps I've been too hasty in wishing her gone. Now might be a good time to discover the cracks in her facade.* He lifted a brow. "Which articles are you speaking about?"

"All of them, although one or two stand out. The paper you wrote for the Royal Society about the sarcophagi, and how you think they were made, had horrid illustrations."

She knows my work very well. Is that a good sign or a bad one? "Neason has a very good hand for rendering, if he'd but slow down."

She regarded him for a moment. "Lord Hawk, would you mind if I ask you a question?"

"Would it matter if I mind or not?"

She gave him a cheeky grin that revealed a dimple. "No, I'm probably going to ask it anyway."

"Then by all means ask. I wouldn't want you to rupture anything by holding in the question that's burning on your lips." He allowed his gaze to drop lower than those lips, which caused a delicious blush to color her creamy skin.

She cleared her throat, but managed to say calmly, "Michael told me that you've never left Scotland to study afield, as most experts do."

He shrugged. "So?"

"He said you do all of your research right here."

"I still don't hear a question."

"Why don't you travel to the places you love to

research?" She leaned forward. "If I had the funds or the opportunity, nothing would stop me from traveling to see the ancient sights. *Nothing.*"

Her bright, eager expression was a disconcerting, almost disorienting contrast to the room.

His study was lined with dark shelves and thousands of massive tomes, the dark wood floors covered with deep red and blue carpets, the furnishings heavy and dark. The room itself was lit by special lanterns so that he could focus on the objects he loved to study, the heavy curtains over the garden doors usually closed.

Today someone had opened them; probably Mrs. MacFadden in her endless search for ways to uplift his spirits. But when the curtains were closed he felt safe here, encased by his tomes and research, the one thing that had gotten him through the pain of his injuries after the fire. Every man needed a sanctuary, and this was his.

Yet now, sitting in a pool of light, was the annoyingly chipper Miss Fortune. She was wearing a pale blue gown, the neckline lower than any he'd seen her wear thus far. Her gold hair caught the sun and seemed to hold it, and her creamy skin had a luminescent quality that made him yearn to touch it.

She seemed to draw the light to her, holding it and reflecting it until it illuminated every dark corner of the room.

Angus hated that. This was his refuge, his sanctuary. This woman changed things, disrupting the very fabric of his home. Her mere presence threw the entire castle into chaos.

He'd vowed not to allow her in here, but after she'd marched in and made herself so comfortable, all he could think about was how to break her calm. If he rattled her enough, surely she'd admit to her perfidy.

She turned her face toward the windows. "The snow has finally disappeared."

"The roads will be passable, which will speed Young upon his way." Angus watched her closely—would she fear that her true character was about to be revealed?

She nodded with satisfaction. "That will speed my journey to Whitby. My brother William will be holding a ship ready to deliver the box. He was once in the navy, and was a captain of some rank, but he prefers being a merchant and is quite good at it."

"That's a lucrative career."

"He is disgustingly wealthy. Father is worried it will turn his head, but I don't see that happening—he has a very steady temperament."

Could this William be a real brother? Her face softened as she spoke of him.

"Now, if it were Robert," she continued, unaware of Angus's scrutiny, "I would agree that large wealth could become a problem. Robert is a man of fashion, and an attaché to the Home Secretary. I don't know what he does exactly, but he is forever dropping references to this prince and that countess until one feels that he never speaks to the common man unless required by ill fate."

Angus had to hide a smile. "Robert sounds like a fribble."

"He would like one to think so, that's certain. But

I wonder if he's playing a deeper game. As a youth, he adored intrigue."

"What do you mean?" he asked, taken with her story despite himself.

She shook her head. "I have no evidence at all, but I wonder if he's doing more than merely serving as an attaché, which is such a tame profession. I cannot see Robert doing something so mundane unless he was also involved in some other intrigues." She waved a hand. "I daresay we'll never know."

Angus eyed her with interest. There was something damnably fascinating about the way she airily discussed her every thought aloud.

She gave him a level, curious look. "I don't know why I told you all of that. I suppose I've been confined to my bedchamber for so long that I yearn for normal conversation."

She faced the garden window and absently stared out, biting her bottom lip.

The way her head was turned was almost the same as Kiera's pose in the portrait. Kiera had been far thinner, of course, almost waiflike. Never strong, she'd been content to sit by the fire with her embroidery or hide in the turret room and paint. There was nothing waifish about Miss Fortune. She looked as hale and hearty as could be—hale, hearty, and *bossy*.

Perhaps that was the biggest difference. Mary exuded confidence while Kiera had swathed herself in fragility.

Angus's gaze lingered on the ripe gold of Mary's hair, enjoying the thick curls that clustered about her neck and trailed over one shoulder to her full, glorious breasts, which lifted with each breath.

His mouth went dry and he forced himself to look away.

"You haven't answered my question," Mary said, returning her gaze to him. "Why don't you travel the world? I see nothing keeping you bound within these four walls."

"It's none of your business whether I travel or not."

Mary knew she was treading on dangerous ground, but she was too intrigued to go without an answer. She'd spent most of her life sitting to the side of the room while everyone else got to dance. Yet here was a person who'd been invited to waltz and refused to do so. Life was so unfair.

She eyed her host. "Are you afraid to answer my question?"

His scowl appeared, darker than before. "I don't wish to talk about this."

"I wonder why it bothers you so to talk about how you confine yourself to this castle as if it were your prison, not your home."

"What I do is no one's concern, least of all yours."

She tried to think of a diplomatic way to phrase her thoughts, but some things just had to be said. She took a breath and blurted, "Perhaps you don't wish to travel because you worry people will notice your scars. If that's so, then I must say that's a paltry reason not to travel."

"We are through speaking about this," he said harshly.

"Fine. I won't say anything else." She looked out the window, and murmured as if to herself, though her words were plainly meant for him. "I still don't think anyone would say a word. People have accidents all the time, and I can't imagine anyone would care—"

"Miss Fortune, when I said I didn't want to talk about it, I also meant I didn't wish to *listen* to it."

She clasped her hands in her lap. "Oh. Well. I shan't mention it again then."

"Good."

Silence reigned, and she twiddled her thumbs. "Of course, if I *did* mention it, I would say that you're much too important to the world of antiquities to let a little thing like a few scars—"

"*Enough!*"

She flicked a truly astonished look at him, then her color rose as she turned away. "I'm sorry," she said in a muffled voice. "I'm home alone with my parents most of the time, and I'm afraid I've gotten quite used to saying what I think. I—I shouldn't have continued like that. Forgive me."

Angus jerked his head toward the shelves. "Find your books, Miss Fortune. I've work to do and you are keeping me from it." He crossed to his desk and pulled an open tome toward him. Within seconds, he appeared lost to the world.

This hadn't worked out at all the way she'd wished. She looked down at her lowered neckline and sighed. It hadn't had the effect she'd wished for. She walked to the nearest shelf but couldn't bring herself to read the titles.

She glanced back and stared at the top of his head, bent over the open book. She supposed she was lucky to have stayed as long as she had. Why had she pressed on about his lack of adventuring and his scars? For some reason, it had mattered. A lot. Understanding neither herself nor her host, she finally selected a book.

She splayed her fingers over the book. Of dark brown leather and soft to the touch, the cover was embossed in noble though faded gold ink with the words, "A Treatise on the Phoenician Wars." She bent to smell the familiar and comforting scent of paper that made reading a particularly satisfying endeavor.

Robert had once said that reading was a sensual pleasure, and Mary couldn't agree more. There was something about a book that—

"Damn it, are you going to read it or make love to it?"

She blinked at the earl, who now stood at his desk, his face a tight mask. "I beg your pardon?"

"What in the hell are you doing?"

"I was just—" She looked at the book and realized how silly she must have appeared. *Heavens, how do I explain this?* "I was enjoying the feel and smell of the book."

"Why would you do that?"

"Don't you *like* how books smell?"

"I don't know, I've never noticed."

"Well, here." She crossed to his desk and held out the book.

After a stilted moment, he bent down and breathed in the smell of the book. His gaze unfocused and he frowned at it.

"It smells good, doesn't it?"

His gaze flickered up to meet hers. For a long moment he stayed right where he was, his eyes on a level with hers. He was so close that she could see every thick black lash, every fleck of gold in his green eyes.

Suddenly, Mary couldn't look away. She loved the shape of his lips, both firm and sensual, and how his eyes darkened when he looked at her, as if he couldn't help but be interested in what she said and did. She wondered if he was interested now, or if she was misreading his expression.

Perhaps she should kiss him and see? Some naughty part of her urged her on, and she slowly leaned forward.

He straightened and returned to his chair. "I don't smell a thing."

"But you had to—"

"I didn't." He resumed his seat. "Go."

"But I—"

"Muir!"

The butler arrived almost immediately, his pale red eyebrows raised. "Yes, my lord?"

"Miss Fortune wishes to read in the sitting room."

"Of course, my lord. Miss, if you'll come this way?" Muir gestured to the two footmen who'd stood guard outside the room and they entered.

Left with nothing else to say, she clutched her book and led the way out. Erroll nodded to the footmen, who escorted her to the sitting room. There she was left to her own devices, though the door was left open and both footmen could see directly inside.

It was better than nothing. Barely.

Mary found a comfortable settee in front of the wide windows and burrowed into the cushions. Yet she couldn't read, because the light fell from the opposite direction she needed it.

She got up, studied the room, then went to the door and smiled sweetly at her jailers.

Thirty minutes later, the two footmen exited the sitting room looking exhausted. Inside, Mary eyed the new furniture arrangement with a pleased eye. Now a person could read while sitting upon the settee, the light falling at the perfect angle. Two chairs now flanked the fireplace for warmth, and a small collection of other furnishings were grouped about the main rug in the center of the room, perfect for conversation.

So much better. She snuggled back on the settee.

She'd gotten into the forbidden study, rearranged the sitting room, and managed to get under Lord Hawk's skin a little. "Not bad for the first day out of exile," she told herself. "Not bad at all."

Letter from Michael to his sister Mary, written from an inn in Istanbul:

We finally arrived in the part of the world that was once known as Constantinople. My new secretary, Miss Jane Smythe-Haughton, has proven herself up to more challenges than I'd imagined. We've been here less than two hours and she's already arranged for us to meet a local tribesman to take us to the furthest reaches of the country to examine the ruins of an ancient city.

Miss Smythe-Haughton's incomparable command of Turkish has already been most useful on many accounts. If I can only bring myself to deal as successfully with her caustic sense of humor.

TWELVE

Two days later, Mary awoke to the sound of a storm raging outside the castle walls. Snug in her bed in the turret, she listened to the icy pelting on the windows. The sound made her smile for she felt warm and cozy and—

She suddenly sat up straight. Would the storm slow Mr. Young from reaching the castle? She tossed back the covers and went to the bell pull. She yanked on it once, then again for good measure before she pulled on her robe.

Several long, long moments later, Abigail knocked and entered, panting slightly. "Sorry to come so late, miss, but I was down in the laundry. Are ye ready fer some breakfast?"

"No, I just want to know if this storm will delay our departure. I must speak with his lordship at once." Mary crossed to the window and lifted the sash. Sleet drove an angry gray sheet across the cobblestones in the court-yard below. Ice was forming on the eaves, and every tree limb was frosted with clinging spikes of ice. Mary's heart sank. "No one could travel in this."

Abigail came to stand beside her. "'Twould surprise me, miss."

Mary leaned her head against the window frame. "I was just thinking last night that Mr. Young was due any moment, and we'd be able to leave soon—maybe even today." She placed her palm on the icy window. "And now this."

"Aye, miss, 'tis a shame to see the weather change again. But I'm glad he didn't come and then this storm hit whilst we were trying to travel." The maid looked out the window and shivered. "Such weather could send yer soul slidin' off a cliff and straight into perdition."

Wincing at the image, Mary supposed the maid was right. "I hope Mr. Young isn't in this weather right now, or if he is, that he's found safe shelter."

"I'm sure the earl's men are accustomed to this sort o' weather and will take good care of the gentleman. Shall I send ye up a bath after breakfast, miss? 'Tis a good morning fer a hot soak."

Mary sighed and turned from the windows. "I sup-pose there's nothing more to be done. I might as well enjoy it while I can."

"Very good, miss. I'll send in one of the footmen to bank yer fire. 'Tis low in the grate." The maid smiled encouragingly at Mary and left.

A footman entered almost at once and bowed to Mary. "Good morning, miss! Ye're up early."

Mary looked at the clock over the mantel. "Seven in the morning! I had no idea."

"Ye might have to wait a bit on breakfast, but no' too much. Cook's a magician, she is, and can make a meal in the time it takes one o' us t' think o' one." He went to stir the embers in the fireplace, adding a log so that the flames sent out noticeable warmth.

Mary watched, trying hard to stave off her disappointment in the weather. As Abigail had pointed out, there wasn't a lot to be done about things. Sighing, she decided to read the book she'd gotten from the earl's library the day before. She walked toward the nightstand beside her bed, skirting around the settee as she did so and—

The footman whirled, the poker still in his hand. "Miss! Ye canno' go through that door!"

Mary frowned. What door? She realized he was staring round-eyed at the door beside the nightstand. She'd noticed it her first night in the castle and then hadn't paid it much heed. It wasn't unusual for larger houses to have adjoining rooms. Her sisters' houses were large— one was even a castle similar to New Slains, though not as modern—and the rooms often connected. "Why shouldn't I open the door?" she asked now. "Who's in there?"

The footman gulped, his eyes wide. "No one, miss. But ye need to not go in there."

"I wasn't going to the door. I just wanted to fetch my book." She went to the nightstand, her gaze drawn to the mysterious door.

Well, it was mysterious now, judging by the pallor on the footman's face.

"Who's in there?" she asked again, moving closer to it. "I thought I heard a noise on the other side last night, but then it stopped and I fell asleep." She frowned. "Does the earl have a guest he hasn't introduced to me?"

"No, miss."

"Hmm." She looked at the door a moment more. "Muir told me his lordship and Mr. Hay both have apartments in the other wing of the castle, so they can't be staying here. I can't imagine who might be there—" She reached for the doorknob.

"*Miss, NO!*" The footman's voice was strangely quiet, though he'd managed to yell.

Mary dropped her hand and turned to the footman. "Whose room is this?"

The footman looked miserable. "Miss, please. 'Tis no one's bedchamber."

She couldn't help but feel sorry for the man. He wasn't very quick on his feet and he was a horrible liar.

She carried her book to the chair farthest from the door. "I'm sure you're right and that there's no one in there. I daresay you just don't want me to open the door because it's filled with stacks of boxes or something that could fall and cause me an injury."

The footman's brow cleared. "Tha' is it, miss! Boxes. 'Tis just a lot o' boxes."

She settled into her chair and opened her book. "How dull. I shall just sit here and wait for my breakfast and bathwater."

"Do ye promise, miss? Ye won't rattle the knob?"

She lifted a brow. "Rattle the knob? So 'tis locked?"

"O' course 'tis locked. But it wouldn't do to rattle the door. It might, ah, it could cause the boxes to shift and—"

"Very well," Mary said, unable to stand the man's poor excuses another moment. "I'll leave the door be."

"Do ye promise, miss?"

She hid one hand behind her book and crossed her fingers. "Absolutely. Now, if you'll excuse me, I think I'll read for a bit."

He bowed and hurried from the room as if released from a trap.

Mary barely waited for the door to close before she rose, tossed her book onto the settee, and crossed to her dressing table. She selected a strong hairpin and went back to the door.

She pressed her ear to the panel, but could hear nothing. She had her suspicions about what—or who—had arranged for the room next to hers to be occupied. There was only one person in the castle who could make the servants turn pale. She didn't for a second entertain the notion that the earl would occupy one of the turret rooms when his own apartments were on the other side of the castle, but perhaps he'd established a spy here, in the bedchamber next to hers?

Her gaze narrowed as she carefully turned the knob, noting where it caught mid-turn. She sank to her knees and slipped her hairpin into the lock and gently worked the tumblers. In less than a minute, the lock gave a satisfying *click*. Mary placed the pin on her nightstand and returned to the now unlocked door, silently thanking

Robert for showing her how to pick a lock. She wasn't
sure how he came to possess such a skill, for he merely
grinned whenever she asked, but it really was a most
useful talent.

She placed her ear to the panel and listened, hearing
nothing, which was a good sign that the click of the lock
hadn't disturbed her neighbor. It was probably some
callow footmen like the ones Erroll had set to guard her
door. How dare the earl set someone to spy upon her!
She'd show the unfortunate individual that she wasn't
about to allow someone to invade the privacy of her
bedchamber.

Slowly, Mary turned the lock and opened the door.
The room was pitch black and it took a moment before
her eyes adjusted. It was a smaller room than hers, but
the heavy curtains along one wall indicated far more
windows. She suspected it would be a pleasant room
when filled with sunlight, unlike now, when everything
was shrouded in darkness but for the gloomy light at the
bottom of the curtains.

She took a tentative step into the room, then stood
still, listening.

Deep, even breathing came from the bed. *There he is!*
The idea of someone listening in on her conversations
stiffened her back. She'd show Erroll that she was not
to be toyed with. Fortunately, she'd had years of practice
giving people rude awakenings. Having brothers prepared one for just such moments as this.

She silently crossed to the curtained bed and
squinted into the darkness, but could only see an elbow
and a dark head.

She quietly bent down and grabbed the offender's sheets, gathering a good handful where they hung off the edge of the bed.

She stood up, gathered her strength, and—

A band of warm iron clamped about her wrist, and with a sudden twist she was hauled through the air and slammed onto the soft mattress as a tall masculine body rolled on top of her and pinned her in place.

For a moment she could only lie there, stunned. Then she began to swing wildly, her fists hitting firm flesh with a satisfying "oof" from her captor.

He immediately captured her arms and lowered his weight upon her. In that moment, she quickly became aware of three things.

First, she'd made a grave error. This was no footman to be cowed by her demand that he leave the premises immediately. That was obvious by the expanse of muscled shoulders and arms that had captured her, and the expensive scent of sandalwood that tickled her nose.

Second, from the sight of those powerful muscles, she realized that her spy was not wearing a nightshirt—a potential complication she'd naively never considered. Thank God there were three layers of clothing—her thick cotton night rail and robe, as well as the sheet—firmly wrapped between them, though she was vividly conscious of the man's leg brushing hers.

Her third realization tumbled hard on the heels of the last. There was only one person who would have the audacity to pin her to his bed while he was naked.

"Well, well, well." Erroll's deep voice rumbled from

his chest where it pressed against hers. "If it isn't Miss Fortune come to brighten my morning. Haven't you heard of knocking?"

She struggled against him, the air slowly being squeezed from her chest. "Let me up! I thought you were someone else."

"Oh really? Who else did you think would be sleeping in this bed?"

"A footman." She panted and tried to press him up so that her own lungs could expand, but he was as immovable as a wall.

"Have you gone mad, woman?" Erroll snapped. "You're lucky I *wasn't* a footman."

"Can you . . . lift up? Can't . . . breathe."

"That's the price you pay for spying on me."

"Me?" she gasped out. "Spy . . . on you? You've been spying on . . . me!" She twisted against him, which only caused him to lower yet more of his weight onto her.

Suddenly breathing became the most important part of her world. She pressed against him, gasping out a weak, "Please!"

"I'll move if you'll promise not to pummel me again."

She nodded, desperate for air.

He rolled to one side and she gasped gratefully as fresh air filled her lungs.

Apparently completely at his ease, Erroll rolled to his elbow and looked down at her. She wished with all her might that she could see his face, but it remained in the shadows. Suddenly, the impropriety of their positions was borne upon her and she twisted in an effort to get up, but he had her pinned within the sheets.

"Not so fast, my little troublemaker. What are you doing, sneaking in here like a thief?"

"I realized you'd set someone to spy on me, and I intended to surprise them."

"I was surprised, all right. But I'm not spying on you—though the idea has some merit."

She blinked up at him. "I would think so. You could discern if I'd found a way to escape."

"I'd already made certain you wouldn't, so why would I need to do that?"

The man was unbelievably arrogant. "I might still find a way," she announced.

He shrugged and the pale light gleamed over his muscled shoulders.

Mary was struck with a sudden desire to touch those shoulders, to feel those muscles under her own fingertips. *Stop that! The sandalwood is making me dizzy.* Which was blatantly untrue, for there was only the subtlest hint of the scent. "Perhaps you thought to listen to my conversations and see if I was really who I said I was—and am."

Angus *had* thought about doing just that, and had tried it a time or two, but while he could hear Mary's dratted maid enough through the door, he could never catch her mistress's more muted tones. "I can't imagine you'd ever say anything of interest."

She looked disappointed, the pale gray light lighting her creamy skin to a pearly sheen against his white sheets.

"So why are you sleeping in this room? Muir told me your chambers are in the other wing."

"They are. We've had one fire in this castle. I would

not leave someone locked in a bedchamber without adequate protection."

"Protection?" She blinked, her thick lashes making her dark eyes mysterious. "You . . . you are protecting me? But—" She lifted on her elbow, her expression earnest. "You wouldn't protect me if you thought I was a thief, as you claim."

"Yes, I would. I will not be responsible for another death in this castle."

She was silent a moment, her gaze flickering over him searchingly. "You feel responsible for your wife's death."

The soft sentence held no question, yet he chose to answer it as one. "The old wing had horrible drafts, and Kiera would never go to bed until I'd arrived home." He paused, trying to make his throat work. "One night, I was late arriving and Kiera had lit a candle while waiting for me. A draft must have blown a curtain into the flame—such a thing had happened before, but I'd caught it." His voice grew cold. "I'd warned her about keeping the candles from the curtains, but she never listened, and when I arrived home smoke was coming from the upper windows. The servants had tried to save her, but the stairwell was wooden and had caught afire very quickly. I ran into the house, but—" He stopped there, then added harshly, "That's all you need to know."

She was quiet, the sound of her steady breathing soothing Angus's ire. He hated thinking about that night. Hated reliving the pain. As the memories and pain had grown more distant, he now fought the guilt of losing those memories. They were all he had left. How could he just let them slip away?

Her warm hand covered his on the coverlet. "I'm sorry."

The words were simply spoken, without any expectation of return or acknowledgment.

"Thank you." Angus removed his hand from hers, surprised when he missed the warmth of those slender fingers. He frowned down at her now. "You were very foolish to come into this room."

"It *has* dawned on me that perhaps I was somewhat precipitate in my actions." She spoke in a dry tone, and he had to hide a sudden grin.

"You were *foolish*."

"I was *hasty*."

He bent over her. "Foolish."

Her lips quirked, but she responded primly, "You can't intimidate me; I'm not going to say it."

Somehow, the air in the room had changed. Where before there had been irritation and anger, there was now amusement and . . . comfort? Whatever it was, he didn't wish it to end. At least not for a few more minutes.

He shifted to his left so his arm was in a more comfortable position.

"So why did—" Her gaze fell on his neck, and he realized she could see the shadows of his disfigurement.

He slapped a hand over his neck and sat up, frowning at losing contact with her soft body. It had been a very long while since he'd had a woman in his bed and his body had reacted instantly, which could be clearly seen. Suddenly, he didn't have enough hands. He always needed to hide too many things when the irritating Miss Fortune was about, which annoyed the hell out of him.

Cursing, he climbed from the bed. Her soft gasp told him that she'd seen his naked arousal. Growling to himself, he reached for his silk night robe and pulled it on, turning the collar up. "That's enough. You will leave."

She sat up, holding the sheet before her like a shield. "But I—"

"Miss Fortune, although you may not be aware of this, it is a gross impropriety for an unwed woman to be in a man's bed."

"Of course I know that."

"Then you need to leave at once." *Before I make that impropriety a reality we will both regret.*

She stared at him, hurt showing in her eyes. "You're right, of course. I'm just—I was surprised and I'm not thinking clearly and—" She gathered herself and rolled from his bed, but not before he was given the most tantalizing glimpse of a delicate ankle and a well-rounded calf.

His body ached at the sight and he turned his back on her, fisting his hands at his sides. "Leave before the servants discover us."

"Yes, but I—I was wondering. The weather has turned. It might make Mr. Young late and I—"

"Miss Fortune," he ground out, sweat beading his forehead. "I will count to three, and if you're not gone, I will pick you up and carry you to your damned bed.

Do I make myself clear?" He turned on the last word and saw the edge of her robe as she disappeared into her room, slamming the door as if the hounds of hell pursued her.

Only it wasn't her they pursued, but him. His entire body was aflame. *What is it about that woman?*

He glumly turned to the window and tossed the curtains open, grimacing at the cold gray light. The day echoed his mood. A long ride in the icy rain would put an end to this endless yearning he felt whenever she was near.

And if that didn't work, then he'd try something more dire. Resting his forehead against the icy glass, he murmured, "Young, you had better be on your way. Because if you're not—"

He closed his eyes and did something he hadn't done for seven long years. Angus Hay said a prayer.

Letter from Michael to his sister, Mary, from an inn near the docks of Tunis on the Barbary Coast:

My new assistant, Miss Jane Smythe-Haughton, has undertaken against all protests to organize my research papers. I explained to her that as we are in transit and have many more weeks of travel before us, order must sometimes be sacrificed for ease of movement. She disagrees.

We shall see who is organizing what by journey's end.

CHIRTEEN

For the next three days, Erroll kept well out of sight. Even Mr. Hay, usually an eager companion, seemed hesitant to engage Mary in conversation.

She'd won the right to spend some time out of her room, only to be denied any company. That was *not* what she'd had in mind.

"Well, Hurst, if you don't like it, what are you going to do to change it?" she asked herself in the mirror as she patted her just-pinned hair. Normally Abigail did it, but the maid had been inexplicably late this morning. Added to that, Mary had awoken early and was impatient to get out and *do* something now that the weather had cleared. Several days of mild-mannered sitting in one room of the house was enough. Her sensibilities, and her sense of adventure, demanded that she change her circumstances immediately.

So far, she'd won changes in her circumstances by not
meekly accepting the rules. Of course, she might have
crossed the line a bit when she'd picked the lock on the
mysterious door in her bedchamber, which explained why
the rules were now being enforced to the final degree.

She sighed. A proper lady would feel regret and
shock at accidentally finding her host naked in his bed,
but all Mary could dredge up was the fervent wish that
the light had been just a wee bit brighter.

Obviously, she wasn't much of a lady. Poor Mother
had tried to raise her correctly, but the lessons apparently hadn't taken.

Erroll had been right about the potential for a scandal, but she'd given no thought to that at the time. She'd
been too distracted by her first sight of his scars and,
even more, by his reaction to revealing them.

She frowned. The fire had to have been fierce indeed to have caused such damage. His skin was horribly
scarred along his neck and shoulder—however, and this
was the part she'd dreamed of every night since, his
form made one quite forget about the scars.

Her face heated, but she didn't think any other
woman would feel differently. The earl possessed a
masculine beauty that reminded her of some of the
Greek statues she'd seen in London. His shoulders were
well defined and broad, his chest powerful and wide;
his stomach was rippled perfection, while his hips were
narrow and his thighs—

She fanned herself, wishing she had a glass of cold
water. *I have to stop thinking about that!* Now was not the
time to be distracted by a mere man.

Mary crossed the room to examine herself in the mirror over the dresser. She'd returned to her usual sedate manner of dressing; low cut gowns were simply not for her. Sighing at her sad lack of fortitude, Mary repinned a riotous curl that threatened to fall, and wishing she were a tad thinner, smoothed her cheery yellow round gown of light wool and tugged her long, lace-edged sleeves to the tops of her hands. She then draped a shawl about her shoulders.

That done, she marched to the door and opened it. Instantly, the two footmen stood at attention. They were both young, and she liked that. Younger men were easier led, as she knew from her experience with her brothers.

She smiled at them. "Gentlemen, I wish to eat my breakfast downstairs."

The footmen exchanged glances. "But . . . it's not yer time for the sittin' room, miss. That's at ten."

"Yes, but I do not wish to eat in my room alone and would prefer to eat in the breakfast room."

The two footmen looked at each other and blinked. The taller of the two cleared his throat. "Miss, I'm afraid we canno' let ye do that."

"Oh, but you must. I am dying for a cup of tea."

Relief crossed his face. "If that's all, miss, I can fetch—"

"Oh, no. It isn't all. I am also tired of eating on a tray and wish for some company. It's nine right now, and I assume that there is food laid out in the breakfast room?"

She came out of the room and closed the door behind her.

The taller footman stepped forward, his face white, his freckles standing in stark relief. "Miss, I canno' allow ye t' pass."

She pretended to be surprised. "No?"

"No, miss. We've orders." He sent a nervous glance to his partner. "Ain't that right?"

The younger footman stepped forward, too, looking every bit as desperate. "Yes, miss. We canno' let ye to pass."

"I'm asking nicely."

"Yes, and we're grateful fer that, but we've orders."

"I see. You don't wish to upset his lordship."

"Nor Mr. Muir, the butler," admitted the younger one.

"I can see your position," she told the footmen, "but it wouldn't be your fault if I did this—" And with a swift move, she ducked around one of the footmen and dashed down the hallway, not pausing until she reached the top of the stairs. There she stopped, both footmen sliding madly in an attempt to keep from running into her.

She smiled. "Do you think they'll have ham?"

The older footman eyed her with a mistrustful gaze. "I dinna know, miss."

"They usually do," the younger one added, which earned him a frown from the other.

"Oh, I hope so," Mary said, and turned to go down the steps.

The older footman stepped forward and placed a hand on her arm. "I canno' allow ye to go any further, miss."

She replied in a frosty tone, "Remove your hand immediately."

He started to do so but then caught himself. He gave a noisy gulp and then said in a voice that shook slightly, "Miss, 'tis my job to—"

"To be a footman, not a goaler. If you do not unhand me, I shall scream."

He gulped, his eyes wide.

"J-Jamie," the smaller footman said, his face as white as a sheet. "She means it, Jamie. Ye'd best do as she says."

She sighed. "Look here, Jamie. I am well aware that his lordship has put you in a difficult place. But I assure you, I can put you in a more difficult one."

He looked so miserable that she took pity on him. "Come. All you have to do is tell people that I ran so fast you couldn't catch me. That part is true."

Jamie blinked. "We *was* catchin' up t' ye, miss."

"I doubt that. I could beat all three of my brothers at footraces, and they were great athletes."

"Miss, ye're puttin' us into an awful spot, ye are. If Lord Erroll sees ye in the breakfast room, he'll dismiss the both of us." Jamie looked to the other footman. "Wouldn't he, Donnie?"

"Aye, miss. The earl dinna like inefficiency."

"Yes, but this is different. It's not as if you forgot to polish the silver. He told you to stand guard, but did he tell you what to do if I came out of my room, other than 'Don't allow it'?"

"No, miss." Donnie shook his head, looking much struck.

"See? You were given instructions on *what* to do, but not *how*."

Pressing her advantage, she went down the stairs. "If you guard the breakfast room door, that will show Mr. Muir that you are not remiss in your duties."

Jamie sighed as he looked at Donnie. "We'll tell the earl or Muir that we never let her out of our sight. Surely that's worth something."

"I hope so," Donnie said as he hurried down the stairs to open the door for her.

Mary entered the breakfast room to find it empty except for Mr. Hay, who was reading a newspaper. He blinked in surprise, then hurried to rise to his feet. "Miss Hurst!"

"Good day, Mr. Hay." She looked around and nodded in satisfaction. "This is a lovely room, especially since it overlooks the garden."

Mr. Hay looked pleased. "It's one of my favorite rooms in the house because it's so bright."

He was right; bright sunshine streamed through the windows, casting merry rays halfway across the large blue-and-gold rug, which echoed the colors in the walls and window hangings.

"Goodness, is that Oriental wallpaper?"

Mr. Hay nodded. "Yes, it is. Lady Erroll—Kiera—ordered the wallpaper from a sample she saw in the Pavillion in Brighton."

"It is lovely." Mary crossed to examine it closer. A profusion of blue, red, orange, and green flowers were artfully displayed against a background of deep gold that picked up the gold antique-style window draperies hung in the French fashion. The gold striping of the rug drew the eye further into the room to the furniture grouped in front of the large, marble fireplace heavily decorated with pilasters. Over the mantel hung a small, amateur portrait of Lady Erroll. She appeared much younger than she did in the huge portrait that hung in the library.

Mary regarded the picture for a moment, admiring how Lady Erroll reclined upon a sofa, her gown artfully draped about her, her dark blond hair in ringlets about her perfect face. She looked as beautiful and innocent as an angel. Mary cast a glance at Mr. Hay. "This is lovely."

He briefly looked at the picture, then away, as if the sight pained him. "Yes, it is. It was done several years before Lady Erroll married my cousin."

"Ah." She glanced curiously at Mr. Hay. It was difficult to believe he was the earl's cousin, for they were so different—the one dark, the other light; the one harsh, the other gentler and more refined. Yet both seemed uncommonly fond of the countess.

Mary ran her hand over the backs of the chairs clustered about the table. The furniture, pleasingly simple against such dramatic backdrop, was made of dark mahogany. "This room is quite different from the library and the salon."

"Yes, Kiera decorated it herself. She had exquisite taste."

"You sound as if you admired her very much."

"I knew her from the time she was five years old. Our parents were quite close and always hoped that Kiera and I might make a match, though we were only children at the time." Bitterness twisted his lips. "But then my parents lost our fortune and died and I came to live here, and circumstances prevented me from seeing her for years."

"A lost passion, then?"

He gave a rueful laugh. "No, not really. It was never something Kiera or I thought of, especially after I returned to my old home with Angus. The second he and Kiera set eyes upon each other—" Mr. Hay shrugged. "I was surprised and—as much as I hated to admit it—disappointed that she didn't fall into *my* arms instead. But when I saw Angus and Kiera together, I knew that it was meant to be."

"I don't know. Sometimes youthful loves can feel even more real than those we feel as we get older."

"Are you speaking from experience?"

"I am speaking from the standpoint of a sister with three brothers who shared their youthful passions with me."

"They were lucky to have you. I've not had that."

"I've heard it said that you and the earl are as close as brothers."

Mr. Hay looked pleased. "He is as close as anyone's brother could be. He's been there for me when things were difficult, and I hope I've been there for him as well."

"Such as when he was injured in the fire?"

"Yes. I didn't leave his side for two months." Mr. Hay took a deep breath. "It was a frightening time."

For a long moment, he seemed lost in thought and sad.

Mr. Hay seemed to suddenly realize he was staring into the fireplace. "I'm sorry. It's just that I think about

Lady Erroll the most here, in this room." He glanced around and smiled. "She would sit in here for hours—whenever she wasn't painting in the turret room."

"The turret room? Where I'm staying?"

He nodded. "That room and the one beside it held her painting supplies. She was a very good painter. But she spent most mornings here answering her correspondence." He nodded to a small secretary that sat in one corner of the room. "She and I and Angus also had breakfast here every morning until—" His eyes darkened. "I'm sorry. In many ways, she was the closest thing I had to a family outside of Angus."

"Of course." His lips trembled, and she turned away to give him time to compose himself. "Ah, what have we for breakfast?" She went to the sideboard to examine the dishes. There was indeed some ham, thinly sliced and steamed, a small plate of eggs, two types of breads, several dishes of sausages and potatoes, and one featuring quail eggs. "This is *much* better than what I've been served in my room." She took a plate and filled it, then sat across the table from Mr. Hay. "You don't mind if I join you?"

He brightened. "Not at all! It's nice to have some company."

"I take it that Lord Hawk has already eaten?"

"He doesn't have a schedule. The man hardly sleeps. I call him Creature of the Night because he wanders the house at all hours." His smile faded. "I think he is glad when the sun's up and—" He caught Mary's interested gaze. "But that's neither here nor there. What brings you to the breakfast room today?"

"The desire for warm eggs."

"There were none on your tray?"

"Yes, but it wasn't warm. It rarely is."

His smile slipped. "You've been eating cold food? I shall tell Angus and—"

"You will do no such thing. The turret room is so far from the kitchens that the staff couldn't possibly deliver it warm. Besides, any man who wishes me locked in a room wouldn't be bothered that I had cold sausage for breakfast and chilled turtle soup for dinner."

Mr. Hay sighed ruefully. "I wish you had met Erroll under different circumstances. He is not usually such a difficult man."

"I'll have to take your word for it. I fully expect him to be angry that I'm out of my room. However, I've come heavily guarded, so I'm still following his rules to the *spirit* of the law, if not to the actual *letter*." She slathered marmalade over her toast.

Mr. Hay's lips twitched and he finally laughed, his blue eyes twinkling. "You are not to be gainsaid, I can tell, so I shall not try." He reached across the table and lifted a teapot. "Shall I pour?"

She slid her teacup his direction. "Thank you very much."

He poured her tea and began to chatter pleasantly about the castle and the surrounding countryside.

Mary watched him under her lashes and decided that he really was a handsome man, when one actually looked at him. It was just that his cousin's strong personality quite eclipsed Mr. Hay's softer one. He was very well formed, with broad shoulders, and though he didn't possess Lord Hawk's height, he would appear to distinction in most other society. He had sandy brown hair, a very pleasant smile, and the nicest eyes, which twinkled when he laughed.

How did he stand his cousin's overbearing ways?

When a pause came in the conversation, she said, "I can see you know everything there is to know about New Slains Castle. I suppose things are quite different since the fire."

Mr. Hay didn't pretend not to understand her. "Angus . . . he hasn't been the same since the accident. I'm sure you saw the west wing when you rode up to the castle. And then there are his scars—" Mr. Hay stopped.

"I saw them partially." At Mr. Hay's surprised glance, she quickly added, "His scarf slipped."

"Oh. Yes, that can happen."

"He is not incapacitated?"

"No, thank God. At first we thought he wouldn't live. His arm, shoulder, and side were burned, all the way down to his hip." Mr. Hay shook his head.

"He was in agony for months as he healed. He's still in pain at times, for the scar tissue is not very forgiving and does not stretch as it should, so he exercises in the stables using bales of hay and—" He looked embarrassed. "I don't know why I'm telling you all this."

"Whatever the reason, I thank you. It's very difficult to be thrust into the middle of a situation with so little information."

"I can only imagine." Mr. Hay leaned forward, his expression earnest. "Miss Hurst, I didn't believe you were who you said, at first, but now . . . I will do what I can to help you."

A rush of gratitude at the simple words surprised her. "That is most kind of you. You, sir, are a true gentleman."

He blushed and smiled. "Had I been a true gentleman, I would have stood up to my cousin earlier."

She shrugged. "The force of habit is strong. I allow my brothers to overspeak me all of the time. It's not that I think they have more to say or more validity, but I'm simply used to them being boisterous and loud, so I let them speak."

"I cannot imagine you allowing *anyone* to overspeak you."

She laughed. "I'm not shy or retiring, it's true."

"No, and I wonder if that's why Angus was instantly set against you. You are a bit outspoken and he does not like that in a female."

Which is what Angus himself had told her when she'd mistakenly thought him a coachman. *Really, of all the bigoted, short-thinking attitudes!* "Such sentiments do not do his lordship any honor."

Mr. Hay appeared regretful. "I hope you don't think poorly of Angus, but from the day he was born, he was the center of life here at New Slains Castle. His every wish was seen to, his every thought guessed and provided for. As a result, he is sometimes unthinking of how his actions might affect others."

"You are saying he is arrogant."

"No! He is merely unused to measuring his conduct in regards to its effect on others."

"Sir, you mince words," she said dryly. "I believe we say the same thing."

He winced. "I assure you, nothing could be further from my intentions. My cousin is capable of great depth of feeling. If you'd seen his agony over losing Kiera . . . and even before; Angus was so alive. He would laugh and tease. No matter where you were in the house, you could hear his voice. He was happy."

A lump rose in Mary's throat, and for the first time in her life, she felt a flash of pure, hot jealousy. She looked at the willowy beauty in the picture who reclined upon the sofa, the secret smile that tempted yet revealed nothing, the delicate neck and slender figure . . .

Mary looked away and took a sip of tea. It was rare that she felt inadequate. A lifetime of being active kept her from such silly thoughts, though it would be a lie to say that she didn't occasionally wish there were things about her that were different—that she were thinner, perhaps, even beautiful.

Of course, part of that was because her twin sisters were renowned beauties who had captured the interest of men of a much higher station than their life at the vicarage warranted. And part of it was her own fault, for try as she would, she could *not* give up her marmalade. Thus she was larger than she should be, and she didn't think her weight would ever change. It was just who she was.

With a small sigh, she picked up her toast and ate it. She had no business feeling regret for something that was simply a part of her. And no business at all feeling regret that she didn't look more like a woman who'd had the misfortune to die a horrible death. Mary silently said a short prayer, asking for forgiveness and requesting that Lady Erroll be well taken care of in her heavenly home.

Feeling better, she turned back to Mr. Hay, who was still staring at the portrait.

He turned to her and said with a small shrug, "It doesn't pay to live in the past, does it?"

"No. Nor does it pay to wallow in regrets. We must all leave our histories where they belong: in a book on a dusty shelf."

He chuckled. "That is a unique way of putting it, Miss Hurst."

"Thank you. I try to dwell in the present so I can face my difficulties . . . like that of the earl."

Mr. Hay's smile faded.

"Miss Hurst, Erroll's work is very important. I wouldn't want anything to disrupt him and you . . . Miss Hurst, you have been a distraction."

Just then a deep voice sounded from the hallway. Mary heard the young voices of her two footmen raised in reply, tumbling over one each other in their haste to answer him. *Poor things, he is reprimanding them.*

She rose and went to the door.

"Miss Hurst," Mr. Hay said in a strained voice, "perhaps it would be best if you—"

She opened the door.

The earl stood in the hallway in his riding clothes. If ever a man had been made to wear the tailored cut of a riding outfit, it was this one. The tight breeches molded to his powerful thighs before disappearing into his top boots, while his shoulders showed to advantage in the smoothly fitting coat.

His black scarf was higher than usual, but she sup-posed that might be because of the cold. "How is the weather," she asked in a bright voice.

"Frigid," he said shortly. He sent a hard glare at the footmen. "I will speak to you two later."

The footmen looked as if they might be ill, so Mary gave them both a smile. "They really had no choice. I ran."

Erroll sent her an unimpressed glare. "You ran."

"*Very* quickly. Neither of the footmen could keep up."

"I can't believe they couldn't catch you."

"I had a head start, for I surprised them. I'm *very* good at surprising people."

His dark gaze fastened on her. "What are *you* doing in here?"

"Eating breakfast. You should try the ham. It's deli-cious. Shall I fetch you some?"

"You won't fetch me anything except the reason you tricked your mindless footmen into allowing you down-stairs. It is not your hours for visiting."

"I am tired of sitting three hours a day, confined to one room. It is hardly sufficient. I am bored and lonely, and I won't have it."

Angus glowered at her, but she merely returned to the breakfast table and took her seat. "Your cousin was just telling me about your wife's death."

Angus stiffened and cast a hard glance at Neason, who turned pale.

Mary raised her calm gaze to his. "And if you're thinking of ringing a peel over the man's head, pray do not. Family history is a common enough topic. I regaled him with some facts from my own life, too."

"All lies, of course."

"No, I was saving those for you." She lifted a plate toward him and asked in a sweet voice, "Would you like some bread?"

Neason stood and wiped his hands together. "I, ah, I think I'll get back to that crate and—" He was out the door before he'd even finished the sentence.

Angus, robbed of anyone to take his temper out on, turned back to his real target.

Which was a mistake, for she was in the process of spreading marmalade on a piece of bread, her attention riveted on her task. As he watched, her pink tongue slipped out and ran across her plump bottom lip.

Angus's irritation evaporated before an onslaught of lust so strong that he almost gasped. *Good God, how does she affect me so much?*

She replaced her knife on her plate and, lifting the bread to her lips, caught his gaze. She froze and suddenly the air grew heavy and thick. Angus couldn't think, couldn't concentrate on anything other than the sight of her damp lip. And he knew then that he must have her—right now. Right here.

He turned and closed the door, then turned back to face her. She'd risen from the table, her eyes bright, her breaths lifting her breasts in the most tantalizing way.

God, I want her. Here. Now.

And somehow, as soon as the thought was made, he was kissing her. Slowly, as if sinking down a soft, seductive, silken spiral, he lowered his lips to her. The second they touched, heat slammed into him with the power of a galloping horse. He'd spent so much time since he'd ordered her from his bed, imagining what *might* have happened, that he no longer cared for "what ifs." He wanted the here, the now, *her.* With the kiss, his hunger roared to a life of its own, and he was suddenly as greedy for her as a starving man for food.

All he knew was that finally—*finally*—after days of torture, days of pretending that he didn't care and that he was in control of his thoughts and feelings, she was back in his arms, pliant and sweet, and kissing him back with her astounding passion.

God, it was sweet to lose himself in her softness, to mold her warm curves to his hardness, to savor her perfumed embrace.

She twined her arms about his neck, her passion fanning his own. She had little to no experience, but what she lacked in finesse, she made up for in sheer enthusiasm. *No one* had ever kissed him with such un-abashed fervor, not even—

Angus opened his eyes and found himself looking directly at the portrait of Kiera.

In the past, looking into her eyes in a cold canvas sent him into a tailspin, but no more. Now, when he looked at Kiera's picture, all he saw was that—a cold picture of someone he hadn't really known. Kiera, for all of her beauty, hadn't allowed him close. She'd kept her passion and her personality locked away, unlike Mary Hurst, who wore her love of life on every sleeve she owned.

But she was his enemy. She might be a thief or worse. It was even possible that she was responsible for Michael Hurst's abduction.

He pushed her away so suddenly that she stumbled and had to clutch the table for support.

"You—you—" He struggled to find the words, to tell her how outraged the situation made him.

Apparently his expression told the story for him, for her eyes flashed with anger. "I did nothing wrong, and if you suggest that I did . . ."

His jaw tightened. "You deliberately place yourself where I am tempted. Say that you do not!"

"Your response to me is your choice. And it's a shame you don't allow yourself to enjoy it the way I do." She resumed her place at the table and buttered some bread, her hands shaking. "I am done with you. You may leave."

"*I* may leave? This is *my* house. *Mine.*"

"Oh! *You*—" She left the table and stomped up to him, her eyes flashing. "You are the most infuriating man I've ever met! One minute you surprise me with a kiss that's so passionate, I think it will never end, and the very next instant, you *blame* me for that kiss! *I* didn't do anything to encourage it."

"You did, too," he snapped in return.

She crossed her arms. "What did I do to encourage your kiss?"

"You—" He gestured wildly. "You looked like—you know."

"No, I don't."

"Don't play the innocent with me."

"I'm not *playing* anything, and if you'd be reasonable for once in your life, you'd know it!"

They were toe to toe now, shouting as if they were on separate floors of the castle.

She plopped her fists on her hips. "From now on, when you try to kiss me, I shall rebuff you."

"As if you've ever rebuffed a kiss in your life."

Her face flushed a deeper red. "At least *I'm* not a stodgy researcher who presents his papers with drawings that look as if they were done by a first-year student!"

He stiffened. "There is nothing wrong with my research."

"No, but if you want people to respect it, then you have to become more cautious about whom you allow to illustrate your work."

"Damn it, woman, you don't know what you're talking about!"

"I know more than you, apparently. *I* would never have allowed one of Michael's articles to leave our house without proper illustrations."

Angus was so angry, he could have happily throttled the woman who stood defiantly before him. He knew this scene well too well. Someone would say something cutting and then someone else would cry and then someone would pack, stopping by the nursery for a tearful good-bye.

Those had bothered him as a child. But then he'd learned that though there had been tearful good-byes, within the week, there would also be tearful hellos. Still, just the memory wore him out and he found himself suddenly deflated, like a child's ball that had been stomped upon. "I am done speaking about this."

Mary pressed her lips together and returned to her place at the table, picking up her knife and slathering marmalade across a piece of bread as if it had offended her.

"Finish your meal, for you are returning to your room as soon as you're done."

Her lips thinned and she dropped her knife onto her plate with a clang, threw her napkin onto the table, and went to stare out the window, her cheeks bright red.

Angus yanked open the door. "Escort our guest back to her room. She is not to leave there until tomorrow morning."

The footmen exchanged glances. One of them cleared his throat. "Pardon, me lord, but, ah . . ." He glanced past Angus to make certain their guest could not hear. Seeing her standing with arms crossed at the window, a mutinous expression on her face, he said in a lowered voice, "What if she dinna listen to us? Are we to wrestle her like a sheep?"

Angus turned so that his voice could be clearly heard by his recalcitrant visitor. "If she attempts to leave her room, you have my permission to wrestle her to the ground, tie her up with the curtain tassels, and stuff a cloth into her mouth. A few hours bound and gagged might do her temper good."

Mary flashed him a contemptuous look. "I shall be sure to tell Michael of your mistreatment. He will never, *ever* share his research with you again."

"Be gone. You've had your few hours of freedom for the day."

She straightened her shoulders and swept to the door, the image of feminine outrage. As she passed him, the faint lavender scent of her hair found him and his body tightened in hard lust in a second. *Damn her.*

Just before she reached the stairs, he said in a stern voice, "Miss Hurst, up until now, I've been patient with your displays of displeasure. I shall not accept it anymore. If you make noise of *any* kind in your confinement, I shall revoke your three hours a day *and* withhold meals."

She stiffened. "You wouldn't dare."

"Try me." He met her gaze, daring her to push him. Oh, how he *wanted* to punish her, *wanted* to show her his displeasure. How dare she tempt him, tease him, and insult him?

She spun on one heel and left, the two footmen eyeing her as if she were a wild beast that needed caging.

Angus strode out the front door and slammed it shut, the sound reverberating through the castle. The only beast that needed caging was in his breeches. What in *hell* was wrong with him?

Restless and unsettled, his body aching and his mind in turmoil, he returned to the stables.

The groomsmen knew his mood from his expression and they emptied the barn. He took off his coat and waistcoat, undid his shirt and cravat, and tossed aside his silk scarf. Then, clad only in his breeches and boots, he began to move the great bales of hay that lined the barn wall. It strained his arms and back and tugged painfully on his scars, but he continued, pausing only to wipe the sweat from his brow as he struggled with the heavy bales. This was how he'd won back his strength after the fire, how he'd defeated the memories that couldn't be tamed, how he'd stretched his burned skin so that he could use his arms the way a man should. It was also how he'd defeat this impossible attraction for Miss Fortune, damn her soul.

He lifted bale after bale, stacking them to one side. He was soon covered in sweat, his back aching, his scars burning as if they were still afire, but he finally accomplished his goal. He no longer burned for Mary Hurst.

"Angus?"

Angus straightened, rubbing his back.

Neason stood in the open barn doors. "Are you . . . are you well?"

"I'm fine." Angus realized he was almost too tired to walk. His legs trembled, and his heart was beating so hard it threatened to burst from his chest.

"I came to see if you wished to work on the new artifacts."

"Once I've had a bath." Exhausted, Angus retrieved his clothes and threw them over his soaked skin. That done, he walked toward the house, annoyed at his cousin's irksome presence.

Neason fell in beside him, giving him a concerned look. "Angus, I can see Miss Hurst upsets you. Perhaps you should leave New Slains for a few days, just until Mr. Young arrives. I can watch over Miss Hurst and—"

"No. I will not leave Slains Castle like a scalded cat. This is my home. Here I was born, and here I'll die." *As others I loved lived and died here.* He closed his eyes, but it wasn't Kiera's face that appeared before him. Instead, it was a rounder face, framed by dark honey-blond hair, a face with deep brown eyes, a piquant nose, and the softest lips known to man . . .

His heart tripped a beat, his chest aching painfully as he lengthened his stride.

Neason had to almost run to keep up. "I know it's a painful memory," he murmured in concern.

Angus shot his cousin an annoyed glance. Neason seemed to think he knew Angus's every thought, but it wasn't a painful memory of Kiera that held Angus in its grip. It was a wave of pure, heated lust, more powerful than any he'd ever experienced.

Angus let out his breath in a painful hiss. It was ridiculous to be so tied up over a woman he barely knew. A woman he suspected of deception. Ridiculous and foolish, and he was not a man to stomach either.

Neason was panting. "Angus, I know you had words with Miss Hurst; I think everyone in the castle knows."

"So?"

"I—" Neason stopped to a dead halt, panting heavily. "Can you slow down, please? I cannot keep up and still talk."

Angus came to a halt and said sharply, "What *is* it, Neason?"

"I—I was just wondering if perhaps we should ask Muir to order breakfast served in the library, the way we used to do before—" *Before Kiera died.* Though his cousin hadn't said the words, Angus heard them nonetheless.

Damn it, was he to never be allowed to forget Kiera? Even after all of these years, must every moment of his life be filled with the bitter taste of guilt? Though Neason didn't mean to, his sad tone reminded Angus of his dead wife far more than the woman residing in the turret room did. Mary washed away all thoughts of Kiera—and anything else, for that matter.

Neason offered a tentative smile. "We can order poached eggs if you'd like. I know you enjoy those—"

"I never liked poached eggs, Neason. Kiera did."

"Oh. We can have whatever you want, then. I just thought . . . Angus, things seem to be changing at New Slains. I wish we could go back to the way things used to be, when it was just the two of us."

Perhaps Neason was just lonely. He'd taken to going out more of late, and Angus had hoped that the young man was finally overcoming his sorrow at Kiera's death.

He put his hand on Neason's shoulder. "Order that breakfast. Afterward, I will come and help you catalog the new crate that arrived so you can—"

"*No.*"

The word was spoken so sharply that Angus lifted his brows.

Neason flushed and shook his head. "I'm not done yet."

"I saw the crate just this morning, and it looked as if you'd already unpacked it."

"I will have it done before you finish your bath. I'm almost finished."

Angus nodded. "Good. Then we can sort through the objects this afternoon and start working on them."

"Fine. I'll bring everything to the library."

"An excellent idea. In an hour, then?"

Neason nodded and they continued on their way.

It was damned irritating the way Neason hovered,

but Angus owed his cousin too much to snap at him. In the months following Kiera's death, Neason had unselfishly devoted himself to overseeing Angus's care, consulting with the doctors and urging Muir to fetch more of the unguent that had lessened Angus's pain.

But he had other things in his life now—his work and, recently, dealing with an unreasonably attractive, intriguingly saucy woman.

Angus rotated his arm, wincing at the ache of his exhausted muscles. It was a hell of a way to fight off an inexplicable passion. Thank God Young was due any day—for then one way or another, Mary Hurst would be on her way.

Letter from Michael to Angus Hay, the Earl of Erroll, about the acquisition of an ancient Egyptian sceptor:

It's an amazing piece, is it not? I wish you could have been there when my guide pulled back the lid on the sarcophagus. My heart literally stopped for a moment.

I know Neason must be shaking in his shoes, for the gold is finely wrought and the ruby easily the size of a man's fist. If cut and polished, it would be of huge value—but not to you and me. We see the world in terms of history, not money. That's the main difference between us and the rest of the world—we appreciate man's foibles, passions, and beliefs, while the rest of the world appreciates their coins.

FOURTEEN

$\mathcal{M}$ary turned the page. She was seated by the fire in her bedchamber, her legs hanging across one chair arm while a thick pillow supported her back against the other arm.

Abigail sighed noisily, dropping her embroidery for the tenth time in as many minutes. "I don't know how ye can read at a time like this."

"What else are we to do?"

"But your brother—"

"Will be fine if we get the box to Whitby by the first of the month. William's ship won't be ready before then. We have two more days before we must panic, and I refuse to do it until then." She turned another page.

It was a surprisingly good book. Actually, all of the ones she'd chosen from Angus's library had met with her approval. One of her favorites was about Napoleon's

Nile campaign, which brought many interesting treasures to England, including the Rosetta stone and other antiquities that Michael had been fairly salivating to see. But perhaps the best of all was a torrid novel called *The Lost Heir*. It was rather overtold, but filled with such adventure that Mary was enjoying it. The fact that the heroine's evil uncle was now holding her captive in a turret similar to the one Mary was now in—though not as luxurious, of course—enabled her to identify with the heroine in a new way.

Poor Esmerelda wasn't the brightest flicker of the candle, which made Mary long to yell at the pages, but perhaps she'd find some ideas in the story on how to get out of her own predicament. One thing was certain: The earl was quite an intriguing—and maddening—man.

Try though she might, she couldn't forget the heated passion she'd felt at his touch. It was so wondrous it begged for further exploration. Not to mention that it seemed to infuriate the earl.

If only she didn't rise to his barbs when he was angry. She needed to exert some self-control in that area.

Abigail stabbed a needle into her neglected embroidery. "When do ye wish to take yer break, miss? Soon?"

Mary turned the page. "At ten, as we've been told."

"Yer going to follow the rules now?" Abigail looked surprised.

"Yes, for the moment. Of course, if we get bored this afternoon, I may try something new."

"His lordship will be upset."

"Lord Hawk can rant all he wishes."

"Lord Hawk? Ooh, that's a romantic name!"

"Nonsense." Mary was many things, but she was *not* a romantic. She enjoyed the occasional romantic gesture, as did any woman, but she did not idealize men or love like silly Esmerelda.

No, men were men. She had watched her three brothers grow from children to men and she knew how they thought—and how they often didn't.

She'd allowed her temper to get the best of her the day before, and had set in motion a reaction that had led to her further banishment. Now, after a night's sleep and a few calming hours immersed in an entertaining book, *voilà*—clarity of thought.

Abigail dropped her embroidery into her lap. "Miss, ye must have a plan a-boilin' in yer brain. Ye're too calm not to."

Mary sighed and closed her book, wondering if she'd ever find out how Esmerelda escaped her turret prison. "I don't have a complete plan, but I'm working on one."

Abigail leaned forward. "What is it, miss?"

"I'd rather not say anything until I've worked out all of the details. I do know the first step, though."

"Aye?"

"I need to find a way out into the garden, right outside his lordship's library."

"The library?"

"Yes. I believe that's where my brother's artifact is being held." Mary placed her book on a small table beside her chair and looked directly at the maid. "Actually, I could use your help with this."

Abigail clapped her hands. "Do tell me what ye wish me to do."

"Get the servants to talk about Lord Hawk. Pretend you're only interested because you're impressed with the castle or you think he's attractive or something."

"He is attractive, but he's too frightening. Now, if Mr. Hay wanted a bit of a squeeze . . ." Abigail grinned. "That I could do."

"You'd prefer Mr. Hay over Lord Erroll?"

"I would, miss. Lord Erroll is just like a hawk, like ye said. He scares me."

"He does possess an abrupt manner. But there is something about him that makes his roughness acceptable."

"If ye say so, miss," Abigail said, looking doubtful. "Don't you find Mr. Hay attractive?"

"He's certainly nice enough. He's also quite handsome, but he's not . . ." He didn't spark her interest at all. Few men did, which was why, at the advanced age of twenty-seven, she'd never been engaged.

It was a rather lowering thought, but one had to be true to one's principles. And Mary's wouldn't allow herself to form a relationship with someone unless she truly fell in love.

"Abigail, there are specific things I need you to find out. What are his lordship's habits? Where does he spend most of the day? Does he read? I know he's a researcher, but he has to have other interests. Also, since his wife died, has he been romantically involved? With who? Is he still involved?"

The last three questions were merely her own curiosity, but since Abigail would be asking questions anyway . . .

"Yes, miss! I'll find out everything ye need to know."

Mary glanced at the clock and stood. "Shall we go downstairs, then?"

With a wide grin, Abigail went to open the door. "After ye, miss!"

Letter from Michael to his sister Mary, from a caravan heading for the Sahara Desert:

My new assistant has finally shown her fangs. I knew it was inevitable, for one cannot travel the world over with a female without being exposed to their worst side. I've been waiting for weeks to see just how long Miss Jane Smythe-Haughton's fangs might be, for she hides them well.

The oddest thing is that *she* is accusing *me* of rampant moodiness. Have you ever heard anything more ridiculous?

Fifteen

*I*gnoring the spill of weak sunshine from the garden, Angus examined his latest paper for the Royal Society, holding an ancient gold necklet beside it.

After several long moments, he sighed and replaced both items on his desk and looked at his cousin, who sat at a smaller desk nearby. "Neason, when you drew the golden necklet, you didn't put the lion's paw in the right position."

Neason looked surprised and came to regard the necklet and the picture. He shrugged. "I hadn't even noticed."

Angus frowned. "And what's this?"

Neason looked where Angus pointed. "That's an ink blot."

Angus shot Neason a hard look that caused the

younger man to flush. "You knew it was there and yet you submitted it, anyway."

"I didn't think it would matter."

"It matters." Angus looked from the necklet to the picture a few more times, then picked up a paper presented by Michael Hurst at the same meeting not six months ago. The article was excellently written, as usual; now he looked at the drawings that accompanied it.

With only one glance, he realized they were far superior to Neason's. The detailing was exquisite and precise, every line in proportion.

Beneath the drawing was the signature of the artist—M. Hurst. Angus had always assumed that stood for Michael, but could it also stand for Mary? Had she been telling the truth?

He pushed the articles aside. "In the future, I wish you to take more time with the drawings. They should at least be accurate and free from blots."

Annoyance flickered over Neason's face. "I didn't realize they mattered so much."

"Neither did I, but apparently they reflect upon my work." Oh yes, Mary's words had stung. She knew just how to get to him.

Had she made a cutting remark about his clothing or his appearance, or even of New Slains Castle, he would have shrugged it off. But to question the quality of his work? That was a different level of attack.

"Though it is obviously unfair, I believe it's possible that one's work could be seen as"—he struggled to find a word, finally spitting out—"*lacking* if the quality of the illustrations is poor."

Neason's mouth thinned into a mulish line. "Who told you that?"

"Our guest, before I banished her back to her room." *And* after *I kissed her . . . again.*

But there was no sense in thinking about that. It was nothing more than a momentary lapse, one he'd instantly regretted and was determined to never again repeat.

Of course, he'd made that exact promise to himself about Miss Fortune before and hadn't been able to keep it, but this time she'd managed to make him so angry that he was certain he'd have no trouble maintaining his distance.

Damn the woman for her interference. His gaze fell on the now crude-seeming drawing that accompanied his article and he tossed it aside in disgust.

If nothing else, that kiss had silenced the quarrelsome female, which was worth something. Now, if only he could convince himself the kiss was worth the frustrated yearning it had left behind . . .

And yearn he did. He couldn't fall asleep without imagining Mary's pouty mouth and generous curves yielding to him in all sorts of carnal ways. Ways that left him awake and panting, longing for things he was better off leaving alone.

Neason frowned at the drawing that Angus had tossed aside. "I find it odd that you care so much about the drawings now. You've barely looked at them before."

"I was remiss. I should have been more exacting, but I was too taken up with the research itself."

"So something has changed your mind. Or should I

say *someone?*" There was no mistaking the accusation in the younger man's voice.

"Yes, damn it. She was right—a fact I like no more than you." Angus shot Neason a hard look. "Think of how often we've looked at illustrations to understand complex textual descriptions."

"Perhaps once or twice—"

"Nonsense. I can think of a dozen times or more. The details provided by the illustrations can't always be captured in words. Those details are the edges of the puzzles we're all working on fitting together."

Neason grimaced. "If other collectors really want to know about the artifact, they'll read your article and take the description from there. Besides, you never want pictures of the really interesting pieces, like those gold and ruby earrings from old Alexandria."

"They aren't significant."

"Angus, how can you say that? They were *gold* and *ruby.* They're *valuable!*"

"They weren't old enough to be of interest to a real collector."

"But the quality of the stones—"

"Neason, this isn't about baubles one can buy at any jeweler's in London! This is about studying ancient cultures and their lives and trying to understand who they were and—" Angus rubbed his forehead. "You don't really understand, do you?"

Neason sent Angus a dark look. "Perhaps your research would be better recognized if you found more pieces like those earrings. Pieces we could sell and—"

"Damn it, Neason! We've had this conversation

too many times already. You don't understand the importance of *history*."

"And you don't understand the true value of the objects that come to this house! People send you things that are nearly priceless, and unless those items have a history of some sort you are uninterested. In *everything!*"

"You have to understand—"

"No, I don't. Unlike you, I'm not hidden away here in this moldy castle. I'm a part of the real world and you're lucky I'm here to—"

Angus stood, his hands fisted at his sides.

Neason turned bright red and an uncomfortable silence settled.

He grimaced and lifted a hand. "I'm sorry. I'm just prickly this morning and tired and— Oh hell. I didn't sleep well at all and I'm taking it out on you."

Angus eyed Neason, then nodded and resumed his seat. "Perhaps you were out too late. I didn't hear you return, and I usually do."

Neason didn't look up. "I met some of my friends at the inn in town and the time slipped by."

Angus raised a brow. "You've been out cavorting quite a bit of late. Who are these friends of yours? You never say."

Neason slipped a glance toward the door and then shrugged. "They are no one you'd know."

"Well, be cautious, will you? I've no wish to be dragged from my bed by the local constable, should you and your friends get in trouble of some sort."

Neason grinned sheepishly. "I will have a care."

"Meanwhile, try to have more care when you do the drawings, too. No more ink blots, if you please."

Neason's smile faded. "I'll do what I can, if you'll promise to keep Miss Hurst from critiquing my efforts."

"I think she thought *I* had made the drawings, so it was a slap in my face and not yours. However, if she says another word about the drawings or anything else, I shall spank her. I've had enough of our troublesome guest."

Which wasn't true at all. The truth was that he couldn't seem to get enough of her.

Neason's irritation dissipated and he chuckled ruefully. "You wouldn't spank Miss Hurst, of course."

"Of course." But Miss Fortune was another creature altogether. Angus looked once again at the M. Hurst neatly written at the bottom of the drawing. What would he do if it turned out that Miss Fortune was indeed who she said she was—Michael Hurst's unknown sister? An apology wouldn't be nearly enough.

The thought sat uneasily on his shoulders. Could he have made such an egregious error? Angus sighed and rubbed his scarred jaw, suddenly tired. "I hope our guest doesn't turn out to be who she says she is."

Neason had returned to his desk, but at this he paused and sent Angus a sidelong glance. "You are beginning to wonder?"

"Perhaps. Hopefully we'll hear from Young soon. It's past time for him to reply, and now that the weather's cleared . . ."

Neason collected the drawing from his desk and slipped it into the top drawer. "If you wish my opinion, I don't believe her."

"No?"

"No. In fact, I've wondered if she didn't expect us to send for Young all along."

"To what end?"

"Michael's letter said not to trust even people you know. Could he have meant Young?"

Angus was still for a long moment. "You think Miss Fortune and Young to be in collusion?"

"It makes sense. He's the closest person to New Slains who has stayed at Hurst's vicarage. He's also very competitive about artifacts."

Angus stirred restlessly. Good God, it seemed as if everyone around him was conspiring against him. "I can't believe that of Young."

Neason gave a little laugh. "I didn't expect you to. I just thought I should mention it." He seemed on the verge of adding something, but then he collected the books he'd carried into the room. "If you no longer need me today, I think I'll retire to my room and see if I can catch up on my sleep."

Angus replaced the necklet into the drawer of his desk, settling it into a velvet tray that held an assortment of other artifacts. "Of course. I'll see you at dinner."

Neason agreed and, glancing at the wall clock, he left.

Angus attempted to settle back into his work, but his mind refused to be contained to the papers on his desk. Somehow his thoughts continued to land on Mary and her lush curves, and how they'd feel pressed to him and how he'd—

He threw his pen down and stood. "Damn it!" he announced to the empty room, grimacing at his own foolishness. *I'm just tired. I should stretch my legs and refocus myself.* He stretched his arms above his head, wincing as the scars on his arm protested. He hadn't been stretching his arm as much as he should. He'd spend some time this evening correcting that.

With a sigh, he picked up a book, opened it to the page he'd marked, and paced the room as he read. The words slowly began to make sense and he'd made several turns about the room, immersed in the details of a late Mesopotamian dynasty when, for some unknown reason, his gaze was drawn from his book to the terrace windows—where he found himself staring directly into Miss Hurst's wide eyes.

He froze. She was seated in the garden, a book open in her hand, a wool pelisse buttoned to her neck as the chilly wind rustled her pages, skirts, and the plump curls that spilled from the edges of her bonnet. When their eyes met, she flushed and immediately turned her gaze to her book as if it were the most natural thing in the world to be reading in the garden on such a blustery, cold day.

"Good God. What is she doing now?" He scowled, then strode to the fireplace and tugged the red velvet bell pull.

Muir answered almost immediately. "Yes, my lord?"

Angus pointed out the window to where Mary sat. She jerked her head to one side and pretended a sudden interest in a statue placed to block the dining room windows from the glare of the direct afternoon sun.

Muir *tsked*. "You've chanced to look outside. I was afraid you might."

Angus turned his back on the troublesome woman and pinned a basilisk stare on his butler. "Well?"

Muir sent a look of regret toward the window. "My lord, I didn't know what else to do. She wished to sit in the gardens and was most insistent about it."

"There are no footmen about."

"She is chained, my lord," Muir said in a pained voice.

"What?"

"My sentiments exactly, but she requested it. Her reason was that she didn't wish to force 'the poor footmen' to stand in the cold, though I assured her that their coats were much thicker than hers." Muir turned a concerned look out the window. "I fear she'll take a horrible chill and come to grief, my lord. I would have informed you, had I thought you could stop her without—"

"Wait," Angus snapped. "You didn't think I could stop her?"

"Actually, my lord, I knew you would find a way to do so. But I didn't wish the altercation to become *physical*."

Angus simmered, turning his gaze back to Mary. Though the sun shone in the gardens and the winter snows had left everything verdant and green, he knew what an early Scottish spring was like. It blew snow one moment, and bloomed with sunshine and roses the next. Yet even when the sun was out, there was a fierce underlying chill that couldn't be seen through sunlit windows.

It was obvious that Mary was feeling this now, for though she was wrapped in her pelisse and sat upon a cushion that protected her from the ice-cold marble bench, the wind whipped the edges of her yellow gown and blew her curls against her reddened cheeks.

He noted with dry amusement that she had to struggle to turn a page of her book due to her heavy gloves. The woman had to be freezing.

As if aware of his regard, she looked up and caught his gaze, smiling for all the world as if she were glad to see him, even though her chin quivered with the cold.

Muir cleared his throat. "My lord, shall I ask Miss Hurst to come inside and—"

"No. Leave her there."

"But my lord, she is obviously cold and—"

"She is a grown woman. If she wishes to sit in the garden, then we will allow her to do so." Angus deliberately resumed his place at his desk, where he replaced the book he'd been reading and straightened his papers.

After a moment, Muir bowed. "Very well, my lord. If you're *certain* that's all."

"I'm certain."

With a stiffness that indicated his unhappiness, the butler left, closing the door softly behind him.

Angus tried to immerse himself in his research. Yet even as he did so, his neck prickled and he looked up. The second he raised his head, Mary's head lowered.

His gaze narrowed.

Her expression was one of carefully schooled interest as she turned a page, the wind flipping several more with it. It said a good deal about how much attention she was truly giving the book when she didn't bother to fix it.

Angus turned his shoulder toward the window and pulled his papers closer. He reread the page he'd been attempting to study, but just as he slogged his way through the first paragraph one more time, his neck began to prickle again.

She was watching him.

He yanked his head up and met Mary's surprised gaze. Her nearly white lips parted in surprise and she dropped her gaze back to her book, her face now red with something other than the cold.

Angus smiled grimly. So that's the way she wished to play the game, did she? Well, he could put an end to that.

He bent his head again, but kept his gaze upon the terrace window.

The second his head was down, Mary's head lifted from her book. She met his gaze through the glass and froze, surprised to find him looking directly at her.

Angus inclined his head in the manner of a fencer acknowledging his own superior parry and winked.

Obviously miffed, she turned her shoulder slightly his direction, the book held up as if to block her view of the world, though it was now upside down.

He should have been satisfied with that, and would have been, had he not been able to see how she shivered from the cold.

The chit will die on that damned bench. He scowled. *Not that it's my problem. She made the choice to sit there.*

He doggedly settled into one of his tomes yet he

found himself peering up at her, noting how she was now rubbing her arms, the wind whipping even more fiercely.

Damn it. I can't work like this. He shoved his papers aside, arose from the desk, and went to the terrace doors. Within seconds he was standing before her, the frigid wind even colder than he'd suspected.

She shaded her eyes against the weak sun with one gloved hand, her chapped cheeks so red they appeared to have been slapped. Still, she managed a numbed-lip smile. "Why, Lord Erroll! What a pleasant surprise."

"What in hell are you doing out here?"

"Reading." She pointed to the book in her lap as if to prove this falsehood.

"Muir informed me that you are chained to the bench."

"Yes. I simply couldn't drag the poor footmen with me any longer. They were getting rather tiring."

"Tired of *you* is more accurate," he said mercilessly. "Lift your boot."

She frowned.

"Lift your boot, damn it! I wish to make certain you are indeed chained."

Her lips thinned, but she lifted her skirts and stuck out her left foot. Wrapped about the kid boot was a thin gold chain. It was on her ankle so loosely that as she held it up, it fell off.

"Oops." She quickly slipped it back on. "There."

"That's not a chain; it's a necklace."

She tucked her boots beneath the edges of her skirts. "It's all we had." She rubbed her arms. "Muir didn't wish to affix one that might scuff my new b-boots. I'm not a wealthy woman, you know. My father is a—"

"Vicar. I know, I know." He raked a hand through his hair, his jaw tightening as a cold wind lifted his jacket. Damn, it was cold.

She smiled up at him and patted the bench beside her. "Stop scowling and come sit. It's beautiful here."

"I'd freeze to death, as will you if you don't come inside this instant." He was quite cold already, his thin coat no match for the swirling wind that danced through the garden and tossed Mary's fat curls about her cheeks.

She perked up. "Are you inviting m-me into your library?"

What? "No."

Her smile faded, though her teeth were now audibly chattering. "Then I'm staying r-right here. It m-may be cold, but it's still b-beautiful."

Yes, she was. Even with her nose red from the cold, her plump cheeks almost purple, she was a beautiful woman.

Irritated at his wayward thoughts, he gestured toward the terrace doors. "Get inside. *Now.*"

"To your l-library?" She repeated the phrase in a stubborn tone.

He frowned. "Why do you want to go there?"

"Because it's where you are." When he hesitated, she added quickly, "If I could just sit there until I am warmed . . . That's all I'm asking." Her brown gaze fixed hopefully on his. "Please. I don't wish to sit in my bed-chamber alone any longer."

Her eyes were dark with sincerity. To his chagrin, he heard himself say, "Very well, damn it! You may sit by the fire until you're warm, but that's it."

She hopped up with alacrity. "Oh, thank y-you!" She tilted the bench to one side and slipped the chain out from under the leg, then pointed her boot so the chain slid to the ground. "There." She scooped it up and placed it inside her book, looking far too happy.

Angus walked back to the library, not even looking to see if she followed. He shut the door behind her, and by the time he'd turned around, she'd already made herself at home in *his* favorite chair by the fire.

He grimaced, but said nothing and returned to his desk. He took a quick moment to organize his papers, and then firmly refused to look up.

His guest was not so restful. After a moment or two of holding her boots to the fire and noisily blowing on her ungloved fingers, she rose and began to wander about. She teased his peripheral vision as she touched this item and that, exclaiming softly over various antiquities, and generally irritating him to the point of explosion. Just as he was about to snap at her to find a seat, she did just that, plopping back into his favorite chair as if it were hers.

She turned her head his way so suddenly that he was unable to hide that he'd been staring at her. She grinned ruefully and gestured to her feet. "The fire is delightful. I can finally feel my toes."

He gave her a curt nod and pulled a book toward himself, pretending to read.

He didn't know why he was so irritated that she was

here, in his library, but he was. As a rational man, he had to admit that his reaction far outweighed the simple circumstances. She was only going to be here for as long as it took for her to warm up, and then he'd banish her back to her bedchamber to await Young's arrival.

Of course, now there might be complications with that aspect, thanks to Neason's suspicions. Could he be right? Was Young the one Hurst had tried to warn them about?

"May I ask you a question?" Her soft voice slid across his senses like silk.

"No."

He found the latest papers from the society and spread them before him, determined not to give her the gratification of his attention.

Mary watched him from under her lashes. He'd initially seemed so angry at finding her outside, yet he'd all but demanded that she come inside and warm herself by his fireplace.

Well, perhaps he hadn't precisely demanded it, but he hadn't protested very much when she'd suggested it. Angus Hay was a difficult man to understand, a prickly and quick-to-anger man who kept people at arms' length by snapping at them, as if he were some king and everyone else a lowly servant.

Well, she was no servant. She stood and stretched, holding out her hands toward the welcoming flames.

Erroll didn't look up. *Blast it.*

Mary wandered to the bookshelves and traced her fingers over the leather bindings. She randomly selected one, winning herself a brief hard look and frown. *So that displeased you, did it?* Apparently not enough that he was willing to engage her in conversation, though.

Stifling a sigh, she paged through the book and then closed it with a thud.

His mouth tightened, but he didn't look up. *Very well, Erroll. If that's the way you want it . . .*

She tucked the book under her arm and wandered near his desk, pretending to examine a globe placed on a low shelf. From there, she could peer almost over his shoulder and see—

"What in *hell* are you doing?"

She pointed to the drawings on his desk. "May I see those?"

His brows lowered. "Why?"

"I frequently do drawings myself, you know, so—"

"Yes, yes, the drawings for your brother's papers. You also write the serial about him for the newspaper. I daresay next you'll tell me you wrote his research papers, too."

"I wasn't going to say any such thing." She plopped down in a nearby chair and scooted it to the desk, gazing at the papers that were within tantalizing reach. "What are you reading?"

He leaned back and crossed his arms over his broad chest, his icy green gaze boring into her. "I didn't invite you to sit there."

She set her book on the edge of the desk, reached over and picked up some of his papers. "Ah, from the Royal Society. This is one of yours." She began reading. After a few minutes, she replaced the article on his desk.

"Well? Are you going to tell me I should have mentioned the Euphrates connection? Or perhaps that I needed to expound more on the evidence supporting that Ramses II was involved?"

"I would never be so rude." At his disbelieving glance, she flushed. "Not unless someone goaded me mercilessly. *Then* I might say something."

He glowered at her. "You've already told me that my drawings are inferior."

She winced. "I was a bit angry."

"You meant it. How did you come to do Hurst's drawings?"

"Convenience, more than anything. I was trained to draw as a child; all of the girls in our family were."

"Yes, watercolors seem to be quite popular with your sex."

"Not by choice," she said, an edge to her voice.

His lips quirked. "Is that so?"

"Yes, and to be forced to draw odiously boring subjects like trees, and flowers, and— Oh, it's too dreadful to think about. But then one day Michael asked me to do an illustration for him, because the gentleman who usually did them was ill, and he thought I did a credible job. So now I do all of his drawings."

"Do you enjoy it?"

"More than I thought I would. The objects are so fascinating, and to think of the history that they've lived through—" She smiled blissfully and said in a low voice, "I once drew a Was-scepter. It was—" She shook her head. "I can't describe it."

He nodded. "But you can draw it."

"I could probably draw it now; every detail was magnificent. That's not the sort of thing you forget."

"I feel the same way about some of the artifacts." He slid a paper across the desk. "See this drawing of a necklet?"

"Yes."

He could tell she was trying not to frown, but was failing miserably. "It's hideous, I know."

"Thank goodness! I was afraid you wanted me to compliment it."

His lips quirked. "No. I just want to see you draw the same item."

She eyed the paper once more. "It shouldn't be too difficult, but I'll need the actual artifact."

He reached into his desk and removed it from its velvet box.

She examined it, holding it reverently. "It's beautiful."

"I thought so, too. So you think you could do better than the original drawing?"

She grinned. "Give me paper and ink, and I'll show you how the drawing should look."

He reached into his desk and withdrew the requested items, then placed them before her.

Finally, a chance to prove herself to Angus!

She examined the object for a few moments, then dipped her pen into the ink, tapped it carefully on the lip of the inkwell, and began to draw.

This was the part she loved—transcribing the minute details of an object so it could be shared with others. Some might see the drawings as an artistic endeavor, and indeed artistic talent was required—but Mary knew the drawings were more. Unlike parlor drawings, these renderings were required to be true to life, precise and detailed.

Her pen began to cross the page, growing in steadiness and smoothness as she became lost in the process.

Angus watched, mesmerized, as her calm gaze seemed to take in the small gold object and measure it, shape it, and then translate it onto the paper. As she became engrossed in drawing, her teeth came to rest on her bottom lip, which effectively stopped his attention from moving elsewhere.

She had the most gorgeous mouth, full and plump, one that begged to be tasted. He shifted uncomfortably in his chair and tried to force himself to read, but again and again his gaze was drawn to her.

It was a relief when she finally placed the pen back in the holder. "There. It's wet, so be careful." She slid the paper across the desk to him, and he instantly recognized the same delicate hand that had illustrated Michael Hurst's papers. His entire world shuddered to a halt.

"Erroll?"

He opened his eyes to find her watching him. "Are you well?" she asked.

"I'm fine," he said curtly, gathering the papers, careful not to smudge her drawing. "Thank you for illustrating this."

Oh God, what will I do? Hurst, I failed you. What a coil. What an ugly, horrible coil. Angus suddenly realized Mary was speaking.

"I could do more drawing, if you'd like. It would be

much more fun than sitting in my room all of the time and—"

"You may come out of your room."

She blinked, apparently uncertain. "Anytime I wish?"

"Yes. I would prefer you kept the footmen with you, though."

"Of course."

He stood, quickly locking his desk, his movement jerky. "I believe I'll finish this paper now."

Mary stood as well, though she didn't know what to think. One moment, she was drawing an illustration and the next, Erroll was looking at her as if she were a stranger. "I—I don't know what to say. Thank you for allowing me out of my room. You . . . do you want me to come back? I could illustrate whatever you're working on now and—"

"Yes. Tomorrow. We'll—" His gaze met hers and she was astounded at the intensity of his expression.

"Erroll, what's—"

"Tomorrow." He bowed, then turned on his heel and left, leaving her alone among his treasures.

Letter from Michael to Angus Hay, the Earl of Erroll, from a carriage creeping through the narrow streets of Paris:

I just spoke to Elgin about the marbles he brought back from Greece and the significance of such a treasure. He was most energetic in his praise of our efforts to break the code of hieroglyphs and said he quite believes that Champollion will have it solved before the year is out. Would that were so! I relish the solution to a good puzzle almost as much as life itself. But then so do you, so I waste my ink mentioning it. You understand that fascination better than most, don't you, my friend?

$\mathcal{S}$IXTEEN

$\mathcal{T}$he next morning, Neason walked into the breakfast room and came to an uncertain halt. "Angus? I've never seen you up this early."

Angus lowered the *Morning Post* and favored Neason with unsmiling regard. "I'm not 'up' for I haven't slept." His night had been filled with far too many thoughts to allow sleep. And the fact that Mary was on the other side of the door from him didn't help, either.

"Ah," Neason said in a knowing voice. "You dreamt of Kiera again. That always keeps you awake."

"Actually, no. Not this time."

Neason looked surprised. "Oh. What kept you awake, then?"

Angus knew exactly what had kept him awake: the realization that the woman he'd held prisoner was, in fact, exactly who she said she was. That was enough to keep any sane man from sleeping.

He'd thought she'd been lying, but why had he been so *certain*? Was it because of Michael's letter urging caution? Or the disturbing fact that Mary looked so much like Kiera, which seemed far too coincidental to his suspicious mind? Or was it something more? *Did I not want to believe her because I was drawn to her? Was I merely protecting myself?*

After a long night of pacing Angus knew the answer, and he didn't like it one bit. He'd been wrong—dead wrong. Now, he needed to find a way to tell Mary that.

Neason filled a plate with food from the heavy serving trays that lined the buffet and then came to sit at the table. As he did so, he glanced at Angus. "Your scarf's—" Neason winced. "I'm sorry. It just reminds me of Kiera."

Angus tugged the scarf back in place, not surprised at Neason's reaction. Few people were comfortable with his scars and it was safer just to keep them covered.

He turned a page of the newspaper, though his gaze was on Kiera's portrait over the mantel. Every day stole away more of her presence, leaving in its place faint wisps of memories devoid of color, scent, and sound.

He tried his best to remember the sound of her voice, but nothing came—not even a whisper. His gaze dropped to the mantel below and he realized that someone had placed some of the French figurines that she'd so prized there. Who in hell had done that?

He frowned. It had never before dawned on him how much New Slains had become a memorial to Kiera.

She wouldn't have liked that. If there was one thing he remembered about her, it was her deep love for New Slains.

"Neason, perhaps it's time we retired the portraits of Kiera to the family gallery. That picture would look well at the head of the stairs: She deserves a place of honor."

Neason turned an astonished face his way. "Angus! You— How could you suggest such a thing?"

Angus frowned. "Easily. It's been seven years."

"Seven years is *nothing.*"

The intensity of Neason's voice made Angus pause. He looked at his younger cousin, who glowered at him and then began to cut the ham on his plate as if he wished to kill it.

"Neason, Kiera would be upset to see the castle turned into a monument. She loved it too much."

"No!" Neason dropped his knife and fork onto his plate, their rattle loud as he threw back his chair and stood. "Don't tell me what Kiera thought or didn't think! You keep forgetting that I knew her first."

Angus's gaze narrowed. He folded his newspaper and placed it on the table. "I know you were fond of Kiera, but she was *my* wife, and I knew her in ways you did not."

"At least *I* never began a flirtation with a woman who looks enough like her to be her sister! A woman who is a lie and a cheat and a—"

"*Enough!*" The word echoed in the room; Neason took a step back at the force of it. Angus scowled. "Be careful what you say about Miss Hurst."

Neason's hands fisted. "Miss Hurst, is it now?"

"Yes." Angus glared at the younger man, daring him to continue.

After a tense moment, Neason's shoulders sagged and he sank into his chair as if exhausted. "You've changed your mind. You believe her."

"I saw her signature on a drawing she rendered of an artifact. It matches the one in Michael Hurst's papers."

"She could have forged it."

"She wrote it right in front of me and without a bit of hesitation. She is who she says she is, and—"

"You don't know—"

"I know enough, and that is all I'm going to say about it."

Neason's mouth thinned. "Angus, I wish you'd listen to reason. There's only one way to make certain she is who she says. Wait until Young arrives to verify her story."

Angus reflected that a few extra days couldn't hurt. And it might be the only way she would stay. His jaw tightened. "Fine. We'll wait for Young."

"Good." Neason leaned back in his chair and tugged on his cravat. "What a coil."

"Precisely. Now you know why I didn't sleep last night. I—" Angus frowned as something flashed. "Is that a new ring?"

Neason's gaze dropped to his hand, where a sapphire and gold ring gleamed softly. "This old thing? I've had it for some time. I won it in a card game months ago at the village inn."

"They must be serving a different style of customer, if that is the sort of wager they make there now."

"It's improving. By the way, a new crate arrived this morning from Lord MacAndrews," Neason said, naming one of their more prolific explorers.

"He has been very busy of late."

"So he mentioned in the letter that came with the crate. They're Roman artifacts; some very well preserved ones, too."

"How many items are there?"

Neason salted his eggs. "Six. Several interesting pieces. There's an old oil lamp, two rather exquisite vases, a small marble statue, a large pot decorated in the Greco-Roman style, and an engraved tile that I suspect you will be like very much."

"Sounds like a very interesting shipment. Was that all?"

Neason paused in the process of putting more ham on his plate. "Yes. Why?"

"MacAndrews sent word two weeks ago that there would be twelve ancient Roman coins in the crate along with the other items. Are you sure there are no coins?"

Neason returned his fork to his plate. "I didn't see them, but—" He frowned. "Perhaps they were tangled in the packing."

"That could be it," Angus agreed, watching his cousin.

The younger man stood, his chair scraping on the floor. "I'll go right now and see—"

"Nonsense. There is no hurry; I'm sure the coins will turn up." Angus stood. "I've been asking for more thorough descriptions from those who send us their artifacts to evaluate and grade. It will help us maintain better records."

"Of course," Neason agreed, looking away.

"Now, if you'll excuse me, I believe I'll go to my library and work on my paper some more. I am almost finished."

"Shall I help with the illustrations?"

"That won't be necessary today. If you'll just examine the packing from the newest crate and see if you can find the missing coins?"

Neason gave a jerky nod. "Of course. I'll do it as soon as I've eaten."

Angus nodded and left, glancing up the stairs as he crossed to the library. Was Mary awake? Perhaps he should send her an invitation to join him in the library. There was no need to tell her of his realization. Young would be here soon, and that would be that.

He stopped just outside the door of his library. *And then she will leave to deliver the artifact and I will never see her again.*

Why did that thought make him feel as if an icy, wet cloak sat upon his shoulders? Thinking was getting him nowhere. Besides, it would be several hours before Mary arose, so he had some time to decide how to approach her. His heart told him he owed her the truth—that he believed she was who she said—but his head whispered that admitting that would just make her angry, and rightly so. But if he just left things as they were, at least they could be pleasant to each other in the limited time that remained . . .

Sighing, he opened the door of his library and entered.

Thirty minutes earlier, Mary had entered the library and organized the small desk near Erroll's larger one. She found several sheets of fresh vellum and had placed them neatly on the desk. Along the top she lined up the pens, a heavy silver inkwell, and two sticks of charcoal. To her immense satisfaction, in the lowest drawer she discovered a small ivory box that held fresh nibs. She placed it on the desktop alongside the other items.

When Erroll entered the library she was sitting at the desk, hands primly folded in her lap, ready to produce illustrations.

He started on seeing her, a surprised smile reluctantly lighting his dark face.

He is happy to see me. For some reason, that sent an answering smile straight to her lips.

As he walked toward her she realized that though he smiled pleasantly, he looked tired. "Good morning, Miss Fortune."

"Good morning." She rose as he paused to examine her desk, his brows rising.

"You're ready to go."

"I'm glad to have something to do. I'm not used to such long periods of inactivity."

"Of course." His gaze flickered over her and she thought he was on the verge of saying something, but his gaze dropped back to her desk. "Do you always line everything up as if you were playing toy soldiers?"

"The drawing process requires neatness. It prevents things like ink blots. Those are caused by both sloppy habits and from having too much ink upon the nib."

"Aha. I can see this is more difficult than I'd envisioned."

"Now I merely dip and tap."

"I beg your pardon? Dip and tap?"

She dipped a pen into the inkwell, tapped it once upon the lip, which sent a drop back into the well, and then displayed the pen. "See how it doesn't drip? Just enough ink to draw a line or two, but not so much as to blot."

"I had no idea there was so much technique involved in a mere ink drawing."

Was he actually . . . *teasing*? "There is if you wish for quality results."

He regarded her thoughtfully. "You take great pride in your work."

"I do when I'm drawing something I care about. My drawings of flowers and such weren't so well done." She wrinkled her nose. "My governess said my only aptitude was for buildings. I filled sketchbook upon sketchbook with etchings of every house within ten miles of Wythburn. My brother used to tease me about those drawings, but they are what led him to ask me to illustrate his work."

"I'd like to see those drawings myself one day."

She looked at him in surprise.

His wistful expression faded and he said in a brisk voice, "Since you're so anxious for something to do, I have an object for you to draw." He turned and strode to his desk.

Mary followed him, eyeing him uncertainly. Something was different about the earl this morning. Gone was his blustery, abrupt manner and in its place was a quiet, almost gentle tone. *It's almost as if he's sad.* But surely that wasn't it. *What does he have to be sad about?*

As if in answer, her gaze was drawn to the huge portrait that dominated one wall of the library. *Ah yes. Although . . . how long should one pine for a loved one? Was there a time limit?*

Her heart whispered, "No." If she'd loved someone like the earl and then lost him—

Stop thinking about such silliness. You will be leaving soon, which is a good thing. She looked at Erroll's dark face, noting how his black hair fell over his brow, shadowing his green eyes. *He is beautiful. Simply—*

He looked up as he opened the drawer of his desk. "I think you will like this."

She forced herself to smile. "What is it?"

He pulled a long object wrapped in black velvet from the drawer and carefully placed it on the desk. With a reverent air, he unwrapped the object.

Mary's heart thumped an extra beat. "You . . . you have a sekhem scepter?"

Erroll's gaze softened as he smiled. "I thought you'd be pleased."

"It's—" She shook her head. "I can't believe it! Michael will be so envious."

A smug look crossed Erroll's face. "I should hope so."

She looked at the carving on the gold handle. "Five registers carved in the back, along with a bull. Hmm. That will be challenging to draw, for the details are so delicate, but—" She nodded. "I'll draw it."

"Good. I've written a paper on it to present to the

society. Neason was going to try his hand at a rendering, but he said it was beyond him."

She looked up at the earl. "Where on earth did you find this?"

"Michael Hurst's not the only explorer out there."

"Don't tell him that," Mary said with asperity.

He flashed a grin that made her melt. "I shall remember you advised against it."

"Please do, for his head is already far too large as it is." She gestured to the scepter. "May I touch it?"

"You may do anything with it you wish except drop it."

She carefully picked up the scepter, holding it in both hands. "Goodness! It's very heavy."

"Gold usually is," he said drily.

"I can almost see—"

"Angus!" Neason strode into the room, a small bag in his hand. "I found ten coins in the packing, as we'd expected. Two of them must have fallen out when—" He stopped and stared at Mary. "Miss Hurst!"

Mary carefully replaced the scepter. "Mr. Hay, how nice to see you."

His astonished gaze moved to Erroll and then back to Mary. "I'm sorry; I didn't expect to see you here."

Erroll shrugged. "I asked Miss Fortune to do a rendering of the scepter that you thought would be too difficult for you."

Neason stiffened, and Mary wished that Erroll would be a bit more diplomatic. She added, "I have much more free time than you right now. I'm sure you'd be doing it if you weren't so busy."

The younger man nodded, though he didn't look convinced. He placed the small bag on the desk. "I wrapped each coin so they won't scratch one another." There was an almost defiant tone in his voice.

Erroll placed the bag in his desk drawer. "Thank you, Neason. I'll look more closely at these this evening. Meanwhile, find the other two coins."

"But I—"

The earl raised his brows.

Neason flushed and nodded. "Of course. I'll go through the packing once again."

"Thank you."

Neason bowed to Mary. "Miss Hurst, if you need anything, let me know." With a disgruntled air, he left.

Erroll pulled a chair to the side of his desk. "I know you have everything arranged on the other desk, but it would be more convenient if you would do your drawing here. Then, if you have any questions, I won't have to come over there to answer them."

"Of course. I'll fetch the supplies." Within moments, she was seated at one side of his broad desk, within arm's length of the earl as he sat writing.

They were quiet for a while and Mary began her drawing, stopping to stare in reverent admiration at the scepter. *What would it be like to be a queen? I would only wear blue silk, make certain that ices were available for all of my subjects in the summer, and hot tea and cake in the cold of winter. It would be fun to order people about . . . especially* one *person in particular.*

She glanced at the earl from under her lashes and watched him write a few lines, his large hand steady, his script strong and purposeful. His brows contracted as he refined the wording of a particular paragraph.

Neason had been correct about one thing; the earl worked hard to always do his best. She could see it in his meticulous research and in the way he'd gone to such lengths to protect her brother's artifact. There was loyalty, and then there was the Earl of Erroll, who took that loyalty beyond what was expected.

Which is why he still mourns his wife. The thought cut like glass. For a wild moment she envied the late Countess of Erroll—which was silly for Mary had a perfectly good, if uneventful, life. The trouble was, she was only now realizing how quickly it was passing her by.

She glanced again at the earl, noting his well-shaped hands as he stroked his chin, deep in thought.

What would he do if I leaned over and kissed him? She wouldn't, of course, but . . . *Would he rebuff me? Or pull me to him as he's done before?*

The idea made her shiver. She wished she dared find out. Mr. Young would arrive any day now, perhaps any hour. Her time to be adventuresome would soon be gone; her time at the castle over, the artifact delivered into William's hands in Whitby. Then she would be home in Wythburn, far away from the dashing, scarred earl.

A lump grew in her throat and she found herself staring at his firm, masculine mouth. *And then what? Can I just return to my old life at the vicarage after I've been here with him?*

Suddenly, he looked up and caught her staring.

Mary blushed. "I—I was just going to ask you a

question about the, ah—" She glanced at the scepter. "The height! Have you measured this? If I have the dimensions, I can . . ."

She stopped, her gaze on the scepter. She didn't want to end up like the artifacts she admired.

She turned to the earl. "Actually, that wasn't what I was thinking at all."

Angus had been trying to focus on his writing, but after only a few sentences he'd been agonizingly aware of Mary sitting only a few feet away, the faint scent of lavender tickling his nose. He'd been so distracted that he'd written the same sentence twice.

He'd glanced up only to sneak a quick look at her so he could return to his work. Instead, he'd found her clear brown gaze locked on him with unmistakable longing.

His body had reacted instantly. "If you weren't thinking of the scepter, what were you thinking of?"

"You."

"What about me?"

She regarded him through her lashes, her white, even teeth resting on her plump bottom lip.

Angus had never seen a more sensual sight, and his entire body flooded with heat as he imagined kissing that plump lip as he—

Stop that! It will drive you mad, and frighten her. To regain control, he forced his gaze down to the scepter as he took a deep, calming breath.

She cleared her throat and said in a husky tone, "To be honest, I was wondering what you might do if I kissed you."

The impact of this didn't even have time to register, for as he lifted his head, the end of his scarf slid down and he realized it had come unwrapped, his scars now in full view.

His heart thudded sickly and he briefly closed his eyes against the vision of her face twisted in disgust as she turned away from him. The thought was like a knife turning in his stomach.

"Erroll, are you well?"

He steeled himself and turned toward her. "I'm fine."

As her gaze met his, she lifted her brows. "You've lost your scarf."

He grabbed the end to rewrap it, but she grasped his arm. "No, don't do that. Just leave it."

Angus's jaw tightened. "Why? Haven't you seen enough?" His voice was harsh, crackling through the air like the snap of unexpected thunder.

"Nonsense. There's not that much to see. Frankly, the scars are far less noticeable than that silly scarf."

He frowned fiercely. "How can you say that?"

"Because it is the truth. But what do I know, not being a woman who's addicted to fashion? Definitely listen to your cousin, the fashion plate."

"I beg your pardon?"

She sat back in her chair and regarded him with a flat look. "Neason *is* the one who told you that fara-diddle about a huge black scarf looking better than a few unimportant scars, isn't he? For I see no other con-fidants running about the castle."

In fact, it *had* been Neason who had suggested the scarf, but Angus was suddenly loath to admit it. "I don't remember how that came to be, but it has stood me in good stead. People don't stare so much as they did."

"I daresay they wouldn't stare now whether you wore the scarf or not, because scars fade and people grow used to them."

"How do you know that?"

She shrugged. "All scars fade, even ones you think won't."

That was true about physical scars. He couldn't vouch for other kinds.

She propped her elbow on the desk and rested her chin in her hand.

He eyed her suspiciously. "Now what?"

"I was just looking at your eyes."

"My eyes?" he repeated, astonished. "What about them?"

"They are a most unusual color. Like a new leaf." At his incredulous stare, her cheeks pinkened. "That is rather forward of me, isn't it? I don't know why I was staring—"

"Don't even pretend you were looking at anything other than my scars. People stare all of the time. I'm used to it." He shrugged. "It's no matter. I know I'm beastly looking."

"Beastly *acting,* I would agree with."

Obviously surprised, he burst into laughter, the rich sound warming Mary thoroughly.

She found herself grinning back, infected by his sudden humor. "That was a bit rude, wasn't it?"

"It was honest."

"See?" she said pertly. "You can trust me to tell you the truth."

His lips still curved with a faint smile, he pointed to her work. "I don't care about trusting you right now. What I *do* care about is getting some of your excellent work for my research."

Her brows lifted, as did her heart. "You think my drawings are excellent?"

"Yes, and so do you."

"What? I never said any such thing."

"Yes, you did, and in this very room. You said it while you were criticizing the drawings that accompanied *my* work."

"Oh, that." She sniffed primly. "I was angry, so I can't be held responsible for anything I said."

His lips curved into a sensual smile. "Is that how it goes?"

She grinned back. "Yes, that's exactly how it goes."

"I see." He tapped a finger on her current drawing. "How long will it take you to finish the scepter?"

"Several hours, at least." More, if she didn't stop wasting her time staring at him. "This is such a detailed drawing."

He nodded thoughtfully. "Can you draw items made of stone? That may be more difficult than metals."

"Of course I can. What do you have?"

He pulled a small black velvet bag forward. "I have some stone pieces here that form into a very interesting hieroglyph. Do you think you could draw them for me in a way that shows the characters, but also the worn state of the stone? For that's an important detail."

She scooted her chair to his side and looked at them. Within moments, they were working together, she drawing, and he looking through his tomes for a reference that had eluded him.

She dipped her pen, tapped it on the edge of the inkwell, and carefully sketched the outline of the stone pieces, a pleased warmth in her heart.

When his guard was down, the earl possessed a surprising amount of warmth and humor. There was something endearingly gentle about him then.

Mary was beginning to realize the many positives that hid behind his gruff exterior: He had welcomed his cousin into his house, knew his many servants by name, and—when not locking her away—was a fascinating man.

How could she find that side of him more often? When she'd first arrived at the castle, he'd been entirely filled with suspicion. It seemed that slowly his fears were being allayed. Once Mr. Young arrived, her relationship with Angus would change altogether.

But how? She glanced at him from under her lashes and watched him studying his tome, his green gaze intent, his expression serious. His very presence made her heart thud in her throat and her skin prickle with awareness.

He was such a handsome man, though not in the classical sense. Except his mouth, which had the masculine beauty of one of the Greek statues she'd seen at the British Museum, his face had a more unconventional beauty—his nose bold and decisive, his brows strong slashes over pale green eyes. He had the raw strength and beauty of a raging storm, one that inspired both fear and fascination.

This was her chance—perhaps her *only* chance—to explore the opportunities offered by meeting this man. Once she was tucked back into her cozy life at Wythburn, chances like this would never find her again.

If she wished to make the most of the adventure life had offered her, she would have to take some chances. She splayed her fingers over the cool mahogany of his desk and leaned toward Erroll.

She knew the second he became aware of her approach, for his brows snapped down and he froze in place—but Mary didn't stop. With the gentlest of kisses, she touched her lips to the ridge of scars that traced along his jaw.

Angus slowly turned to look into her eyes, awakening an instantaneous answer. She *wanted* him to come to her, to pull her from her chair, to lift her into his arms and—

He stood, looking down at her from his great height.

Her heart stuttered, then burst into a flurry of yearning. Her entire body ached with the need to be touched—her breasts peaked, her skin tingled. She was holding the ink pen so tightly that it threatened to snap.

"Mary." There was quiet command in the voice, laced with a definite promise.

She suddenly knew he would not reach for her. If she wanted him, she had to reach for him first.

Should I? her calm sense of honor whispered.

Then she realized she was already moving toward him. *I have to. I'm leaving soon, and if I don't explore this attraction, I may never understand it.*

It *was* an exploration, as thrilling and fraught with danger as any adventurer had ever experienced. She didn't know the outcome, didn't know the cost—all she knew was that her soul refused to respond to the calm voice of reason, but was intent on answering passion's call.

She went straight into his arms, closed her eyes, and absorbed the instant heat of his body. Even separated by clothing, his simmering sensuality caressed her. She shivered as his hands slipped about her waist and, with a low groan, he pulled her to him.

Angus had never tasted anything so sweet as the woman molded against him. He'd tried to fight this, to resist it. Yet every day she was under his roof, he'd succumbed even more, slipping into her arms as easily as one could slip under water.

God, she was intoxicating. He loved the feel of her, the fullness, the way her breasts filled his hands and her generous curves fit against him as if made for him alone. This was a woman made for loving, proved by her enthusiastic response, the way her hands clutched him, pulling him closer as she—

A sharp thud made him lift his head.

She looked up as well. "What was that?"

"Someone closed the door." *Damn it, I should have closed and locked it.*

But it was too late now. It had to be either Neason or Muir; the footmen never came unless summoned.

Angus looked down at Mary, whose wide brown eyes were shimmering, her creamy skin flushed with passion. She looked mussed and . . . happy.

Happy? From a mere kiss? But it had been far more than a mere kiss. And she was more than a "mere" anything.

His fingers went to his scar. She'd kissed it, accepting

it as well as himself. But she hadn't seen them all. She didn't know how far his scars went, how they still hurt and ached and sometimes burned as if on fire.

Yet, somehow, he knew it wouldn't matter. She was made of stern stuff, was Mary, and unlike Angus, she faced life without flinching.

Since Mary had come to his household, Angus had come to some rather unflattering realizations about himself. Those very realizations had kept him awake last night. Mary seemed to thrive on challenges, welcoming each new experience with a relish and creativity that had at first astonished, and then captivated him.

Angus hadn't met the challenges in his own life nearly so well. And last night, awake in his own bed, he realized that since Kiera's death, he'd been living a coward's life, hidden away safe among his books and research. He could have gone exploring, had his own adventures like his fellow historians, but instead he'd stayed here at New Slains, not because he loved the castle—though he did—but because here he could avoid the reality of his own scars, both inside and out. *And until I face those, I'm in no position to further a relationship with Mary.*

The crystal clear thought gave him pause and he wondered when he'd started thinking about having a relationship with this woman and he knew the answer. *It began the second I met her, though I fought it because I wished for no more pain, and as I'd thought her a liar and worse, I could see no other outcome. Now that I know that's not the case, I must fight this attraction again, but because I am not who she needs.*

His heart ached at the thought, and he let his arms drop to his sides like weights. "I'm sorry."

"For what?"

"Mary, if we continue with this"—he hesitated to use the word "flirtation," because somewhere along the way it had become something more, but he could think of no other term—"this flirtation, we will make decisions that could alter our lives—your life."

"You don't know what my life is like. Perhaps I *wish* to alter it."

"Not this way. When—if—we come together, it will be on our own terms, and not because we were careless with your reputation. I suspect it was Neason who walked in on us just now; I'll speak with him and make certain that what he saw goes no further. But we can't keep dancing so close to the fire or we will get burned. It has to stop. Fortunately for us both, Young will be here soon and you'll be leaving."

"You . . . you want me to leave?"

He nodded curtly. "It would be best for us both."

"But what if I want to return here after I deliver the artifact?" Her words were hushed but sincere. "What if someone—someone who'd never even seen a fire before—what if they *liked* dancing too close to it? What if they thought the fire was exciting, and didn't care that dancing around it might lead to pain later? What then?"

Angus's chest ached, and he was overcome with a mad desire to sweep her up and carry her to the settee and take her, as his body demanded. She was so tempting, so desirable, and so damnably pure. "Mary, when Young arrives, you will take the artifact and go at once to Whitby. I have decided to ask Young to escort you; he's an experienced traveler and will be a great help along the way."

"You are determined that I should leave?"

"Yes."

His voice was harsh and brittle, his expression forbidding, but Mary couldn't help feeling that his eyes were saying something altogether different. "And after I've delivered the artifact to my brother?"

"You will return to Wythburn and your family, and you will forget me and this place." A bitter smile touched his mouth.

"And if I stayed?"

He was silent a long moment, his eyes closed. Mary breathlessly awaited his answer.

Finally, he looked at her. "You know what would happen."

Her heart leapt. "Perhaps that's what I want."

"It doesn't matter what you want, damn it!" he snapped. "Mary, don't you see how this will turn out? We will succumb, and then society—and your brothers, I've no doubt—will demand that we marry, which will benefit no one. You deserve more than what I've become. You deserve someone who lives out in the open, someone who will answer the wanderlust you have. You deserve someone other than me."

"Angus, stop this. Don't shut another door! In so many ways, you're just as locked away here as I was at the vicarage." She stepped forward and placed her hand on his chest, feeling the racing beat of his heart. "Why don't we begin our new lives of adventure *now*? Why don't we at least taste this passion that's been offered to us, so it doesn't go to waste?"

Angus tugged his scarf back into place. "The trouble

with a taste is that it's never enough. Not where you and I are concerned."

Though Angus had only pulled the scarf over his lower jaw, Mary felt as if the gesture had placed an additional barrier around his heart, as well. "Erroll, all we've shared is a kiss. Was that so bad?"

"Don't push this, Mary. My life is comfortable the way it is and so is yours, if you'll just admit it."

"But I don't want 'comfortable.'" She almost glowed as she spoke. "I want excitement, happiness, adventure and—"

"No, you don't! You don't want any of that. If your time at New Slains has done anything, it should have shown you that adventures are not always good things." His gaze flickered to the portrait on the far wall and then away, a deep sadness in his expression. "I am through discussing this. It's not safe for me to be alone with you, so I'll leave you to finish the drawing in peace."

"But—"

"No, Mary. Ring the bell if you need anything." He turned on his heel and left, leaving Mary standing in the center of the library, her eyes wet, her heart aching.

She glared at the open door. *We are not finished with this, Angus Hay. You were right in saying that I've learned something by being imprisoned here, but it is not to fear adventure. I learned that adventurers never quit and I am now, and will from now on, be an adventurer. And nothing—and no one—will ever stop me.*

Letter from Michael to his sister Mary, from a ship docked in Venice:

Soon I'll be leaving for Egypt. It's an odd thing, the beginning of an adventure, almost as odd as the ending. In one case you're excited to be gone, and the other, excited to return. The beauty of living the life of an adventurer is that for every end there is a beginning, and thus we continue on and on and on.

Seventeen

"M ary?"

She whirled from where she'd been standing looking at the rapidly worsening weather out the
sitting-room window. For the last three days, the earl
had avoided being alone with her. "Mr. Hay! You
startled me."

He looked contrite. "I'm sorry. I saw you earlier
today in the hallway, and you looked upset. Is there
anything I can do?"

The kindness in his voice made tears spring to her
eyes. She forced her lips to smile. "No, no. I'm fine."
Which wasn't true, but she refused to share her disappointment with anyone, especially as there was no
way she could explain what had really happened. She'd
practically thrown herself at Angus, and he'd rebuffed
her without a second thought.

She turned back to the window so Neason couldn't see her lips quivering. She tried to focus on the view, noting that the wind was stronger, the large trees surrounding the garden waving their heavy branches, the sky now obscured by hazy clouds. "Do you think it might rain?"

"I suppose it could. In Scotland the weather changes minute by minute."

Just like Angus. "I wish Mr. Young would arrive." The second she had the onyx box, she would leave.

"We expected to have word before now. Angus sent out another footman this morning, to see if they had trouble on the road."

Mr. Hay chuckled. "He's as anxious for you to be gone as you are to leave."

The words pained Mary, but she managed a nod. She only wished she'd left earlier, before she'd come to— Did she dare say it? She *cared*. She wasn't sad her adventure was turning out the way it was; she was sad because she felt that she was losing something very important.

"Pardon me, Miss Hurst, but are you well? You look pale. I hope you haven't allowed my cousin to upset you. He can say the most shocking things at times."

"No, I was just thinking of taking a walk."

"I just took a turn about the gardens myself, and it was quite invigorating."

"I may do that."

"Before you go . . ." Mr. Hay hesitated. "Miss Hurst, I have a favor to ask you. My cousin has been unstinting in his praise of your drawing skills. He says you're the best he's seen. Before you leave, could you show me how to go about the drawings more properly?"

"Of course. I'll fetch the ones I began earlier from the library."

"Thank you. I'll get some paper from the escritoire. Any hints you could give would be greatly appreciated, and it will help pass the time."

"Of course." She turned toward the door.

"Oh! And Miss Hurst, I almost forgot. Until I saw you sitting here, I'd thought to take a short ride and I ordered a horse brought round. Could you please tell Muir that I won't need it after all? I would rather stay indoors with you and work on my drawing abilities." He gave a rueful grimace. "I know Angus would appreciate it."

Mary agreed and went down the hallway, but saw no sight of Muir or a footman. *I will find one on my way back and let them know Mr. Hay doesn't need his horse.*

She walked into the library and came to an abrupt halt. There, sitting on the desk as if asking to be taken was the onyx box. She knew it instantly from the drawings she'd made of it for Michael.

Michael's freedom. She was across the room and reaching for it, her fingers sliding over the cool, hard surface. It was unexpectedly heavy.

She traced the hieroglyphs with the tips of her fingers, wondering what they could mean. Mr. Young would know; she was certain of it. But where *was* he and why hadn't he arrived yet?

The late-afternoon light broke through the clouds, shining on the box and setting it agleam.

She glanced at the open door. She had the box, and
there were no servants about. In addition, Mr. Hay had
ordered a horse saddled and— She frowned. Mr. Hay
wished her to escape. There was no other explanation for
the fortunate stream of events.

She looked at the onyx box. *Should I simply take it?* She
thought of Michael as a captive, and had her answer. *I
can't allow myself to get distracted by the earl.* Heart thudding,
she slipped the box into her pocket, where it hung heavily. She'd have to walk carefully so that it didn't bruise
her thigh. It was unfortunate that she couldn't wait for
Mr. Young to arrive and explain some of the secrets of
the artifact, but time was running short, and the trip
to Whitby to meet William would take at least a week,
more if the weather turned. She went to the window
and peered outside. It was cooler now, the wind rat-
tling the glass panes. If she left soon, there would still
be light.

She hated to go without saying a word to Erroll.
But would he want her to? He'd made his feelings clear.
He was attracted to her but wished to be no part of
her life. She rubbed her throat absently where an ache
grew. It would be better for everyone if she just went.
She'd need her pelisse and heaviest cloak and boots,
and she should call for a tray of food—some bread
and cheese that could be easily tucked into a pocket. If
she could reach the inn in the village, she could hire a
conveyance with her few coins to take her the rest of
the way and . . .

Her mind racing, she hurried upstairs.

Letter from Michael to Angus Hay, the Earl of Erroll, from the British consulate in Greece:

I'm awaiting approval to remove my goods to a British ship, which may take weeks. It's not a difficult process to gain the approval—you just need one stamp here, another there. But like all simple things, once you add the human element, all hell breaks loose.

$\mathcal{E}$IGHTEEN

The thunder crashed and roiled, so close that Angus could feel it shake the floor. He crossed to the window of his bedchamber and looked outside. The rain blew almost horizontal, the trees bent in battle with the wind. A blinding light flashed, almost immediately followed by a booming crack that rattled the windowpanes.

It wasn't snowing yet, but it was perilously close, the rain almost sleet already. It clung to the window, frozen in place by the wind. It would get colder before the night was through, though the rain would cease, and in the morning there would be layers of ice on every ledge and tree branch. It would be beautiful and haunting and was one of the times he most liked to ride.

Another brilliant flash of lightning lit the raging

North Sea, touching upon the white-capped fury of the waves and the crooked road leading to the castle. Huge puddles sat on the cliff road, turning to icy traps for the unsuspecting.

He dropped the heavy curtain back in place and crossed to the fire to warm his hands, glancing at the connecting door between his bedchamber and hers.

Hers. His chest tightened and he rubbed it as if scars bound it, too. Walking out of the library this morning had been the most difficult thing he'd ever done.

He leaned forward and pressed his bare cheek to the door and listened, but he could hear nothing over the drum of rain upon the rooftop. Was Mary afraid of lightning? He found himself shaking his head at the thought. If there was one thing he knew about the little Hurst, it was that if she did fear something, she'd die before admitting it.

He left the door and poured himself a drink, his gaze returning to the door as he sipped the mellow whiskey. Mary had been absent this evening, which had concerned him until Neason had said she'd sent word that she wasn't feeling well and needed to rest.

Angus knew how she felt. He rubbed his chest again, taking a deeper pull on the Scotch, his gaze locked on the door. He could imagine her on the other side, dressed for bed, perhaps, or maybe even looking out the window as he'd been doing.

At least she now had furnishings and could sit before the fire, should she wish to. Good God, he'd been a fool when she first arrived, so suspicious and untrusting. How confused and frustrated she must have been.

His lips twitched when he thought of her campaign to win her freedom. *You never give up, do you?* He walked to the door and placed his hand on the panel.

He knew she was Hurst's sister, knew it without a doubt. If he were honest, he'd admit that he'd known it even before he'd seen her drawing.

When had the change occurred? When had he gone from disbelieving every word to accepting that she was indeed Michael Hurst's sister?

He set his glass aside and leaned against the door. It was so silent. What if she was hurt? Injured, perhaps? Lying on the floor in a puddle of her own blood?

His stomach tightened with an ill feeling, and somehow, some way, Angus found himself turning the knob.

With a soft click, the door opened. Angus stared at the knob. *How long has this door been unlocked? What might have happened if I had known that?*

He swallowed and slowly pushed it open. The room was in total darkness. He frowned, surprised there wasn't at least a candle lit. He peered through the dark and could just make out her bed, the curtains closed against the cool night air.

She's not injured, then. I can return to my own room. And yet he lingered, looking at the bed. *Did she miss dinner because of our conversation? Is she more distraught than I thought?*

He needed to know.

He went back into his room to fetch a small lamp, then carried it to her bed. The bed curtains were drawn and he reached to open them, hesitating a moment . . .

He shouldn't be here. He knew it, yet he couldn't

convince himself to leave. His fingers closed about the heavy velvet drapery. *No*, he told himself.

He dropped his hand and turned away—and then halted. Suddenly, with a surety that was frightening, he *knew* what he'd find behind the curtain, knew it with every fiber of his body.

He whipped back the curtains and stared down at the empty bed. His hand curled about the red velvet and he yanked it, ripping it as he turned back to his own room, yelling as he went.

Followed by four footmen and Muir, Angus ran down the steps to the foyer.

Neason came out of the library, blinking sleepily, a book in his hand. "Angus! Where are you going?"

"Have you seen Mary?"

"Mary—you mean Miss Hurst? Not since this afternoon. I was just reading about the Punic Wars and fell asleep in the library—"

Angus brushed past him. "Muir, send for my horse. It sounds as if the rain is slackening, thank God."

Muir snapped his fingers, and a footman ran from the foyer.

Neason blinked. "Angus, where are you going? It's dark and the weather—"

"I know what the weather is, damn it! I can see it for myself! But someone must go after that foolish, stubborn, short-sighted, lack-witted—" She was beyond any frustration he'd ever experienced, and his emotions ranged from raging lust to bloody fury within moments. She tied him up, twisted him in knots, and then did something like this, where he didn't know whether he should shoot her or strangle her.

Angus realized Neason was staring at him with concern. "Our guest has left us," he told him.

"In this weather?"

"Yes."

Neason frowned. "That is most unexpected."

"I know. Only a fool would travel in such horrid weather. If she hasn't already come to grief, I will be surprised." The thought of Mary's lifeless body at the bottom of a cliff was unbearable. The force of the image staggered him, and he had to close his eyes.

"Angus?" Neason grasped Angus's arm.

"I'm furious, that's all," Angus said harshly. "She's a fool to leave in this weather."

"Do you know why she went? Did you argue?"

"We had a disagreement days ago, but—" *It had become something much more. Good God, why didn't I explain to her why I have to stay away from her? Did my seeming coldness frighten her off? Good God, what have I done?*

Neason shook his head. "This is so odd. I can't imagine she'd leave without the artifact. She's been so adamant that she had to have it for her brother's release. I wonder . . ." Neason looked at the open library door.

Angus followed his cousin's gaze. "How could she get inside the desk? It's always locked."

Neason gave an uncertain laugh. "You're right, of course. I just couldn't imagine her leaving without accomplishing her goal. She seems so determined in her efforts." He shrugged. "Perhaps something else occurred to send her off into the night."

Angus found himself looking at the library. *Could she have? But how?* He stalked inside to his desk, took the key from his waistcoat pocket, inserted it into the lock, and yanked the drawer open.

It was gone.

"Well?" Neason asked, following after. "Did she—"

Angus slammed the drawer closed. "I don't give a damn! We must find her." He stalked back into the hallway just as a gong sounded. Muir opened the front door and a man entered, followed by a swarthy servant.

The slender gentleman was dripping wet, his hair plastered to his head, his coat soaked at the shoulders. "Good God, Erroll! What sort of weather do you people have? I nearly drowned just getting from my carriage to the door."

"Young!" Angus started forward. "I didn't expect you in this weather."

The gentleman looked surprised. "You asked me to come and so I did. We had a bit of a problem on the way here with a broken axle, but Rajid took care of things, as ever."

The silent servant bowed and placed a heavy-looking portmanteau on the ground.

Young peeled off his gloves and handed his wet curly-brimmed beaver to a waiting footman. "So, Erroll, you sent for me? Something about Hurst's youngest sister."

"You know her?"

"Lord, yes. Who doesn't?"

"Hurst never mentioned her to me," Angus said grimly.

"Odd—but then, Hurst doesn't often talk about anything other than work. Daresay you might not notice it, being the same yourself, but he's remarkably one-themed in his conversations." Young handed his multi-caped greatcoat to another footman. "What do you wish to know about Miss Hurst? She's a dashed good artist, and does a good bit of research for her brother's finds as well. Daresay she could put us all to shame if she decided to take to the life. And I— Why, blast me, look at that." He turned an astonished gaze to Angus. "Why do you have a portrait of her hanging in your library?"

Angus followed Young's pointing finger toward the open doors to the library to the portrait of Kiera. Young tilted his head to one side. "No, silly of me, that's not her, but it could be one of her sisters. Blond hair, brown eyes,—ravishing smile, too. I—"

Stalking to the door, Angus grabbed his coat from the footman and shrugged into it.

Neason followed. "Angus, you can't go out in that weather!"

"Young made it to the house."

"He has Rajid." Neason glanced at the personal servant who stood beside the door, watching every move with interest. "Besides, Miss Hurst could have left hours ago. You don't even know where she's headed!"

"It doesn't matter. I will find her and bring her and that damned box back, if it's the last thing I do."

He buttoned his coat, wrapped a muffler about his neck, and slapped his hat upon his head. "And when I find her, only God will be able to save her."

"Erroll, what the deuce is going on?" Young asked, looking from Neason to Angus. "I just arrived, and off you go and—"

"Miss Hurst came to request an artifact consigned to my care by her brother. Unfortunately, Hurst sent a letter warning that someone might come for the object and to guard it closely. So when Miss Hurst arrived, I didn't believe her."

"He locked her in her bedchamber," Neason added.

Angus shot his cousin a hard look.

"Pardon me, my lord," Muir said, drawing himself up to his full height, slight as it was. "I believe there is something you should be aware of."

"Whatever you know, be quick."

"Yes, my lord. Miss Hurst left on a horse that was requested by Mr. Hay." Muir shot a dark look at the younger lord, who'd paled. "Now that I know she is gone and didn't return, I wonder . . ."

Angus turned on Neason. "*You* ordered her horse?"

"No, no! I ordered one for myself, but I asked her to let Muir know I had changed my mind and wouldn't need it. I didn't know she'd taken it for herself, though I suppose I should have thought of it."

"Muir, when was this horse ordered?"

"At four this afternoon, my lord. Miss Hurst must have left a short time later."

Angus frowned. "If that's true, then—Neason, you told me that Miss Hurst couldn't join us for dinner because she felt unwell. If she left close to four, then how could she have told you such a thing?"

Muir's reddish brows drew down as his gaze pinned on Neason.

"I—I didn't see her then. I just assumed that when she didn't come down to dinner that she was feeling ill—"

"My lord, if I may?" Muir interjected. "Mr. Hay informed me an hour *before* dinner that Miss Hurst would not be available, though at the time he didn't mention that she was feeling ill."

"Dear me!" Mr. Young said, his brows arched so high they almost disappeared under the damp edges of his bristled brown hair.

Angus glowered at Neason. "What have you done?"

The younger man backed away, his hands palm up. "I didn't tell Muir—Angus, you know me. I would never—"

"If you value your life, you won't say another word."

Neason blanched.

"We will sort this out when I return. I must find Mary."

Angus strode out the door and down the steps, glad that the rain was just an icy drizzle now. A groom huddled beside the black gelding held a lantern, which he handed up to Angus once he was mounted.

Holding the lantern aloft, Angus turned the horse down the smooth drive, careful not to hurry though every instinct screamed at him to do so. He didn't dare risk the horse, or Mary would indeed be lost.

The icy drizzle dampened his clothes thoroughly by the time he reached the end of the drive.

Damn this weather!

Fortunately, the lantern was well shielded from the rain, its glass panes keeping the wetness at bay.

Angus slowly picked his way down to the cliff road and beyond, looking for signs that Mary might have left the main road in search of shelter. There was precious little to be had, though he knew of one or two places. He refused to look over the black edge of the road where it broke over the high cliffs. One stumble of a horse, one slip on the road and—

He ground his teeth and rode on, careful not to tire the horse. About an hour from the house, just as the road grew its most treacherous, he came upon a horse standing in the center of the road, the broken rein telling its own tale.

Mary! Where are you?

Heart thudding against his throat, Angus climbed from his mount and examined the horse closer, noting the animal's nervousness and a long, angry scrape on one fetlock. "What happened?" he murmured. "Did you bolt? Or slip on the ice?" He had an image of Mary broken and bleeding, and instantly dampened the thought. He couldn't afford to be distracted. She was a strong woman—she'd proven that again and again. She wouldn't bend to circumstances; she'd bend the circumstances to *her*.

He tied the mare's reins to the saddle on his horse and pressed grimly on. He'd find her. He had to. Still, the rain came down, and his chest ached now with both fear and the cold.

Somewhere in the middle of this horrid icy night, on foot and perhaps injured, was Mary. Head down against the weather, Angus Hay said a prayer.

Letter from Michael to his sister, Mary, from a tent on the outskirts of the ancient city of Jafar:

Whenever things are at their bleakest, I always pay a little extra attention to my more immediate creature comforts. It's amazing what a drink of water in severe heat, or a cup of hot tea in icy cold weather, can do to revive the spirits and focus the mind. Sometimes the little things are the big things.

NINETEEN

$\mathcal{M}$ary opened her eyes, aware of the icy mist. She was shivering, her teeth chattering. She wiped water from her face and wondered for a moment where she was.

The memory came seeping in. She pressed a shaking hand to her head, feeling the large knot over one ear. Her hair was so wet, it was difficult to tell if it was bleeding or not, but it didn't really matter. Right now she had to find a way to get warm. Thank God she'd found the old sheepherder's croft. It was half caved in, the roof leaking from a dozen places and water pooling on the mud floor, but at least half of it held out the rain.

She gathered herself and stood, pulling her wet pelisse and cloak tighter about her. She wiped her face and looked around, noting a few pieces of wet furniture. *Think, Mary. Think.* She struggled to make her numb brain work, but she was shaking so hard it was difficult to even finish a thought.

She rubbed her arms. *What happened when I fell?* A rumble of thunder overhead reminded her.

Ah, yes. Lightning had struck so close that she'd been able to smell it. The blinding strike had panicked the horse and it had reared, throwing Mary from the saddle. Then, with a terrified whinny, it had run away into the night.

Mary prayed that the poor, terrified animal hadn't run off the cliff road.

She shivered uncontrollably, her teeth still chattering. "I have to get warm," she announced. "What would Michael do?"

No answer came, and she grimaced. "What should I do?"

She forced herself to look about the small hut again. Two broken chairs were stacked in one corner, and household items were littered about the floor— several bowls, the remains of a straw mattress, a bent candleholder, and a rusted knife. Mary picked up a half-broken chair, wedged one leg in a crack in the small fireplace, and began to break the wood into smaller pieces.

That done, she piled it into the small opening and added some straw from the mattress. She then collected the rusted knife and the candleholder and carried them to the fireplace. Sitting cross-legged, her wet skirts shoved to one side, she began to scrape the knife along the candleholder, showering sparks on the damp hay.

Mary held her hands to the warm fire. "Mary Hurst, you are an *excellent* adventurer. Michael would be proud."

But even though she knew he would applaud her efforts, it wasn't Michael her mind kept returning to. Rather, she thought of a tall, dark, green-eyed man who had the ability to make her feel warm even without a fire.

She scooted a little closer and looked around. She was stuck here until morning came, and luckily, she could make herself a bed. She cleared all the broken pottery pieces out of the way, then moved what was left of the mattress close enough to the fire that she wouldn't freeze to death.

That done, she undid her cloak and removed it, shivering mightily, and hung it by the fire to help hold in the heat. Within a few moments, a faint warmth gathered about her.

Mary crossed her arms and rested them on her knees. Her entire body ached, though whether from the fall or the cold or exhaustion, she didn't know. All she knew was that the faint warmth had stilled her shivering. Now she had to plan her next action.

She slipped a hand into her pocket and felt the reassuring weight of the onyx box. She was halfway through with her adventure, though it still felt as if she had a long way to go. She released the box and used a chair leg to stir the fire to a better height. It didn't burn any more brightly, but the faint heat increased.

She sighed and replaced the chair leg on her small stack of wood. It wasn't enough to burn all night, but it would last a few hours. Her stomach growled and she wondered what was being served for dinner at the castle. She could picture Angus at the head of the long table, his green eyes crinkling when he smiled.

A swift pang of homesickness rippled through her. Though the image was lovely, she doubted there was a pleasant meal being had at New Slains. Angus would know by now that she'd left, and he'd be furious.

Well, let him be furious then. I don't owe him anything. He wished me gone and now I am. A cold drop of water fell on her nose and she scrubbed it away, noting that a few hot tears had leaked out as well. It wouldn't do to keep thinking about New Slains and Angus. She dropped her head to her arms and closed her eyes, focusing instead on the pleasant warmth before her. She was just dozing off when the sound of a horse whickering made her look up.

A moment later, she heard Angus's deep voice curse.

"Angus?" Mary called, unable to quell a stab of relief.

"Wait there," he answered gruffly. He pushed on the door, but it refused to budge.

"Angus, you don't need to—"

With a splintering thud, the door gave way and Angus lunged into the hut, tripping over the broken door and landing on Mary's makeshift bed.

She had never been happier to see anyone in her entire life, but she had already been rebuffed once and she wasn't going back for seconds. So instead of giving him the welcome that sang through her veins, all she said was, "Finally."

He frowned as he rolled to his feet. He was so tall

that he couldn't stand, so he knelt across from her and eyed her warily. "Finally *what?*"

"I thought you'd never get here."

"You knew I was coming?"

"Of course."

She suddenly realized that she had, too. Somewhere deep in her heart, she'd hoped, prayed, *wanted* him to come for her—so badly that she'd been afraid to admit it, even to herself. But now that he was here, she could say it out loud. "I knew you'd come because I needed you."

His gaze darkened and for a delicious moment she thought he might reach for her and envelop her in a wonderful hug, but then she noticed that the hands he held out to the fire were shaking with cold.

"We must get you out of those clothes!"

He lifted his brows, a humorous glint in his eyes. "Oh?"

"At least your coat."

He obliged, rising to hang it over the opening where the door had been. "The door was stuck. How did you get in?"

"Through the broken window. I tried to tell you, but . . ."

"I was in a hurry." He slipped off his waistcoat and hung it near her pelisse. Then he removed his cravat as he came to sit beside the fire, his open wet shirt plastered to his broad chest. "So . . . did you take it?" His green gaze locked with hers.

She reached into her pocket and pulled out the box. "I suppose I should have asked first—"

"You damn well should have."

She flinched at his icy tone, but tucked the box back into her pocket. "You have no right to be upset. The box belongs to Michael and you know it. Besides, you told me I should leave and so I did." She hunched her shoulders. "I really didn't have a choice. There was the box, right out on your desk, and a horse waiting in the drive—"

"Wait. The box was on my desk?"

"Yes. Neason came to the sitting room and said you'd been telling him how well I did the illustrations, and he asked me to show him how. I went to fetch the ink and pen from the library and when I did, there it was."

"I see," Angus said, looking grim. "I see quite a lot, in fact. The horse was there for you, too."

"Yes, Neason had called for it, but then didn't wish to ride after all. He asked me to tell Muir that he didn't need the horse and—" She frowned at the anger she saw on Angus's face. Slowly, the truth dawned. "He didn't do all of that to help me. He wanted to make you angry with me."

"And it worked, too. I could have throttled you. Do you know how dangerous this weather is?"

"I found out."

"You are a stubborn woman, Mary Hurst."

She looked shocked. "You admit that I'm Mary *Hurst*?"

"I've known it for some time."

"Yet you didn't give me the box?"

"I wanted Young to accompany you to Whitby. It's

not a journey a woman should undertake alone." He shrugged his powerful shoulders. "I couldn't trust myself to take you, so . . . I was waiting for Young. Just not for him to identify you."

"I see." She considered this and could find very little fault with it, except that he hadn't confided in her. "You didn't believe me at first."

"No." He shook his head. "Oh, Mary. I'm afraid I've been a fool in every way you can imagine."

"Yes, but do you think Neason . . . I can't believe that."

"I wonder." Angus stared into the fire. His world seemed upside down.

A warm hand tucked over his cold one, and Angus looked up and met Mary's open brown gaze. He'd come so close to losing her. *Too close.*

He rubbed a hand over his eyes, aware that his fingers shook. "I thought I'd lost you."

She flashed a crooked smile. "I thought the same about you, and yet . . . here we are." As if for emphasis, a fat drop of water hit her on the nose, making her giggle. She was soaking wet, her golden hair a light brown because of the rain, clinging to her cheeks and neck and straggling over her forehead. She'd gotten so wet that her eyelashes were spiked about her wide eyes, her skin gleaming. She had to be every bit as cold and hungry as he, yet there she sat, her eyes crinkled in laughter.

Without thinking, Angus leaned over and kissed her wet nose.

And that was all it took. He couldn't think of a single reason not to show her how he felt, and he felt so much. His body sang with it, his soul soared, and his heart pounded with love.

She placed a hand on his cheek, and leaned her forehead to his. "Angus Hay, I want more than a kiss."

Her soft voice stroked and cajoled, and he knew what she wanted. His heart raced. "Mary, are you sure? You're a virgin and I—"

"I know what I am." Her fingers slipped up his chest to his open shirt and threaded through his hair.

He caught her hand and pressed it flat to his chest. "Mary, we can't."

She slipped her other hand to his cock, where it pressed against his breeches, and bent close to whisper into his ear, "Can't we?"

He closed his eyes and shivered.

Her hands continued to stroke and touch, to tease and torment. His cock grew harder and harder still. "Mary, please . . ."

She cupped him through his breeches and he groaned.

"Angus, I don't care about propriety. I've spent my whole life taking care of people, and I've had all that a staid, proper life has to offer. This trip to fetch Michael's artifact has shown me that I'm done with that phase of my life. Now I want adventure and passion and all of the joys and pains that come with those."

She undid his shirt and placed her hand on his bare chest, her expression earnest. "Angus, I *want* this. I want to experience *this*—right *now.*"

With another groan, he pulled her against him and then covered her body with his own. She sighed with happiness and wiggled against him, making his body burn.

Angus captured her mouth with his own, showing her all of the myriad of things he felt but couldn't find the words to say.

She twined her arms about his neck, straining against him, her tongue seeking his. Her hips lifted in an unconsciously wanton invitation and he had to fight the urge to immediately bury himself into her, so intense was the pleasure.

He pulled back and looked into the smoky passion that deepened the color of her eyes. "Easy, my love," he whispered, then gently nipped her full bottom lip. She shivered and closed her eyes, her thick lashes lying in crescents on her cheeks.

He lifted on one elbow and ran his hands past her waist, to the curve of her hip, and on to the firmness of her thigh.

With an impatient tug, he pulled her skirts up until he could cup the roundness of her leg in his hand. She was made for his hands, he thought possessively, kissing her with renewed passion.

Mary gasped as his hands touched her leg and began a smooth ascent past her knee. Just as she tensed, his warm, demanding mouth was again on hers, his tongue seeking, questing. She threw one arm around his neck and placed the other on his back, running it up and down his rippling muscles, her fingers finding and tracing the lines of his scars.

He paused.

Mary bent to kiss his scarred shoulder, his neck, and

the line upon his jaw. She loved him, this man with his tempestuous ways and his rough scars. She loved him as he was, for who he was, and as he was.

"Take me," Mary whispered, the words wrenched from her secret heart.

He slowly lowered his mouth to place an almost reverent kiss on her lips. She moaned and kissed him back, her whole body writhing with urgent passion. His hands sank into her hair and he plunged his tongue into her mouth in an insistent, seductive rhythm. Unconsciously, she ground her hips against his, her hands tugging senselessly at his clothing.

He began to loosen her dress. As her skin was exposed to the cold air, her nipples hardened. His mouth, hot and insistent, covered one taut peak as his hand cupped the other. She gasped, arching into him, her hands grasping at his hair.

"Don't stop," she breathed, and somehow he managed to free her dress without ceasing his heated caresses to her breasts.

He lifted himself to look at her, his burning gaze lingering with exquisite torture until she thought she would burst into flames from desire. "You are so beautiful," he murmured.

She tugged at his breeches. "Undress," she whispered, pleading.

He did as she asked, then wrapped himself about her. She moaned and writhed as he nipped at her ear, his hand sliding up her thigh to brush ever so lightly against her moistness. Mary gasped with surprise at the rush of sensation his touch caused, arching against him.

Hot, molten liquid rushed through her veins. She was afire with want. She threw an arm about his neck and ran her other hand over his shoulders, down his back and lower, kneading his firm muscles. She reached to cup his manhood and he groaned into her mouth. She wanted to touch him, to hold him. Angus moaned again as she stroked him.

He pulled her legs apart and positioned himself above her, his eyes gazing directly into hers as he lowered himself into her. There was an agonizing second of fullness as he pressed his hips against her.

"By the saints," he whispered between clenched teeth. Before he could withdraw to sink into her again, she tensed, then threw back her head as wave after wave of pleasure rippled through her, and she clutched her legs about him. He couldn't withstand the pressure of her reaction. Spiraling through heaven, she sent him over the edge without even moving.

For a moment they lay spent, their legs intertwined as their breathing returned to a more normal pace. Angus lifted himself to look down at Mary's flushed face and couldn't resist placing a kiss on the corner of her mouth. It looked like a dewy cherry, ripe for a taste.

She smiled at him from beneath heavy lids. "Now, *that* was an adventure."

He chuckled. "Aye, so it was." He kissed her eyelids as she closed them and she smiled, her face a study of contentment. Angus curled about her, tucking her against him, his leg crossing hers, his arm over her shoulder. She sighed as she snuggled against him and he settled a cloak over them.

The scent of lavender rose from her hair and he nuzzled her neck, seeking the sweetness of her bare skin. She chuckled sleepily, which made his heart do an odd flip. He closed his eyes and breathed in the moment, the feel of her, the rightness of it all. Never had he felt this way. And if he let her go, he knew he'd never feel it again.

He tightened his hold and listened to her steady breathing as he watched the flickering fire.

Much later, Angus watched as Mary slept. Her dark blond hair was tangled about her shoulders, her lashes resting on the crests of her cheeks. He traced the line of her jaw with the back of a finger and she stirred in her sleep, a slow smile curving her lips before she sank back into deep slumber.

God, what passion she had. He'd never experienced anything like it, so heated and earthy.

He loved her ability to embrace life so joyously, to throw herself into the moment—not letting life just happen around her, but joining in every chance she had.

Perhaps he could learn that from her. He sheltered her with his warmth, noting that the rain had stopped. Tomorrow he would settle his future one way or another. The thought made him smile.

Letter from Michael to his sister Mary, from a caravan heading for the Sahara Desert:

If you ever find yourself presented with a fork in the road of life and you do not know the correct direction, close your eyes and listen to your heart. I have found more adventure, more love, more happiness, and more life by listening to who I am, rather than attempting to tell myself.

TWENTY

The next morning, Angus walked into the foyer at New Slains Castle, Mary's hand tucked securely into the crook of his arm.

Mr. Young, who'd entered the foyer looking for a footman to order some tea, hurried forward. "Thank God! I've been worried sick about you both!" He came forward to hug Mary. "My dear girl, are you well?"

"Perfectly fine! Just a bump on my head and a bruised hip from a fall from my horse. Nothing worse than that."

"Thank God." Mr. Young looked curiously at Angus. "So you found her this morning?"

She sent a glance up at Angus, unsure what she should say.

She'd awoken this morning to find the horses already saddled and packed, and Angus ready to go. He'd given her some privacy to wash, using rainwater that had collected in a cracked bowl, then they'd saddled up and ridden to New Slains. Angus had been suspiciously quiet, and Mary found herself unable to mention the events of the previous night. It all seemed so far away, yet so inevitable.

She swallowed a lump of emotion and fought to keep her smile in place as Mr. Young patted her hand. She saw his gaze go to her hair and she put a self-conscious hand to it. "My horse bolted and I was thrown and—"

"And I found her and we spent the night in a sheepherder's croft not far from here," Angus finished smoothly.

Mr. Young blinked. "Last night? Then—" His gaze met Mary's and he blushed. "Oh, dear."

Angus slipped an arm about Mary's waist. "Which is why we shall be marrying immediately."

She looked up at him. *"What?"*

"That's not the only reason, of course." His green eyes quizzed her gently. "Mary, we've a few things to settle. I was hoping to speak with you after a bath and a meal, but adventurers don't always have every comfort, do they?"

Her heart tripped an extra beat. "No. No, they don't."

"So I will just have to make do, as a good adventurer would." He took off his wet coat and handed it to an astonished Mr. Young. Then, with great solemnity, Angus dropped to his knee and took Mary's hand in his. "Mary— What's your middle name?"

"Charlotte."

"Mary Charlotte Hurst, will you marry me?"

"But . . . I *stole* from you."

"Oh, my!" Mr. Young murmured.

"No, you didn't. Neason set the box out for you to take. You were tricked into taking it. Besides, I had locked you in the turret room, so I think we're fairly even."

Mr. Young shook his head.

Mary sent Angus a hard look. "You also threw all of my furniture out into the courtyard. *Good* furniture, I might add."

Mr. Young looked in astonishment at Angus, who was still on one knee. "You threw it?"

"Yes," Mary answered for him. "And it all crashed upon the cobblestones. Ruined. All of it."

"Good God," Mr. Young exclaimed. "Erroll, why would you do such a thing?"

Angus sighed and climbed back to his feet. "It's a long story, but if you must know, she was making a great deal of noise with that furniture."

"A *lot*," Mary agreed, rather pleased at the memory. "That was how I got him to release me, by making horrible noises."

"The worst was the singing." Angus looked at Mr. Young. "You can't begin to imagine."

Mary's smile faded. "I was signing very loudly, but not off key."

Mr. Young wisely changed the topic. "By the by, young Mr. Hay left shortly after you did. Judging by the amount of baggage he took, I don't believe he plans on returning any time soon."

"Oh, no!" Mary cried. "Angus, you must go after him! No matter what he did, he has been like a brother to you."

Angus sighed. "Fine. We'll save the proposal for later. As for Neason, if what I suspect is true, he left because he's been stealing from me for a long time and he knew he was about to be caught."

"Sorry, dear man," Young said, shaking his head. "Hurst and I discussed our suspicions on that many times, but we knew you were close and, well, it never seemed like the right time to bring it up. Besides, I always thought you knew."

"I did."

Mary blinked.

Angus added, "He was obsessed with making money, so I made certain he only had access to the pieces that weren't of historical significance."

"But . . . why did you allow him to do that?"

"I was hoping he'd realize he didn't need to, that he had other talents that could be of better use."

Young nodded. "Self-redemption is the only talent that lasts."

"But . . ." Mary rubbed her temples. "Why did Neason want me to have the onyx box?"

"Because he wanted you to leave, and he knew that was all that held you here. I believe he feared I was coming to care for you and if you were here, especially if you were assisting me with the drawings, it would be that much more difficult for him to steal from me."

"Good heavens."

"I daresay he was right about that," Mr. Young

observed, smoothing his mustache. "Miss Hurst has a way with the illustrations. She would be in your library all of the time."

Mary frowned. "But Angus, if you knew Neason was stealing, didn't you worry he'd take the onyx box?"

"I told him it wasn't valuable, though it was. And then, just in case, I replaced it with a fake."

She blinked, then reached into her pocket and removed the box. "This one is *fake*?"

"Allow me?" Mr. Young took it and peered at it through a monocle he'd produced from his waistcoat. "It's a fake, and a rather crude one, I must say."

"It served its purpose." Angus grinned. "I had the true one hidden away. Would you like to see it?"

Mary nodded and she and Mr. Young followed Angus into the library. He went to the bookshelf, pulled out two large tomes, and withdrew a small black bag. He took this to the table, opened it, and there, gleaming softly, was the onyx box. "Watch." Angus reached down, rubbed his finger along one side, pausing to click a hidden latch. With a soft pop, the box opened. He unfolded it until it lay flat. "It's not a box at all; it's a map etched in gold."

Young's eyes widened. "That's— Good God, I've never— Wait until we tell—"

"No." Mary took the box and closed it. "Michael needs it."

Young frowned. "Oh, yes. Where is Hurst being held?"

"Egypt." She turned to Angus. "Can we—"

He pressed a kiss to her forehead. "We'll leave

within the hour. Once we've delivered the onyx box, we'll ask your father, the vicar, to marry us."

"But—I can't just—"

"Yes, you can. Mary, I know you've been responsible for your parents; that won't change. But we will do it together. I had a marriage once and it wasn't all it should be. I don't want that again. I want you and that means sharing everything—the joys *and* the burdens."

"Oh, Angus, that's—you're too—" Her eyes grew cloudy with tears. "But I can't just—you haven't even—"

"Oh bloody hell, I haven't, have I? That's what happens when I'm interrupted. Young, if you'll excuse us."

"Of course." The other man wandered off to one corner of the room and stared at the ceiling.

Angus once again dropped to his knee. "Mary Charlotte Hurst, will you marry me?"

"I . . I *might.*"

He frowned. "Might?"

"I need to know *why* you wish to marry me, Angus. I can't marry for just any reason, and—" Her voice caught in her throat.

"Ah. That's easy. I want to marry you because I love you. Have loved you. Can't *stop* loving you." His eyes shone bright. "Mary, you are my future. May we begin it today?"

The sun seemed to brighten the room, and Mary, her heart so full of love, suddenly knew why adventures were so wonderful. "We've found an amazing treasure, haven't we, Angus?"

He laughed, stood, and scooped her up, holding her

so tightly that she could barely breathe. "Yes, we have! Forever and ever, Mary."

She cupped his face between her hands. "And we'll have more adventures than anyone else you know. I love you, Angus. Forever."

And with that, she kissed him.

Turn the page for a special look

at the next delightful

Hurst Amulet novel

from *New York Times* bestselling author

Karen Hawkins

SCANDAL IN SCOTLAND

A letter from Michael Hurst, explorer and Egyptologist, to his brother, Captain William Hurst:

William,

I doubt this will reach you before you set sail, but letter writing is one of my few diversions while locked in this Godforsaken place. I shall endeavor to send this on the next English ship that sets sail and hope it reaches you.

I received our sister's communication that the artifact is now in your care. William, as soon as your ship is ready, please make haste. My captors are growing more impatient as the days pass and while I'm perfectly capable of dealing with their rude treatment, being forced to remain in such close confines with my assistant, Miss Jane Smythe-Haughton, has not made my captivity any more enchanting. She's removed all of my good brandy and has now implemented an exercise regime. I feel as if I've returned to boarding school.

I will not taste freedom until I deliver the object my captors have demanded. To be blunt: my fate is in your hands.

Sincerely,
Michael

*W*illiam Hurst strode onto the *Agile Witch*, the salty wind swirling his cape as he crossed the gangplank, his boots ringing with each step. He paused upon the deck and squinted up at the rigging, then gave a satisfied nod. Every brass hook and ring had been polished until they shone and every sail was freshly patched.

Good. An idle crew was a troublesome crew, and he had no time for such nonsense. He hadn't been captain for almost fifteen years without garnering a clear idea of how a ship should run.

"Cap'n!" The first mate hurried over, saluting as he came to a halt. "Ye're early."

William slipped a hand into his pocket, his fingers closing over the wrapped object there. "My sister was on time, which I didn't expect. I believe I have her new husband to thank for that."

"Do ye like him, Cap'n?"

"He seems to be well enough. One thing is for certain; my sister is enamored of him." Which had surprised William. Mary wasn't usually a romantic, something he'd always liked about her. But whenever she was in the same room as her new husband, the Earl of Erroll, she went from common sense to nonsense all in the flicker of an eyelash. It was ridiculous.

"Women," MacCready said with a note of disgust.

"Exactly." William took a last look about the ship. "She looks to be in fine fettle."

MacCready beamed. "Och, so she is. I put Halpurn in charge whilst I purchased supplies. He did a fine job keepin' the crew on task, except—" MacCready hesitated. At William's pointed look, the first mate added, "There was one item, but I've taken care o' it. It won't happen again."

"Excellent." William lifted his face to the breeze and eyed the distant horizon. "I taste a storm."

MacCready stuck out his tongue and then smacked his lips. "Ye're right. Do ye think it'll break tonight?"

"I think she'll take her time building, but when she comes, she'll be a worthy one. Plan on setting sail with the morning tide. Perhaps we can miss her altogether."

"Verra guid, Cap'n."

"Give Lawton a copy of the manifest. We make this journey at my brother's behest; he can damn well repay the expenses."

MacCready chuckled. "Aye, Cap'n! Consider it done."

William headed below deck to his cabin. Michael had gotten himself into quite a mess, and all over an object small enough to fit into a man's pocket.

But that was Michael. He'd been a sickly lad, and had only found his health and strength after childhood, which had made him far more reckless than the average man. Thank God he'd found the redoubtable Miss Jane Smythe-Haughton to keep up with his belongings and schedule and . . . William wasn't exactly sure of the woman's role, only that he'd never met a more capable—and frightening—individual in all his days, even when he and his crew had happened upon cannibals while resupplying ship at a supposedly deserted island.

Michael's recklessness had been somewhat curtailed by Miss Symthe-Haughton's iron rule until this crisis had occurred. *Where was Michael's assistant during all of this? Surely if there was a way for an escape, he and the redoubtable Miss Smythe-Haughton would have already found it.* William had to assume that there was no way out and thus the artifact in his pocket had to be delivered as soon as possible.

In his cabin, William removed the ancient Egyptian artifact from his pocket and placed it upon his desk. "Michael, you will owe me more than funds for this little favor," William murmured.

He withdrew a chain from his neck where a small golden key was hung, unlocked the desk, then placed the artifact inside and locked it away.

He returned the chain and key to his neck and tucked it out of sight before reaching for his map case. His fingers had just closed on the stiff leather tube when he caught a faint whiff of the purest essence of lily.

The scent was so real, so immediate, that it made him freeze in place, held there by a scrap of a memory— one he'd thought he'd forgotten years ago. A memory of exotic lavender eyes set with thick, black lashes; of hair that slid through his greedy fingers like black silk; of golden skin that held the sun's fragrant kiss; and of a lush mouth, ripe for kisses that—

"Hello, William."

The throaty voice yanked him from the memory. He closed his eyes, his hand still on the map case. The voice possessed an unusual resonance that made even a whisper clear. It was a rich voice, deeper than usual for a woman, yet feminine and richly wanton.

William knew the voice as well as his own. And it was the last voice he expected to hear coming from inside his own cabin.

"Aren't you going to return my greeting? Or are we still not speaking?" The voice lilted playfully, running up and down his spine, as sensual as a warm hand.

He gritted his teeth against his traitorous body and released the map tube before turning.

There, sitting in a chair at the head of the captain's table, was the one woman he never wished to see again. The one woman whose gut-wrenching betrayal had left him hollow, a fact he'd managed to keep her—and everyone else he knew and loved—from knowing by taking his ship to sea and staying away for more than two years.

He'd vowed to never, ever trust another woman . . . especially this one. He'd promised himself he'd never again lay eyes upon her.

Yet here she was, the fading sunlight caressing her golden cheek and tracing the line of her graceful neck. A black cloak was tossed over the back of the chair in which she sat, her red gown as wanton as her nature.

He removed his own cloak, turning away and breaking the spell of her beauty. He hung the cloak on a brass hook by the door, taking a deep breath as he did so. He didn't even bother to turn back around as he said, "Get out."

"You're not even going to ask me why I'm here?"

"I don't care why you're here. Just leave."

A faint rustling told him she'd stood. "William, I must talk to you. I had hoped you weren't still upset about us—"

"There was no 'us.' We were an illusion. A puff of fog in a long and cold winter." He turned to face her, his gaze pinning her in place. "That's *all* we were, and you know it."

She flushed, her creamy skin pinkening as if he'd slapped her. "I'm sorry. I was wrong to have acted as I did and—"

"Leave." He had to grit his teeth. There was something about her that was simply breathtaking, mesmerizing, that made it almost impossible not to watch her. *Damn it, I should be over this! It's been years. . .*

Her hands fisted at her sides and she sank back into her chair. "I can't go. I came all of the way here and I—" Her voice broke. "William, I am desperate."

Another man would have been moved by her tears, but he ignored her obvious manipulation. "Find another fool, Marcail. This one isn't available."

She gripped the arms of the chair. "You *must* hear me out. No one else can— William, *please*."

"What could you possibly want from me? Has Colchester finally come to his senses and kicked you from his apartments?"

At the name of her protector, her gaze narrowed. "Of course not. Colchester appreciates me . . . as others never did."

"If by 'appreciate,' you mean 'give large sums of money,' I'm certain that's true. The marquis is a wealthy man."

She managed a smile, but it was strained, and he took pleasure in knowing he was testing the limits of her acting skills, considerable as they were.

That was how she earned her living: by treading upon the boards of Drury Lane. Marcail Beauchamp was beautiful, accomplished, and reportedly the finest actress England had ever produced. Her name and her beauty were spoken of with reverence in far countries. He knew what so many others didn't; that her beauty was not due to artifice. No, that she left entirely for her own soul.

His gaze flickered over her, noting that her elegant gown was a trifle too low cut for true modesty. *And that is the* other *way she makes her living,* he reminded himself harshly. *She gives herself to the highest bidder.* "Colchester can have you."

"Whatever you may say of the marquis, he is not involved in my coming here." She hesitated and he saw a flicker of uncertainty. But was it real? "William, I came to ask for a favor."

William gave a bitter laugh. "No."

"You don't even know what it is."

"I don't need to know. If it has to do with you, I want nothing of it."

Her smile was completely gone now. Not that her expression truly mattered, for she changed it as she changed hats, selecting them to augment whatever aura she wished to project. *What was I thinking, to believe the words of an actress?*

He knew only one fact for certain, and it was a damningly inconvenient one; she was just as beautiful as before, perhaps more so. Over the years her beauty had matured and ripened. Gone was her slender, almost coltish beauty and in its place was a seductive, mature woman, one who moved with an assurance that could not be faked.

It was fortunate that he was no longer under her spell.

"William, please, don't look so—" She waved her hand, the movement as graceful as she. "This is not easy for me, either."

"I don't care if this is easy for you." He pulled a chair from the table—the farthest one from her—and dropped into it. "I didn't invite you. How did you come here? The crew didn't alert me that I had a guest and they would have, had they known."

"I came onboard before it was light."

"There is always a guard by the gangway."

"He was asleep."

So that was the issue MacCready had alluded to. I should have asked more questions. "I sense some trickery here. I know you, Marcail Beauchamp, and you are not telling me everything."

"You don't know me. You never did." She spoke with such quiet dignity that he was almost taken aback.

Almost. "I suppose you'll eventually tell me what you want; I could use some merriment before I set sail."

She frowned. "You're leaving soon?"

"In the morning."

Her lashes dropped to obscure her true expression. "I see."

She leaned back in her chair, her deep red gown a perfect foil for her upswept black hair, the thin white ruffle at her décolletage pretending a modesty that was betrayed by the way her full breasts swelled above it. She was a master at looking innocent and wanton at the same time; it used to make him crazed for her. Fortunately, he now recognized the artifice written all over her beautiful face.

She caught his stare. "What?"

"You look older. What has it been? Six years?"

"Eight."

"A pity it wasn't eight more before we had to meet again."

His cool, harsh words didn't even cause her to blink. She merely shrugged. "I will make this short. William, I need your help in locating something that's been lost. It's— Oh Lord, this is difficult to say, and I—" She stood as if restless, her lush figure on display as she crossed to the port window. She peered out of it before turning to him. "I didn't wish to ask for your help, but I have no one else to turn to." Her gaze fell on the decanter and glasses that sat on a sideboard. She gestured toward it. "May I?"

He shrugged.

She went to the decanter and unstopped it. She took a delicate sniff, looking at him with raised brows. "Very nice. You didn't use to be so discerning in your port."

"I'm far more discerning in *all* of my likes now."

Her lips thinned, but she merely poured out two glasses.

"It's from Napoleon's private supply." William wasn't sure why he'd felt the need to mention that inane fact.

"That monster. I'd heard you were with the navy then."

"I've been many places since we parted."

"I shall enjoy the port all the more since it was taken from Napoleon." She replaced the stopper and brought him a glass.

He made no move to take it from her, so she placed it on the table before him, then carried her glass back to her seat. She sat and delicately swirled the liquid. "I wonder, am I wasting my time by coming here?"

"If there's one thing you taught me, it's to never trust an answer that is in fact another question."

"I taught you that?"

"Oh, you taught me all sorts of things—none of it good." He took a drink of the port, the sharpness clearing his throat. "Enough of this. What in hell do you want? You have two minutes to tell me and then you're going overboard."

She pushed her glass away. "Fine. I came to you because someone is blackmailing me."

"What does that have to do with me?"

Anger flashed across her face, so swift that he believed it real. "William, I am *desperate*. I don't know who is doing it or why or— They must stop."

"Ask Colchester for his help. Isn't that his place as your 'protector'?" William watched Marcail over the edge of his glass as he took another drink. At her closed expression, he lowered his glass. "Ah. You don't wish him to know this secret, whatever it is. What happened, Marcail? Did you stray? Is that the secret? That you can no more be true to a man than a dog can stop himself from chasing a squirrel?"

Her eyes flashed fire. "Dammit, this is important! If my secret were revealed—and no, it's nothing so tawdry as that—it wouldn't be I who would pay, but others."

"What others?"

After a moment's obvious struggle, she said, "It doesn't matter. You aren't going to help me, anyway. I should have known better than to ask."

"Yes, you should have. I am done with secrets and hidden lies." He pushed his empty glass away, suddenly tired of it all. Tired of the deceptions that had left him so beaten all those years ago. "I think you should go."

"I will. But first, I wish to tell you something." She rose and came toward him, pausing just shy of where he sat.

"Say what you will and then leave."

"Oh, I shall leave, but not until you've helped me."

"I've already said I wouldn't help you." Dammit, was he slurring his words? He looked at the glass of port. He'd only had one glass. Normally it took far, far more than that to—

He slowly looked up at Marcail. "You put something in the po—" His mouth wouldn't make the words, his vision suddenly wavering. He gathered every ounce of his strength and forced his numb arms to push him to his feet, where he swayed dangerously.

She frowned. "William, don't! You'll hurt yourself and—"

He toppled forward.

She tried to catch him, stepping into his fall and wrapping her arms about him, but he was too large. She managed only to keep him from buckling face-first into the table, her slight body only tilting him to one side so that he instead landed upon the hard floor.

Why in the hell has she drugged me? He was too numb to feel anything, his emotions as muted as his body. He watched with cool, unemotional interest as she took his cloak and made a pillow of it and gently placed it under his head, her hands warm and sure.

Then she gently slipped the chain from around his neck and took the desk key. The lowering sunlight cast her in a golden glow that made her seem ethereal, an angel of purity and beauty and such exquisite grace that it almost pained one to watch her.

It was that grace that had won him in the first place. Not her face nor her figure nor her rich voice, all of which had helped catapult her to fame from the boards. To him her crowning jewel had been her innate, unconscious grace. When she walked, she drew the eye and held it almost as if she were dancing to music that only she could hear.

She bent over the desk, her dark hair agleam with

the golden haze of the final lingering rays of light. She unlocked his desk and reached in. He tried to remember how much gold he had in the cubbyhole. *Two hundred guineas? Three? Why does she need funds so badly? Colchester spoils her with his wealth. Has she garnered debts she can't tell him about? Perhaps she's taken to gambling or—*

She removed her hand, holding the ancient artifact that would free his brother. *God, no!*

Even in his drugged state, fury trickled through. *I must have that artifact. I cannot free Michael without it.*

She tugged open the sack and glanced inside, her brows lowering as she slid the slender onyx box free from its velvet pouch. She traced the tip of a finger over the edge of the box, her expression perplexed. Uncertain, she glanced his way and met his gaze.

Her cheeks darkened as if she were blushing and she hurried to tuck the artifact away.

William wanted to cut her to shreds in word and deed, but all he could do was glare at her with all of the force of his anger, which was burning through the drug's haze.

He suddenly realized he could move his toes, which had been impossible just two moments ago. The drug was already wearing off. Soon he'd be able to rise, and woe betide the wench then. He'd teach her a lesson she'd not soon forget.

She collected her cloak and tied it about her neck before she slid the onyx box into a deep pocket. She paused as she walked past William, the edge of her skirt brushing his hand.

Unexpectedly, she stooped and placed a hand upon

his cheek, her dark gaze bright as if with unshed tears. "Don't try to follow me when you can move; I won't be where you can find me." Her long silky hair brushed over his cheek in a gossamer caress, the faint scent of her exotic perfume making his heart pound faster.

She lowered her lips to his ear. "I am sorry to do this, *mon chere*, but I have no choice." She brushed her lips over his, the kiss as gentle as sea mist. Then she brushed the hair from his forehead and said in a voice tinged with remorse, "To you, this is a trinket. To me, it is freedom."

With that cryptic statement, she rose and pulled the hood over her head, tucking her hair out of sight. "I must have the box. I wish it were otherwise, but—" She shook her head and stepped toward the door . . . but William's fingers had closed about her hem.

He held tightly to the skirt, but only his fingers and toes were capable of moving.

"Oh, William. You never let anything be easy, do you?" She gathered her skirt and with a quick yank, freed it from his grasp. "Good-bye."

She left the cabin, quietly closing the door behind her, leaving William in the growing darkness.